WORLD WAR TWO WILL NOT TAKE PLACE

Bill James

severn
House

This first world edition published 2011
in Great Britain and the USA by
SEVERN HOUSE PUBLISHERS LTD of
9–15 High Street, Sutton, Surrey, England, SM1 1DF.
Trade paperback edition first published
in Great Britain and the USA 2011 by
SEVERN HOUSE PUBLISHERS LTD.

British Library Cataloguing in Publication Data

James, Bill, 1929-
    World War Two will not take place.
    1. World War, 1939-1945–Diplomatic history–Fiction.
    2. Secret service–Great Britain–Fiction. 3. Undercover
    operations–Germany–Berlin–Fiction. 4. Berlin
    (Germany)–History–1918-1945–Fiction. 5. Great
    Britain–History–George VI, 1936-1952–Fiction.
    6. Alternative histories (Fiction)
    I. Title
    823.9'14-dc22

ISBN-13: 978-0-7278-8003-1 (cased)
ISBN-13: 978-1-84751-330-4 (trade paper)

All Severn House titles are printed on acid-free paper.

Severn House Publishers support The Forest Stewardship Council [FSC],
the leading international forest certification organisation. All our titles that
are printed on Greenpeace-approved FSC-certified paper carry the FSC logo.

Typeset by Palimpsest Book Production Ltd.,
Falkirk, Stirlingshire, Scotland.
Printed and bound in Great Britain by
MPG Books Ltd., Bodmin, Cornwall.

For a good deal of factual guidance on this period I am indebted to *Munich, The 1938 Appeasement Crisis*, by David Faber (Simon and Schuster), and *The Climate Of Treason,* by Andrew Boyle, though what I've made of this guidance is, of course, my own responsibility. As the title would indicate, this book adjusts some history.

La Guerre de Troie n'aura pas lieu
(The Trojan war won't happen)
– Jean Giraudoux

BOOK ONE

ONE

Mount flew to Berlin-Templehof in the afternoon, passported as Stanley Charles Naughton, businessman. Section kept a service apartment under the S.C. Naughton name off Hindenburgdamm in Steglitz, a sedate, tree-lined suburb to the south-west of the capital. Mount had used it several times in the last couple of years and considered the address still reasonably anonymous. The apartment itself was on the second floor in a very modern, New Objectivity – *Neue Sachlichkeit* – style block, built in the late 1920s or early 1930s, Mount would guess, though much of the district's imposing grey stone and red-brick property went back to mid nineteenth century. It was a suitable kind of prosperous, developing area for the *pied-à-terre* of a British company's visiting executive. But no matter how right it might be, Section wouldn't lease this kind of accommodation for more than three years. An unusual pattern of usage – or more a *non*-pattern – might get it noticed. There'd be a change soon.

Mount knew what his mission was, of course. Stephen Bilson had briefed him earlier today in that painstaking style of his. But Mount had wondered (1) whether the objective was achievable; and (2) whether, even if it were, it would make much difference to the general international condition of power and politics.

Mount often wondered if his journeys and various activities for the Section had much point. But, as Stephen Bilson told him not long ago, 'In this kind of work little is absolutely plain, Marcus.' The suggestion here was that, looking back later on, Mount might hindsight-understand how seemingly useless operations fitted into a master plan. And Mount would admit SB's hint usually turned out true – or as true as anyone could expect in this kind of work, where so little was absolutely plain, or absolutely true, or absolutely anything. Bilson had served in France throughout the war and was at the Somme. He may have often wondered how – or if – some slaughterous spell of combat contributed to a general strategy. During such bloody fighting he'd picked up two medals, even if, at those moments, he hadn't properly understood this or that battle's objective.

Just the same, Mount continued to think his present mission especially dud and doubted it would ever be proved otherwise. Bilson's decision to send him to Berlin had been too rushed, too impulsive. These were untypical words to use about SB, who habitually displayed absolute calm in all weathers, and whose thinking was methodical, sane, clear; except, obviously, at those times – fairly frequent – when it had to get professionally serpentine and, or, fog-producing, in the nation's interest.

There'd been an episode at another airfield yesterday: Heston, not far from London. Mount and Bilson had gone there together. Would it be exaggerating to describe SB's reaction to events at Heston as near panic? Mount didn't want to call it that. He needed something to believe in and, often, SB and his level-headedness and medals had been it. However, standing with Stephen Bilson then, on the rim of the crowd at Heston, Marcus Mount had thought he detected a quite swift, painful change of reactions in his chief: a move from satisfaction bordering on relish, towards anxiety bordering on despair. Mount had tried to work out what caused this, and when. Bilson had seemed fine, and more than fine, while they waited for the Lockheed to appear out of the clouds and make its descent. This seemingly bland mood persisted right up until the plane completed its landing and the Prime Minister appeared at the top of the steps, waving his peace piece of paper. But, surely, that's what SB had schemed for. Why should it distress him now, offend him now?

Chamberlain had done the job that Stephen, in his devious, oblique, commanding style, must have managed him into doing, or helped manage him into doing, at any rate. Shouldn't Bilson feel and display delight? Some details of the PM's performance *were*, on the face of it showy and vulgar – did Chamberlain need to beam so manically, flourish the document so frenetically? – but that, surely, could not cancel the central, core worth of what he'd achieved in Munich. Politics would always be vulgar, and war politics especially. Chamberlain had the kind of face that found excitement or enthusiasm difficult to register. There seemed to be something permanently cowed and nervy to him, even when he talked as if he had nothing to be cowed and nervy about. At Heston, in fact, he had a kind of triumph to report, didn't he? Did he?

When the next morning – this morning – Mount had spoken in the Section to Olly Fallows and Nick Baillie, about the Heston events, he'd said: 'Of course, I might be wrong about a swing of attitude in SB. He's not easy to read.'

'Harder than *The Waste Land*,' Fallows said.

'He's sending me to Berlin at once – "Sub rosa, entirely sub rosa." But the whole thing at Heston should have been a celebration,' Mount said. 'He'd actually created the scene.'

'Well, yes, in a sense,' Baillie said.

'I'm sure Chamberlain wouldn't have gone and acted compliant, except for him,' Mount said. 'And wouldn't have come back with promises for the adoring crowd and the relieved country, but for him.'

'They're known to have private conclaves, yes,' Baillie said. 'Stephen hates war.'

'He was good at it,' Fallows said.

'He wouldn't want more,' Mount said.

'But he'd also realize that war might be inevitable, and a delay would give us more time to stock up on the arms and barrage balloons and gas masks and blanco,' Baillie said.

'That's presumably why he wanted to be there for the PM's return at Heston,' Fallows said. 'He'd like to see the completion of his work at first hand. He took you with him, Marcus, to learn in a very vivid way what his purpose was, and what the Section's purpose should be – and perhaps to pass on that message to the rest of us young underlings. Did he say, "Marcus! Come along, sonny boy, and witness the sterling results of our work?"'

'Normally, he'd hate to join any public display for fear he'd get identified,' Baillie said. 'But he must have thought the PM's mission exceptionally, uniquely, successful – demanding his formal presence at the welcome home. He's persuaded Neville to stop a war.'

'Or, at least, postpone a war,' Mount said.

Perhaps Fallows and Baillie had it right. Possibly Bilson *had* wanted to educate Mount via the drama of Heston. And nobody could say it wasn't dramatic. The happy tension could be felt, in fact, long before Bilson and Mount actually reached Heston yesterday in the car. The narrow approach roads to the airport were jammed with vehicles and people on foot determined to make a joyful reception for Chamberlain. And when Bilson and Mount did reach the airfield they found a huge gathering of excited folk had assembled. Mount felt a kind of carnival spirit. Among the crowd he saw what he judged from their formal clothes to be a party of Eton schoolboys. Good God, there would be more than a hundred! They'd obviously been given leave to witness these triumphant moments. News of the Prime Minister's success in his talks with the Führer had, of course, reached Britain a good while ahead of his plane.

Like everyone else there, the boys continually stared up into the grey skies, looking for the airliner with the Prime Minister aboard. Such a turnout! And perhaps Chamberlain deserved it. Yes, perhaps, Mount decided. In a little while, he'd heard the aircraft's engine, and then, after a couple more minutes, he spotted the plane descending majestically towards Heston. The Super-Lockheed 14 landed, taxied and came to a stop. Airport staff placed steps in position. The door opened, and Neville Chamberlain appeared and waved happily to the people. Instantly, a cheer of response erupted. The Etonians, in a group and obviously organized, yelled his name, with the accent heavily on the first syllable: *Nev*ille, *Nev*ille, *Nev*ille. He came down the steps and turned to where microphones had been placed on the tarmac. He waved a piece of paper. 'This morning I had another talk with the German Chancellor, Herr Hitler, and here is a paper which bears his name upon it as well as mine. It asserts the desire of our two peoples never to go to war with each other again.' He waved the paper once more. The crowd gave a huge, prolonged cheer.

It was not long after this that Mount thought he noticed the abrupt and huge change in Bilson's mood. Mount wondered whether SB objected to that noisy claque of Eton schoolboys. But Bilson himself had, of course, come from one of the top public – meaning private – schools or he'd never have been invited into his present job. He'd know – just as Mount knew from his own school days – that the kids of well-heeled families could be especially excitable and loud. Bilson's attitude on social class might be complex, though. Apparently, he'd insisted on joining up as an ordinary soldier in 1914. The commission didn't come till well into the war – late 1916.

He and Mount had watched the Prime Minister's Daimler eventually move off on the way back to London. Other cars tagged behind in a triumphal procession, some carrying Press and broadcasting people, but most simply enthusiasts and sightseers. Several drivers blared their horns repeatedly in salute. At least this made sure the string of vehicles couldn't be mistaken for a funeral cortège, though the misery Mount sensed in Bilson might suggest a funeral was what it definitely was. Perhaps his sadness came from a larger cause than the schoolboys' behaviour. Did Stephen think he'd suddenly glimpsed the end of that vastly variable and internationally disputed quality, British honour? He'd wanted proper recognition of what the PM had achieved, but not on such a noisy, delirious, unthinking, reverential scale.

This morning, the Press was almost uniformly enthusiastic about the Munich trip. *The Times* had headlined its report of the meeting 'A Cordial Welcome From The Führer', and the Labour *Daily Herald* had sent him off with the large type message 'Good Luck' and spoken of united, cross-party support for his efforts.

At Heston, yesterday, SB gave the Daimler and its tail of admirers and news hounds half an hour to get clear, then followed. 'He'll report to the king now and most probably to the Cabinet in the morning,' he'd said. 'Delight all round. Out on the palace balcony with all the majesticals for the crowd, I expect. Our monarch, Edward, and his wife, Wallis, are fond of Adolf, aren't they? It's part of their affection for Europe. She's American. To her, Europe is Europe, whether it's Hitler's bit or someone else's. They have minds that generalize – are not good at differentiating. They'll be delighted with the outcome – pleased that the Prime Minister has preserved good feelings between the two countries. Come to me at noon tomorrow, Marcus. I'll want you to get over *sub rosa*, entirely *sub rosa*, to Berlin immediately.' He spoke it all in the same, matter-of-fact tone, as if Mount's trip must naturally follow the PM's encounter with the king and the Cabinet and all the majesticals – a natural, inevitable part of the same sequence.

Mount said: 'May I ask what is the—?'

'Noon. Silence on this, please, Marcus.'

But Mount had mentioned it to Nick and Ollie the next morning, this morning, as part of his account of the Heston sequence. 'At first, Stephen seemed happily caught up with waiting for the Lockheed,' Mount said. 'Then, only minutes afterwards, it's as if he suddenly had massive second thoughts.'

'A revelation had hit him,' Baillie said. Nick was usually quick and definite in his judgements. 'SB might be the sort for epiphany-type revelations: super-balanced most of the time, but if that balance is disturbed by some epiphany – some massive revelation – his mind becomes very, very disturbed. This could shove our master towards breakdown, temporary or worse. It's a familiar psychological pattern. It would be made worse, perhaps, when he heard the PM had been invited to the Palace to get the king's thanks face to face. And the crowd outside yelling, "We want Chamberlain! We want Neville!" Then, later, much the same at ten Downing Street.'

'Suddenly, this very unlogged, false-papers mission to Berlin,' Mount said.

'To do what?' Fallows said.

'He'll brief me personally later today. For my ears only,' Mount said. 'I'm packed.'

'Skulduggery?' Fallows asked.

'I assume no weaponry,' Mount said. 'How does he get me something from the armoury if I'm not just *sub rosa*, but entirely *sub rosa*?'

'Think you'll need something?' Baillie said.

'It's Berlin,' Mount said.

'Well, yes,' Baillie said.

'Maybe he'll draw a handgun on the face of it for himself and let you borrow,' Fallows said.

'You think so?' Mount said.

'No,' Fallows said. 'You might go and kill someone and the gun could be traced to him.'

'*Who* might I go and kill?' Mount said.

'That's for you to decide,' Fallows said. 'Some SS thug giving you bother? How can I tell? You're skimping the information, Marcus.'

'I'm skimping because I haven't got any,' Mount said. 'Not till I see him, and it might be half mystery even then.'

'Be severe with him,' Fallows said.

'With SB?'

'Come right out with it: "How's about a pistol, plus fifty
rounds and a silencer, then, SB?" And he'll see the reasonableness of this and say, "Glad you asked, young Marcus. Have
a brace and a hundred." And you'll reply, selflessly, "Won't
this leave you light on one gun hip, sir? I wouldn't want to
be responsible for that. A single will do, and the fifty."'

'I do love humour,' Mount had replied.

Now, he took a taxi from Templehof Airport to the empty
apartment. It was neat and spruce: the building management
sent a cleaning firm in once a fortnight whenever the place
stood unoccupied for a while. The wallpaper always struck
him as William Morris-y: mostly dark green, plenty of lively
leaves and stalks and gleams of sun through the foliage, very
much pro-Nature, especially jungles. Mount could put up with
the furniture. It had been bought to chime with the modern-
ity of the apartment. A nest of three very black Bakelite tables
sickened him a bit, but he liked the tall, slim hall mirror on
a stand and the wide laminated birch and metal armchairs.

Several bronze and ivory statuettes of limbs-flung dancing
girls cheered things up in the living room. This had two
windows looking over the street. He raised the Venetian blinds.
He'd leave these windows uncovered. The lights made an
announcement: someone had arrived and required a visitor. It
had been important to get an apartment on at least the second
or third floor, so the message could be obvious, and so people
walking the pavement couldn't gawp in. This signalling
mimicked brothels, though their lights would be red, of course.
It was one of the most primitive taught procedures for getting
in touch with an agent, and fairly safe, although lights on in
the day could cause curiosity. Telephoning would not have
been primitive. Nor would it have been safe. Calls were
randomly listened in on. Telegrams, even coded telegrams,
could be a giveaway. Perhaps someone would wonder why
they needed to be coded.

Mount sat down for a while away from the windows and
thought back. During the chat with Baillie and Fallows this
morning, Baillie had asked: 'Have you considered the
Etonians?'

'Considered how?' Mount said.

'*The Times* said a gaggle of senior boys had been allowed
to cut school and get to the Heston party,' Fallows said.

'They intoned his name,' Mount said. 'At least a hundred.'

'Yes, *The Times* reported it as "Neville" over and over,' Baillie said. 'This could be crucial for SB's state of mind.'

'"*Nev*ille" over and over,' Mount said.

'The paper estimates 120 Etonians,' Baillie said. 'Might that have shocked SB? Perhaps made him wonder if he'd led Neville into a terrible error by humouring Adolf?'

'I don't follow,' Mount said.

Fallows clapped his hands twice. 'Ah, I believe *I* do. Very clever, Nick. Insightful. Look, Marcus, consider Sir Henry Newbolt.'

'"A breathless hush in the Close tonight"?' Mount said.

'It's public school cricket under way – probably Eton cricket,' Baillie said. 'We have a needle game, the result touch and go. And Newbolt proudly declares that because these schoolboys learned how to battle well at cricket, they'd be able to battle well as officers in a war and magnificently rally the ranks at bad moments. It's where Britain traditionally got its army leaders: our public schools. They were first over the top out of the trenches. Why so many got mown down. But didn't these braying Etonians at Heston turn all that inside out? They'd come to robot-bellow their support for murky deals, for appeasement, and their adoration of the PM and his bit of paper, gloriously wrung from Hitler and his troupe – by handing Hitler and his troupe everything they asked for. Did this sudden, shocking revelation appal Bilson, bringing on a collapse into confusion and regret, shame and a vast change of mind?'

Fallows said: 'Or think of Rupert Brooke, public school poet and a First War officer, chortling at the start of hostilities in 1914: "Now God be thanked who has matched us with His hour." These lads at Heston hailed a cowardly, feeble, eat-dirt hour. That's what *they*'d been matched with. They exulted in the country's humiliation. We imagine, don't we, that SB's purpose must be to get Chamberlain to keep Hitler quiet for, say, another twelve month, perhaps more, so we have time to build up strength. But what use is that if the potential officer class don't want to fight – if the potential officer class flagrantly idolizes someone who's cravenly dodged out of fighting? Might that shred SB's strategy? And shred his morale?'

'But if Chamberlain and Stephen had decided we *should*

fight now, *should* try to block Hitler now, the situation would be entirely the same, wouldn't it?' Mount said. 'If you're right, the so-called officer class, the Etonians and Old Etonians, wouldn't want to go to war tomorrow, any more than it would in a year or so's time.'

'The trip to Munich and early reports from there hatched a timorous, poltroon spirit,' Baillie said. 'Then it developed at a terrifying rate, overwhelming rate. True, we had the Oxford '33 union vote: "This house will in no circumstances fight for king and country, thank you very much." But that was only powerless, mischievous undergrads wanting to shock, and before we really knew very much about Hitler. Now, we have the Prime Minister seeming to back the students' attitude five years later when Adolf's aims are a good bit clearer – and bloody alarming. Think of that Reich Chancellery meeting with armed forces chiefs last November, where he said Germany's legitimate desire for more space for her people could only be realized through force. *Only* through force. He actually named Czechoslovakia and Austria as territorial hindrances, didn't he?'

'November fifth. Bonfire night!' Fallows said. 'Couldn't be more apt. Try not to let any of them use that force on you, Marcus, even if you are gunless. Maybe at Heston SB saw the link with that Oxford Union idiocy, despite all these subsequent developments, and it devastated him. And you, in your intuitive way, Marcus, sensed the devastation in him, diagnosed the *volte face*. Bravo! And now, off to Berlin! Weird.'

'Yes, fascinating, but not, not at all, unexplainable,' Baillie had said, explaining. Mount's description of SB's sudden mood change at Heston had handed Baillie a chance to try a spot of amateur psychology. And so, the reference to that mighty, officer-quality cricket match in Newbolt's Close. After this, Baillie had categorized SB as a probable stoic, and then discussed what might happen if stoicism fractured. Nick fancied himself as a psychologist/psychiatrist. It could get tiresome. But, although he had no training in such mysteries – his degree was modern languages: double First, Cambridge, in French, German, Italian – now and then he would come up with a believable X-ray of someone's mind and motives. Perhaps he had SB right, Mount thought.

Stephen Bilson said, at the start of the noon meeting in

Section earlier today, 'I'd like you to get over to Berlin and see friend Toulmin. Russia. I'm interested in Russia, Marcus. Toulmin works mainly on Jerry's Russian desk at their Foreign Office, doesn't he?' No mention of a handgun came throughout their conversation.

'See friend Toulmin.' Hence the signal with the living room lights now, in the Steglitz apartment. Instead, Mount might have loitered near the German Foreign Office, where Toulmin worked, and tried to intercept him on his way home, but that could be dangerous, too: Foreign Office staff came under routine surveillance periodically, like most government employees who possibly knew things worth knowing, and who might secretly hate what Hitler was up to, and try to undermine it, also secretly.

Of course, Toulmin was not Toulmin. SB collected antique clocks and took cover names for the Section's foreign agents from famous old makers and styles. Apparently, there'd been a Toulmin in the eighteenth century, a dab hand at ebonized, bong-bong-bong-striking models. SB had one. The arrangement with the current Toulmin required him to check the Steglitz windows at least every other day and call in immediately if he saw the lights. He had a key to the apartment. His stipend took account of these little reconnaissance trips, with payments generously credited for sixteen days in every month, regardless of their length. He operated as second string in Berlin. The Section's major voice had been dubbed Fromanteel, after another ancient clockman. SB had one of his, too. Fromanteel would spill only to Stephen Bilson in person, or so Bilson said: all secrets people loved to feel they *owned* an agent, monopolized his or her disclosures.

In any case, SB thought Toulmin more likely to be right for the kind of queries required now – the Soviet area – and Toulmin would talk to anybody from Section. Mount had dealt with him before. Oh, yes. Toulmin knew a couple of girls from the Toledo Club, and they brought them back to the apartment after drinks last time Mount was in Berlin. Toulmin had always used his cover name with them, so Mount considered the security risk very minor. One of the birch wood and metal armchairs had collapsed under Toulmin and Olga, a hearty brunette, when she so playfully straddled him on it. Neither seemed too badly hurt, although unprotected by clothes.

Afterwards, Mount divided up the chair wreckage into three lots and shared them around other apartments' bins. That seemed to him the wisest solution: he didn't want cleaners to find the fragments in the living room and speculate. When the lease ended there would certainly be inventory questions about the missing chair, possibly of a valuable design, so he'd put in a note to Section explaining it gave way under him – him alone – and must have had a weakness. He did not claim for injuries, saying he suffered only bruising and shock. There was no question of docking money from Toulmin's little salary for the destruction, and, in fact, Mount had paid for both girls and the drinks under 'reciprocal entertainment of various special contacts' on his expenses account. 'Various special contacts' as a species did not reach agent status, but might provide miscellaneous items of information. No names needed to be given for them, not even as ancient clockmakers.

'Yes, Toulmin, a reliable lad, I believe,' Stephen Bilson had said at the private Section meeting with Mount earlier today. He looked as if he was pretty much recovered from whatever undermined him at Heston yesterday. Mount still found it difficult to read his face, but he'd thought it did now show the doggedness and resolution that was customary for SB, but which seemed to slip for a while at the airport. Baillie had often suggested to Mount that SB's army experience in the war shaped his psyche, or reshaped it. Of course, this might be said about many who came back from the trenches in 1918. Baillie had done some research. SB started in the ranks as a rifleman, became a no-man's-land sniper, then corporal in charge of a machine gun unit, then sergeant and sergeant major and, by 1916, had been commissioned in the field. He left the army in 1919 as a lieutenant colonel with the Distinguished Service Medal, earned as a corporal, and the Military Cross, as an officer.

Baillie, this would-be psychologist, but not a stupid would-be psychologist, reckoned that stoicism – the magnificent, unflamboyant ability to keep buggering on – was what carried Bilson forward in the war and remained his chief strength. This had been Baillie's argument after the poetry babble about Sir Henry Newbolt yesterday. There might be something in it. 'The point about stoicism,' Baillie had said, 'is it works well, as long as it works well. But if it weakens, or fails altogether, there's not much left. The ex-stoic may become a breakdown case, his behaviour either fallen into paralysis, or gone wild, irrational, incoherent.'

Had this happened to SB? Was the Berlin assignment for Mount wild, irrational, incoherent? 'You're concerned about Russia? In which respect, sir,' Mount had asked him.

'Moscow cuddling up to Adolf. A potential pact. That respect. I want to know if it's happening.'

'Is it likely?'

'We in our little game don't necessarily deal in likelihoods, Marcus.' He said this mildly enough, but it was severe, instructional, a right-hand jab at naivety. 'Possibilities are our meat. We have to guess at which way things might go. We pick through these possibilities until we reach what looks as if it could be a likelihood. Or we hope we do. And *if* we do – and that's not at all guaranteed, Marcus – we then tell our leaders about it. I'm afraid we might have overlooked a possibility. Or that *I* might have overlooked a possibility. And a possibility that could develop into a likelihood. My error. A bad one. I think I know how it happened. Get over there, will you, and send Toulmin sniffing.'

'For what in particular?'

'This love affair I mentioned. Stalin and Hitler.'

'An alliance between Moscow and Berlin?'

'An alliance, a treaty.'

Mount felt left behind. 'Excuse me, sir, but don't most people see Germany and Russia as out-and-out political enemies: one fascist, the other Commie?'

'Yes, perhaps most people do see Russia and Germany as natural enemies. But I'd like you to ask Toulmin to find whether there've been any private dealings, or preparations for dealings, or soundings-out for preparations for dealings, or soundings-out for soundings-out for preparations for dealings, between Moscow and Berlin. That is his objective, and yours, Marcus. Discover whether a new agreement is being cooked up.' Some of Bilson's army experience poked through there. Troops had to have clear, simple objectives. Mount and, via him, Toulmin, were SB's foot soldiers. 'This is not an unhazardous one for Toulmin,' SB said. 'I hope we're always careful in what we ask our agents to do for us. Make it plain that we'll try all we know to protect him and get him, and any family, out of Germany if matters turn rough. And we'll up his retainer, of course. Go very cagily, Marcus. Jerry is improving his counter-us operation all the time. Matters, when they do turn rough there, turn very rough. The Third Reich is a new Reich and still feels vulnerable. Therefore, it defends itself ferociously.'

Then, Bilson seemed deliberately to move away from the perils of the operation. He said: 'An earlier German leader, Bismark, asked those around him, "What's the secret of politics?" Answer? "Make a good treaty with Russia." Perhaps Hitler believes likewise. You and Toulmin will, I know, find out. Off you go, lad.'

In the evening, after making himself a meal in the Steglitz flat, Mount went to the nearby huge Titania-Palast cinema, also built in that New Objectivity mode. Hitler and the Nazis disliked the style's plainness, coolness, lack of the ornate. They were Romantics – dark Romantics, but Romantics – driven by dangerous, passionate nationalism, dangerously boundless ambition, dangerous, master race, *völkisch* myth. Buildings should tally – should be something beyond the serviceable. Architecture should not just stand there and get used, it should assert, it should proclaim, the new, formidable, bold spirit of modern Germany.

There'd be no more New Objectivity architecture. In one aspect, Mount found this odd: an alternative translation of *Neue Sachlichkeit* was 'New Sobriety', and surely the teetotal Führer should have approved.

Mount watched *Der Blaue Engel – The Blue Angel* – part of a Marlene Dietrich festival: the first German sound movie, and mesmeric. He'd left the apartment blinds up and the lights on. Good job Hitler had got the electric industry working well after some bad interludes. Compare Musso's success in making Italian trains run to time.

TWO

When Mount returned after the film, he saw from the street that his windows no longer showed lights. But this was all right, wasn't it? This was positive, wasn't it? For a moment, he'd felt shocked. Why, though? Toulmin must be there, obediently waiting. He had lowered the blinds, reversed the signal: clever. Blinds up meant: 'I, alias Naughton, am here in Berlin and want to see you, Toulmin.' Blinds down meant: 'I, alias Toulmin, am here in your snuggery, Stanley, or most likely alias Stanley, awaiting your return.' Perhaps, also, he felt more secure with the glass covered, even on the second floor. Toulmin would occasionally get nervy. Well, of course he'd get nervy. He spied. Nerviness went with this game. So did a vengeful death for those who played it. All regimes detested spies and being spied on. This new-Germany regime would probably detest spies more than most, as Bilson had hinted, and would show it if they caught one, also as Bilson had hinted.

Of course, Mount, also, spied. But for him it was a profession, and a fairly decent profession, with sterling people like SB running things, some of them medalled, and Cambridge double firsts as rankers: a sought-after, pensionable, classy career, hard to get into. But spying was not Toulmin's profession or career. No. In fact, Toulmin actually spied on people *in* his profession and career: on foreign affairs deskmen who knew him as a colleague, not as Toulmin, an agent working to Mount. As Fallows had said not long ago, 'One man's agent is another man's traitor.' Toulmin's behaviour would strike many as disgustingly corrupt and due no mercy if discovered. He'd be termed a renegade rather than a spy, although he spied for Mount. Toulmin had to live permanently among the people he spied on, bringing non-stop strain. On the other hand, Mount could go home now and then, resume normality, become simply and purely, for a time, Marcus Mount, known by friends and relatives as having 'some tidy government job in London with a lot of travel'.

Despite these contrasts, Mount often grew very nervy, too. He felt especially anxious now, even though the dark windows could be regarded – *should* be regarded – as simply a message board, and a message board that had been considerately kept up-to-date. Was his jumpiness stupid, perverse? He thought he might have been seriously pushed off-balance by SB's seeming plunge into crazy haste. Projects built in that kind of rushed, gimcrack way often failed. Also, he felt he might have been idiotically casual, over-relaxed, in drifting off to the cinema tonight. He was here to do a job for Stephen Bilson, not to drool over Dietrich.

Mount approached the apartment gingerly. *Procedures for clandestine penetration of occupied premises* had taken two full days in his training. Plentiful caution had been preached, and that stuck with him. But determination to get into the occupied premises regardless had also been part of the instruction. Normally, it would not be one's own premises that were involved, but those of a target. The same conditions applied, though. He couldn't be thoroughly sure lowered blinds accounted for the absence of light as he gazed up at the building. The windows might be dark because the room behind was. Why would Toulmin switch off, suppose it to *be* Toulmin? And, then, suppose not – who, for God's sake?

The wariness taught for *clandestine penetration of occupied premises* focused above all on doors and how to go through them. On the face of it, that's what doors were for – to go through when open. But an open door into the wrong kind of area carried some perils. Standing in a doorway even for half a second meant you were nicely framed, a simple potshot for anyone inside and waiting for you. Techniques on how to manage doors and passing through them in these special conditions differed, depending on whether the officer had a firearm or not, and, if the officer did have a firearm, differed again depending on whether it was '*blatant*' – that is, in the officer's fist and visible – or '*latent*' – that is, holstered, handbagged or waistbanded, and out of sight. Neither the blatant nor latent approach concerned Mount. He had no gun. To draw a weapon from the armoury would have required signatures and a proper record. SB didn't regard the visit as that kind of operation. The Berlin jaunt was unofficial – unknown, except to Mount and Bilson, plus, illicitly, Fallows

and Baillie. The Section had an unaudited and unauditable
emergency cash store, which SB must have used for the flight
costs and Mount's spending wad. So, his ticket had been taken
care of, and his working cash. But no pistol.

Mount saw the Berlin flit as an untypical SB impulse, a
twitch. He would have to try to compensate through special
prudence and organization. But, of course, special prudence
and organization couldn't eliminate every risk. He'd shown
the Stanley Charles Naughton passport at Templehof, as usual,
and said the purpose of his visit was business, as usual. That
had seemed to be accepted by the squat little officer who let
him through. And it had always been all right when S.C.
Naughton had made his previous visits. Would there come a
time, though, when an officer started wondering what kind of
business this businessman, S.C. Naughton, did in Germany?
'Welcome to Berlin!' this officer had said, and gave a very
genuine looking smile. That disturbed Mount.

The training warned against lifts, and Mount did not use
one now on his way back to the apartment. Lifts made a noise.
And, when they reached your floor, and the doors automatically opened, there you were, cosily presented in a well-lit
metal box for someone with an automatic. He went quietly
and swiftly up the stairs. When he reached the apartment door,
he didn't attempt a subtle, almost silent, use of his key. Training
manuals recommended hard against this. No matter how subtle
you might be, the enemy inside, if it *was* an enemy, could be
expecting you and alert to the slightest sound. He would
deduce from your flagrant delicacy with the lock that you
expected trouble and that you were ready for it. Therefore,
your enemy would act first, before you could counter. That
is, you might be neutralized at once – given no chance to
defend yourself. The danger would obviously be greater if the
space you wanted to penetrate offered your enemy a cover of
darkness – possibly like the apartment – while you were fully
illuminated by your background when trying to enter, as Mount
might be: this was an expensive apartment block with good
amenities, including well-lit corridors. Against this, if you
rammed the key in as normal, and shoved the door back heartily
as normal, your enemy would think you unprepared and unsus-
picious. He might marginally delay. And that could offer the
opening to neutralize *him*. Or, of course, *her*.

Obviously, this bit of optimism only worked if you had a gun to neutralize him with before he neutralized you with his. But the manual and the training did cover occasions when the officer might have *no* gun, like Mount now. In such instances, key the door as noisily as you liked and swing it open as forcefully as you liked. But do not, DO NOT, attempt to go through it at this point, nor stand in the opening. Get to the side of the door space immediately, and out of sight from the hallway or room, no target. Perhaps like that you have won a fragment of surprise: he wouldn't know to which side of the open door you've gone. An unarmed-combat jugular chop blow might then be possible when he pushes his head out to see where you are, especially if he chooses to glance the wrong way first. Or she. But even if he – she – doesn't, you might have a chance, as long as you hit fast and hard, and on exactly the correct patch of neck. This correct patch of neck was, of course, also taught in training.

Mount opened the door wide and stood to its left, his back against the corridor wall. After a while, Toulmin called out in German from the living room: 'Is that you, Mr Naughton? Come in, do. No need to be shy in your own quarters.'

Mount stepped into the apartment and closed the door behind him. Toulmin was standing in the middle of the living room floor, plump, flushed, russet hair in retreat, fine tailoring, high-grade black shoes. Although he had sounded relaxed and jokey when he shouted just now, Mount felt some of that nervousness radiating from him, as he had occasionally in the past. But, after Mount's rigmarole with the door, perhaps *he* radiated nervousness, too. The room seemed pretty well as he had left it, but he sensed a difference, though he couldn't fix on what. Well, he knew he ought to have been able to fix on what: he was supposed to be a qualified spy, and spies were supposed to notice things.

He went to the kitchen and made coffee. Then he and Toulmin sat in a couple of the birch and metal armchairs. The door to one bedroom off this lounge was closed, the other slightly ajar. They'd been like this when he left for the cinema, hadn't they? Hadn't they? Oh, God, he ought to be certain about such details. The doubt showed pathetic slackness. It clashed with his decision to be extra watchful. In spying, you were always watchful. That's what spying meant. But at times, and quite frequent times, you had to pile on the watchfulness if you wanted to be alive and fit enough and free enough to go on being watchful, and possibly extra watchful, tomorrow.

What was it he feared? What he feared was simple and obvious. He feared what he and all other secret intelligence functionaries always feared: that one of their agents, while still apparently one of their agents, had in reality been turned and now served the other side. It would happen like this: the agent had been detected by a counter-espionage unit and arrested, interviewed, probably tortured, but, instead of getting immediately hanged, shot or garrotted, was forced to help trap someone bigger – the officer-spy he'd previously fed his insights to, such as Mount. If that worked, or if it didn't, the agent could still be hanged, shot or garrotted, but later: his captors had the penny and the bun.

Suppose this had happened to Toulmin. Had he brought people with him to eavesdrop on their discussion through a part open bedroom door, then make the more important catch – Mr Stanley Charles Naughton, so called? Was the yelled, wordy, formal, agreed, genial greeting from Toulmin meant to tell a reception group to get ready, safety catches off? Naturally, Toulmin would appear tense if he'd been recruited for that kind of plot. Mount saw no rough-house signs on Toulmin's face or hands. But it would be a basic precaution in this sort of catch-a-spy programme to concentrate interrogation brutalities on parts of the body normally covered by clothes, and to make sure nothing was broken, so that normal walking, talking, hand-shaking remained possibles. The agent could then be presented to the world and his espionage contact as undamaged, and false in only a two-faced way, not the three of a double agent: his normal workaday face; his secret face as an agent informing to an enemy, or potential enemy; his other secret face as an agent in reverse, and now informing against the alien officer-spy who had first recruited him as an informant.

'I've been to the cinema,' Mount said. He wanted some banal, unincriminating conversation, at least to start with while he went on assessing. This was how a businessman might talk. If he'd been to the cinema he'd say he'd been to the cinema, as explanation for his absence.

'Ah.'

'*The Blue Angel.*' He was Stanley Charles Naughton, a British businessman, and so spoke in English. Too much fluency in German might be unwise.

'This is a famous film.' Toulmin also used English.

'Marlene Dietrich,' Mount said.

'Indeed.'

'It's not new, yet it is still very effective.'

'I concur entirely.'

'It was the film that brought her to the attention of Hollywood,' Mount said.

'From being a German actress, she became an international star.'

'The first German film with sound.'

'Her voice – exciting and full of romance. It could be heard in this film, and that gave her additional opportunities to impress,' Toulmin said. It was as if he, also, wished to limit the conversation to harmless drivel. But that would be useless for an entrapment. He must get Mount to damn himself by talking spy matters. Of course, Mount had gone right through the apartment after his arrival from Templehof; an elementary drill. He struggled to remember how the place had been when he'd left for the cinema. Had he closed a bedroom door and left the other slightly open? The bedroom with the closed door now was the one he slept in. He had put his suitcase in there for unpacking later. His memory would take him no further than this.

'They made *The Blue Angel* in German and English,' Mount said.

'It contains the famous number 'Falling in Love Again'. A nightclub singer marries a professor, doesn't she? Another German film with "blue" in the title is *The Blue Light*. This was directed by the famous Leni Riefenstahl and concerns mountains, but I have not seen it.' Abruptly, he turned his head and yelled at the part-open door in German, "Come out now! Now!"' Both 'now!'s crackled with urgency, the second more.

At once, Mount stood, to be better able to defend himself. Not *much* better. Maybe worse: standing, he'd be a bigger target. Toulmin began to laugh very loudly, all stress seemingly gone, the treacherous sod. But in a treacherous trade, cater always for treachery. And Mount had, more or less. It should have been less of the less and more of the more, though.

The bedroom door was tugged fully open from inside and the two girls who had been here with Mount and Toulmin last time came slowly out. It had to be slowly because they carried an armchair between them, above their heads, both with two hands on it. Getting it and themselves through the door space and under the lintel demanded skilled manoeuvring and adjustments of height. They had all their clothes on. Now and then, despite the effort needed to hold the chair steady, they, too, laughed, but not an outright laugh like Toulmin's; rather, slightly breathless giggles. The chair matched exactly those Mount and Toulmin were sitting on tonight, and the one that collapsed under the weight and vim of Toulmin and the rounder of the girls, Olga, on that previous visit. It had furls of gift-wrapping here and there on its legs and armrests. They gazed up at the chair with a kind of reverence, as though it were a throne or a dear one's coffin. The girls did a lumbering dance with it to the spot in the living room where they'd decided it should go, like a burlesqued ballet scene by a couple of liquored stagehands. Now, they lowered the chair to the floor and stood proudly behind it.

'This is a gift,' Inge said in German. 'The three of us have bought it for you. We feared you might be in trouble with the apartment owner because you were one chair short. Or with the head of your business company who rents the apartment for you.'

'We will not put the chair to such use again,' Toulmin said. 'That previous occasion was deeply pleasant, but perhaps a little unwise.' He spoke German, too, now. 'Tonight, we will be more civilized, with your permission, Stanley.' He pointed to the bedrooms in turn. 'The same couples as before, I think. It would be deeply unromantic, otherwise, and take away some significance from the relationships.'

'This is true,' Olga said.

'You will not object to this sameness, Stanley?'

'How could I?' Mount replied.

'Yes, how could he?' Inge said. 'How could any of us?'

'There are some people who, in this type of situation, would wish for change.'

'Fortunately, we are not of that kind,' Olga said.

'We seek the meaningful,' Toulmin said.

Mount saw why Toulmin's chatter had been so safe and

ordinary: the girls believed he and Mount were business colleagues, only business colleagues, and the pretence must be nurtured. Mount felt comforted and a little guilty. Toulmin was not a tool of the *geheime Staatspolizei* – the secret State Police. It seemed offensive now to think he might have been. Perhaps he had come to the apartment during Mount's absence from Berlin to check the design label on an armchair so they could match it perfectly. Mount didn't feel happy about that, though Toulmin's and the girls' intent was entirely kind and good. And if you gave someone a key to your apartment, perhaps you should expect him to use it.

They had several drinks and danced a little to the gramophone. Mount had bought some Roseland, Carroll Gibbons and Woody Herman records on earlier visits. They did swap partners for some of the numbers, and Olga got a leg up hard into Mount's crotch for most of the slower, blues-style tunes she danced with him. Perhaps Inge did the same with Toulmin. But interchange went no further than this. Mount thought the girls would regard these dry rubs as simple friendliness, on an international basis, in his case.

It became very late. Mount decided the three should stay the night. He'd regard it as inhospitable to turn them out after such generosity about the chair. As Toulmin had suggested, Inge went to bed with Mount, and Olga with Toulmin, so as to preserve and develop the romantic nature of things, and their meaningfulness.

Next day, Mount got up early, hoping for a chance to talk to Toulmin alone before Inge and Olga awoke. Inge opened an eye as he left the bed and put trousers and a shirt on; then she surrendered to more sleep. Toulmin would have to go to his office at the normal morning time, but the girls probably didn't start work until evening. Mount made enough scrambled egg for four and a large pot of coffee. He considered eggs sustaining, and scrambling the easiest way to serve them.

While he was having breakfast in the kitchen, Toulmin appeared, already dressed, and asked if he could use Mount's electric razor. 'Have something first,' Mount said, pouring coffee and helping him to food. Toulmin sat opposite. 'These are girls who greatly help with relaxation and up to date are guaranteed clean,' he said.

'Their thoughtfulness concerning the broken chair is remarkable,' Mount replied.

'It is very typical of their character.'

'I need to know about Russia,' Mount replied as Toulmin ate.

'Russia? Yes, I thought that might be it,' he said. They spoke English.

'You know something of this?'

'I can see where a curiosity about such matters comes from. You wonder if there might be a future non-aggression treaty between Germany and the USSR – on top of the 1926 Neutrality Agreement?'

Mount wondered why Toulmin was considered only number two of the Berlin agents. 'My chief wonders. And what my chief wonders, I feel I'd better start wondering about myself.'

'Your chief is smart. Yes, there have been visitors to the Auswärtiges Amt.'

'To the Foreign Office. From Moscow?'

'Not of any great eminence. Not so far. Middle rank.'

'But you've seen or heard about these visitors to the AA? Perhaps clearing the way for other, more important visitors?' Mount said. 'Usual diplomatic procedure.'

'I wasn't sure you'd be interested, as they weren't major people. They are not people with power, no real power. They can't produce any immediate result.'

'Yes, interested.'

'I'll look for more on it, shall I?'

'Please. I know it might be very delicate.'

'Yes, delicate,' Toulmin said. 'That's one word for it.'

'Risky.'

'Yes, risky. The counter-spy experts from two countries, not just one, will make it so.'

'We'll work on arrangements to bring you out of Germany if things become difficult.'

'Yes, they might become difficult, as well as delicate and risky.'

'This will be very much in our mind,' Mount said. Toulmin would never speak about money. Mount had to show he knew the dangers and would see they were properly paid for, and in sterling or dollars, not the chaotic German mark. 'What about telegrams? Memoranda?' he said.

'Yes, some. I don't see everything, of course.'

'I think you're at Level Two for Confidentiality Clearance,' Mount said.

'Your index cards are very accurate. Yes, Level Two, and this is strictly applied. We Germans do apply regulations strictly, don't we? We are laughed at for that. However, I see some telegrams and so on.'

'And these would be from, and to, what you call "major people"?'

'State Secretary in the AA. Ambassadors. The Foreign Minister himself. But most of it vague, so far. I didn't think—'

'Friendly messages?'

Toulmin had a think about this, maybe unsure of the full implications in English of the word 'friendly'. He said: 'Constructive. Forward-looking. Each side suggests there could be even greater amity, greater commercial cooperation. Russia wants armaments from the Czech Skoda works and an "understanding" about her "sphere of influence". Russia would like to regard that sphere as fairly immense – the Baltic, the Black Sea, the Baltic States, Finland. Obviously, political and ideological differences have to be kicked into touch, as I believe you say. Communists and fascists don't normally fraternize much. But now, several telegrams from Berlin argue that the real enemies of both National Socialist Germany and the Soviet Union are not each other, but corrupt, imperialistic, aggressive capitalist Western democratic states. AA communications point out that Russia was dragged into the last war against Germany and suffered almost catastrophically for it. Now, says Berlin satirically, Western countries would like Russia to become an ally with them in a new war, also against Germany. Surely, our Foreign Office declares, the Soviet Union cannot really want that.' Toulmin stood. 'Now, I must shave, get myself looking presentable and go. This is important in the office. I have to be a model employee. Thus, the good suit, custom-made shoes. Thank you for breakfast. I hired a van to bring the chair. It's outside.'

'But Russia's Foreign Commissar, Litvinov, seems very pro-West. Does he favour this new sweetness towards the Reich?'

'Ah, Litvinov.'

'He shows no hostility to Britain. The reverse. Or am I being naive?'

'I get the feeling from some of these telegrams and from rumour in the office that Litvinov might not be there for much longer. A year? Less? He and Stalin disagree on fundamentals. It's extremely unprofitable to disagree with Stalin on fundamentals.'

'On anything.'

'Molotov will probably take over. Stalin favours him. Both of them suspect the West. Litvinov less so, as you say.'

Mount kept the eggs warm. At about nine thirty both girls got up. Mount had another cup of coffee with them while they took breakfast. 'He paid most towards the chair,' Olga said. 'Sam. He is a good man. I expect you know that.'

'Yes,' Mount said.

'What is his other name?'

'Toulmin.'

'Is that a German name?'

'I think a long time ago his family made clocks,' Mount replied.

'And we don't know *your* name,' Inge said. 'Except for Stanley.'

'I am in Germany quite often,' Mount said.

'You speak German very well.'

'My work requires it.'

'But some questions you don't answer,' Inge said.

'Probably this is true of many people,' Mount replied.

'Is that to do with your work?' Inge said.

'What?'

'Not answering questions,' Inge said.

'Naughton,' Mount replied. 'Stanley Charles Naughton. It's no secret, not at all. Why should it be?'

'I don't know why it should be,' Olga said.

'Germany today does not like people with secrets,' Inge said. 'Sometimes, the government will send officers to find out people's secrets. It's best not to have any.'

'I agree,' Mount said. 'Whether it's in Germany or elsewhere.'

'Elsewhere, secrets might be all right,' Olga said. 'Not here.'

'I'll remember that,' Mount said.

Not long after they had gone, someone knocked at the apartment door. A man's voice called: 'Naughton? Delivery.'

Mount checked through the judas hole. A couple of elderly, manageable-looking men in dungarees stood there alongside

a birch and metal armchair. He opened the door. They brought
the furniture in, carrying it in an unidolatrous, waist-level way,
very different from Inge and Olga, and as if a chair were only
a chair. They put it down near the one the girls had placed
there yesterday evening. In London, Section must have passed
on Mount's note about the disintegration of the original to
Overseas Accommodation and Equipment. Perhaps they had
complained to the manufacturer or the seller. Now came a
replacement. 'You are very fond of this kind of armchair?'
one of the men said, looking around the living room and
counting.

'I do a lot of entertaining,' Mount said. 'In the way of
business.'

'It's good to be comfortable. Our instructions were to ask
the caretaker to open the apartment if it was unoccupied. But
fortunately you are here.'

'Yes. Here I am. It *is* fortunate.' And it was: Overseas
Accommodation and Equipment wouldn't have known he'd
be in residence. It was an on-the-quiet visit, after all. He tipped
the men and they left.

On previous stays in Berlin, he'd noticed a high-quality
furniture shop near the Steglitz town hall, and he walked there
during the afternoon to ask if they'd come and take the newest
chair away. They could have it free. It seemed the simplest,
least bothersome way of dealing with the glut. When he
reached the shop, though, he found it closed down. A yellow
star had been stuck on the window alongside a notice saying
the business had temporarily ceased trading but would reopen
shortly under new ownership. He went to a hardware store
and bought a good sized screwdriver, a shifting spanner and
a saw. He wanted to make the job easier this time. In the
evening, he dismantled the fifth and newest chair and, as previously, disposed of the pieces in others' refuse bins. He felt it
would have been cruel to treat Toulmin's and the girls' chair
like that. 'Unromantic', to use Toulmin's word.

THREE

'I saw your lights from the street, Stanley, so I thought you might be here.'

'Well, yes,' Mount said. He'd been reading the *Völkischer Beobachter* newspaper – the *People's Observer* – when she rang the doorbell. It reported the likely invitation to the Führer from Britain's king Edward VIII and Wallis, his consort, to make a London state visit early in 1939. The half column piece said the Führer would be inclined to regard the invitation favourably. The paper ought to know. His party ran it. Mount felt totally sure that, if the abdication had gone through, as had seemed more or less certain for a while at the end of '36, there would have been no possibility of such an offer to dear Adolf from Eddie's successor. Actually, Mount had heard that Edward liked to be called by one of his other first names – David. Certainly not Eddie. As SB had said, the king and Wallis were very fond of Europe, and Adolf was a notable part of Europe.

'I wondered if you had seen him,' she said. 'Or even if he might be here.'

'Toulmin? Well, no, he hasn't returned. Not since you three brought the chair, and so on.'

'I worry about him.'

'But it's only been a week.' Mount was worried about him, too, though. He might have started those Russian inquiries and, as they'd agreed, these could be 'delicate'.

'Usually, he comes to see me or Inge every few days, never more than three. It's necessary for him – his health. He gets congested.'

'That can be very nasty.'

'The way he's built. Not tall. Stuff can build up. It has been made worse by the incident with the chair. Not immediate, obvious injuries, but his ribs. I feel some guilt. He was underneath. It had seemed quite a natural celebration at the time.'

'Undoubtedly. So he hasn't appeared lately?'

'Not since that same night you spoke of. But perhaps, as you say, it's not important.'

'I think he might be busy,' Mount said. They talked in German.

'Yes, perhaps.' But it was clear Olga didn't think much of his reply. Not quite a frown and not quite a grimace took over her face for half a second. 'I would like to explain,' she said and put patience into her voice, like a teacher to a dullish pupil. 'You speak German very well, yes, almost like a German, but this does not mean you know everything about our country.'

He thought he probably knew more about her country than she realized, and more about some aspects of it than herself, but he said: 'No, indeed. I am only a temporary visitor, and my interests are narrow – are concentrated in a particular commercial area. This is why it is so helpful to meet German friends such as you and Inge. From you I can learn things about Germany that I might not otherwise discover. You widen my view, and I'm grateful.'

'In our country at present, Stanley, if someone stops doing what he usually does, such as a regular meeting, and a necessary meeting for his well-being, you have to begin to wonder about him – about what has happened to him. This is a man who often seemed very nervous. I don't know if you noticed that.'

'Nervous? No.'

She waved a hand, as if to knock this objection and denial into a corner somewhere to be eaten by the cat. 'In our country at present, if people seem nervous, there is usually a reason for this. Events make people nervous. People fear that such events may happen to them. This causes nervousness.'

'It would.'

'Events occur quite often now.'

'I see.'

'Events of a particular kind,' she said. 'Obviously, there have always been events. But events now are different.'

'This is the kind of thing where I would need your guidance.'

'You won't see anything about such events in the newspaper you were reading, but these events take place all the same. We have to ask whether through carelessness or overboldness he has put himself into circumstances where he might suffer such bad events.'

'Toulmin?'

'We like him, both of us. It's not just the payments.'

'I like him, also.'

'He is your business colleague.'

'Yes, business, but also a friend,' Mount said.

'He is a man who has enough money to see us in an active manner quite often, but who also worried about your chair. This is not always the case with men. Some would regard the chair's collapse as of no concern to them, or even amusing, or a proof of their manly force, despite inner, chronic congestion. It is the type of thing they might talk about to their friends with a guffaw. No tact.'

'Yes, he is kindly. I don't regard him as of the guffawing sort. He definitely has never guffawed to me.'

'He is generous. But, I would say again, it is not just the fees and gifts at festivals and other holidays, especially Easter.'

'No.'

'We feel a bond.'

'I can see how that would come about,' Mount said.

'We thought that, because he is a business colleague, you might know where his workplace is, and you could, perhaps, telephone to see if he is in his office – merely to find if he is well. We think his job would be in an office because of the fine clothes he wears, and his hands are soft. Or you might know where he lives. You could inquire there. It would be quite natural for you to telephone his office or his home and say, "This is Stanley Charles Naughton, and I would like to speak to Mr Samuel Toulmin, please, if he is there. I am a colleague." We don't know where he works, or his home. This is quite usual about the men we see. It's how they prefer things to be. They do not want us to get in touch with them. It has to be the other way. That is, *they* get in touch with *us*, usually through the Toledo. To approach his place of work or his home would not be right for Inge or me, even if we knew where they were. Parts of people's lives have to be kept separate in some cases. This is what is known as tact and proper procedure. We are from a certain side of life. For instance, he might be married, or living with his aged mother, and it would be wrong to inconvenience her. Are you married?'

'No. And my mother spends most of the year in Cannes.' The second part was untrue. His mother spent most of the year in Italy. He wanted to seem friendly and conversational and informative, though not tense about Toulmin. But never overdo truth. That advice did not come from a training manual; Mount had worked it out for himself. Perhaps he'd write a training manual himself when he retired and, if so, he'd include the warning about excessive truth. In this trade you soon learned that truth could come back and bite you, even what seemed inconsequential truth. Don't believe that Keats wind-baggery about truth being beauty and vice versa. Truth could be ugly and murderous. A careful mix of *some* truth and lies usually served well to keep you out of reach, as long as you could remember which was the truth and which the lies. Mount thought he usually could. Some said that human and animal intelligence could be measured according to the ability to tell differences between things. Pretty often Mount could tell the difference between truth and lies; his own, that is. It was a kind of flair.

They drank tea. Olga had called on him at the apartment in the early evening, probably before she went to work. The demolition of the laminated birch and metal chair might become one of those trivial incidents that could by ludicrous misfortune threaten the security of an operation, and his own. Although SB would probably not object to Mount and Toulmin bringing girls back once to the apartment, he would be very perturbed to know they'd turned up for a second night, and that one of them had now come back again, and with a difficult request.

Well, SB *wouldn't* know – or not from Mount, at least.

'Which business is your business, and your colleague's?' Olga said. 'Or is this another of those questions you do not answer?' She had on a long, navy blue, admiral-style great-coat over a scarlet low-cut blouse and tight black skirt.

'Yes, I could certainly do some asking round and about concerning Toulmin,' Mount replied.

'It might be nothing at all, or that he is ill. Or requires someone new. There's a French phrase for this: "*Avoir besoin d'un changement.*"' She said it in squeaky French, then resumed in German. 'To need a change. Men can be like that. Excuse me – I speak in general. Men in general, as a species, not necessarily you.'

'Yes, I suppose so,' Mount said. She'd be about twenty-two

and seemed young for such big insights and sexual finesse.
He thought she must have briefed herself very thoroughly,
preparing her material well into the afternoon.

'We would not regard it as disloyal if he went somewhere
else. He might have decided he wants unusual, spicy activities from a girl. Or what he would regard as unusual and spicy.
We could offer that, yes, but if things have always gone in a
certain fashion with us he perhaps thinks this is all we wish
to do, and he would look somewhere else now and then for
novelty and bodily adventure. Although he and I broke the
chair together, despite its metal legs, he might like something
even more unusual than that. I believe your country has a
saying: "A change is as good as a rest."' For that, she switched
to English momentarily. 'This may be very true. The same
sort of view as the French.' She gazed at Mount, her squarish,
broad nosed face alight with reasonableness. He saw worry
there as well, though. She seemed to feel a responsibility for
Toulmin – in the conditions of 'our country at present'. She
was emotionally advanced and various. Maybe jubilant anni-
hilation of the chair showed only one strand of her character.
Inge might be equally serious.

'It's good of you both to feel so . . . well . . . tolerant about
where he chooses to go,' Mount said.

'If you should find him, please say we can do anything he
chooses. Anything. Pain infliction is by no means excluded
if wanted – and *only* if wanted – and imprisonment by rope
or chain. Location on the body for pain entirely the client's
choice, as in an à la carte menu. Because you are friends, he
will not object that such a personal matter comes from you.
We could make suggestions to him in a creative sense. He
should not regard Inge and me as limited or merely traditional. And Inge has certain extra amusing accessories,
humane, not ugly, hygienic and laboratory tested.'

'I'll mention that.'

'Do these interest *you*?'

'What?'

'Accessories.'

'Thanks, but I'm going to be very taken up with business.'

She rose to go. They had been sitting in the birch and metal
armchairs. She looked around. 'A beautiful room,' she said.
'The four chairs – this number is exactly suitable.'

'I think so.'

'Three was not right. The room lacked . . . lacked spirit. But now, a delightful wholeness.'

'Yes.' What about five?

'Great care should be taken when it is a matter of chairs in a room.'

'*Great* care.' He walked with her to the apartment door. 'I think it would be best if you and Inge let me do all the searching for him.'

'Oh, why is that?'

Because if something bad had happened to Toulmin they shouldn't risk showing they'd known him well and often. There might be a search out for his acquaintances. Something bad could happen to them, too. Some of those 'events' could happen. That's how the system worked in her country at present. Did she understand that dangerous concept, 'guilt by association'?

'Yes,' he said, 'it would be best if I looked for him solo.'

'Is there something unusual about your kind of business, and his?' she said.

'Unusual in which way?'

'Yes, unusual.'

'Businesses do have some unusual aspects, certainly,' Mount said. 'All kinds of businesses.'

'Which kind of business is yours?'

'Every business is ultimately about buying and selling.'

'I'm a business,' she said. 'Men come to buy, and if the price they offer is a fair one, I sell. I sell some of my time, and so on.'

'That isn't how Sam Toulmin and I think of you. Or Inge.'

'You have some of that quality I mentioned – tact. And *your* business? What is it you buy or sell?'

'Some travel is often involved in commerce,' Mount replied.

'Is it strange to have lights on so early? Is this meant to say you are here, or will soon be here, as it said that to me? Also for him? Perhaps it is not so easy for you to be in touch, after all.'

'And I know where to find you – the Toledo bar,' Mount said. 'I'll come and report anything I discover. But, of course, he might have returned to see you or Inge himself before then, on account of his congestion, and, because, more than that, I'm sure he enjoys seeing you very much.'

'You don't like me visiting here, for fear of your neighbours forming an opinion? Yet, this call might be only to do
with simple business details. I *am* a business, as we've just
found out. Nothing has been bought or sold today, it's true,
but I always have with me what can be sold, always, so this
could have been a simple business matter.' She pulled the big
coat around her, concealing the other clothes, as if to indicate
that a business woman should be ready for all conditions, all
weathers. A coat like this would be good for concealing some
of Inge's accessories when visiting as a pair to cope with
special tastes.

Olga left. Mount heard the lift come up and then descend.
Almost as soon as the noise of it stopped, he found he wanted
to go after her and repeat that neither she nor Inge should try
to find Toulmin. Olga had seemed casual about his advice.
'Oh, why is that?' she'd said in reply, as if he'd need to prove
it would be dangerous, and hadn't proved it so far. Mount felt
a duty to emphasize this warning. If he ran after her now in
the street she would realize how anxious he must be. Although
she knew something of what her country was like at present,
she might not know thoroughly enough what her country was
like at present. On the other hand, *he*, the professional, was
paid to know what her country was like at present, and he
had been expertly trained to discover what this and other countries were like at present and to record fully how they were.

The girls should not make themselves noticeable by seeking
information on Toulmin, in case his absence did result from
. . . from something dark. As her country was at present, it
had become easy to make one's self noticeable in it. He felt
protective, just as Olga seemed protective of Toulmin. People
were drawn together for reciprocal help when a country was
like her country was at present. And he believed his attitude
to be simple, genuine worry about her and Inge's safety. It
was, wasn't it? Was it? Of course, if they started getting attention themselves from the authorities because, connected with
Toulmin, they might also supply a link to this apartment and
to Mount, as Stanley Charles Naughton . . .

Despite Olga's queries just now on the lights as signals,
and the nature of the business, she and Inge would have no
real cause to think the apartment secret, nor Stanley Charles
Naughton secret. Hadn't he told them his name was not

confidential? Even without pressure they might talk about it and him, though; if they were pulled in as suspicious, there probably *would* be pressure.

But this concern for the apartment and himself came only second to his concern for the girls personally, didn't it? Didn't it? Did it? He hoped so. His thinking would be dismally selfish – dismally and ruthlessly job-based – otherwise. And damn cowardly.

By the time he had chewed all this over, he realized she might have gone out of sight in the street, or one of the side streets. He went down, anyway, and stood outside the apartment block looking for her. He could spot no long, dark, quarterdeck-style overcoat below dark hair. He realized he might appear a bit frantic, and therefore conspicuous. It was not wise to get himself or the apartment block noticed. Stephen Bilson would have roasted him for this kind of panicky, flagrant behaviour. Mount wondered whether his attempt to spot Olga and talk to her again was not much more than a token, anyway: he'd known he'd be too late.

This pathetic mental shiftiness made him think back to his earliest days in the spy trade. At the end of training, officers were entitled to see their assessment reports. These contained three areas of appraisal: Physical, Intellectual, Psychological. He could recall some of the phrases word-perfect. His 'Psychological Silhouette' had said Mount liked sometimes to 'make a show of moral concerns' as they affected his work, but luckily this was *only* a show and probably wouldn't mess up 'his effectiveness in the Service'.

Did they have this right – disgustingly, blazingly right?

The silhouette had gone on to state that Mount probably was not cut out for the higher ranks in the Service because of his 'excessive, unwise, compulsive self-questioning and enfeebling doubts', but might be OK 'when rigorously supervised' at a middle or lower level. Without much relevance that Mount could see, the profile had added that he seemed 'predominantly hetero at present (see, Physical Silhouette)'.

Was his concern for Olga and Inge only a show? Mount recognized that too much human sympathy could be a weakness in this career; could even have a touch of absurdity about it. You didn't join to help old ladies cross the street. And you couldn't put the welfare of a couple of Jerry tarts before the interests of the Service, even if the present interests of the Service did seem to him woolly and too hastily picked. The Service had its eye on what was comfortingly known as 'the greater good'. That is, the safety and continuance of the nation. These did not come as the natural, God-given state of things. They needed looking after. Only if that safety and contin-uance were properly guarded could pleasant qualities like human sympathy have any chance. Put more starkly, 'the greater good' meant the end might justify the means, and ends often did in this occupation. Only the ends came to be known about. The means usually stayed secret, especially if they were dubious or worse, and frequently they were.

On his way back up the stairs he met a hefty middle-aged, anxious looking woman coming down, most likely from a third-floor apartment. 'You are another one who does not trust lifts,' she said.

'I try to avoid them.'

'May I ask you something?'

'Certainly.'

'It is of a personal nature. That is how it could be regarded.'

'Very well.'

'Pieces of a broken chair have been put in my bin and the bins of several others. Have pieces of a broken chair been put in *your* bin?'

'I haven't looked.'

'You should look, in case pieces of a broken chair have been placed there.'

'Well, I will,' Mount said.

'This is the second time pieces of a broken chair have been placed in my bin. On each occasion they are pieces from the same kind of chair. What is happening in these apartments if chairs of this type are being constantly broken and put into residents' bins? I do not want those who empty the bins to think I am always breaking chairs of a certain type.'

'Which type are they?'

'Birch and metal. Laminated.'

'One would have expected chairs of that sort to be strong.'

'The question to be asked is, are the pieces of chair put into the bins by somebody who lives in these apartments, or does an outsider bring them?'

'I should think almost certainly an outsider,' Mount said.

'It would be disturbing to think anyone in the building might do it. A resident should surely put the pieces in their own bin if a chair became broken.'

'Or chairs. You believe someone, or more than one, would carry pieces of chair in the street and bring them to this apartment building?'

'Perhaps not obviously pieces of chair. They could be wrapped. Other people carry parcels in the street after shopping, or on their way to someone with a gift, so that a wrapped piece of chair brought to the bins should not be noticeable. The bins are very accessible.'

'But may I say what I believe?'

'Please.'

'There is a furniture shop not far from here.'

'Yes, I know it.'

'This shop has been closed down.'

'Yes.'

'For a long time. The reason is plain.' She glanced about, up and down the stairs.

'Yes, plain,' Mount said.

'Perhaps someone who bought chairs from that shop before it was closed down is now ashamed, even frightened, about that, and wishes to get rid of them in a gradual, secretive manner, so as not to be discovered owning chairs from such a tainted shop. It is said the shop will reopen, but this has not happened. Therefore someone who bought chairs from the shop as it was previously could not claim to have bought the chairs from the reopened shop. Dismembering the chair or the chairs would be a final solution. But, by putting these pieces in other people's bins, whoever does it might bring blame on those other people, such as myself, and perhaps you, as if *we* had bought the chairs. This is a disgraceful slur.'

'There will be many theories about the pieces in the bins, I expect,' Mount replied.

'Soon, there might be more pieces of chair in bins. Usually, people have more than one or two chairs in their apartment, either here or elsewhere, because of visitors sometimes wishing to sit, at least one chair being required by the host or hosts.'

'An apartment without enough armchairs always seems to me to lack spirit,' Mount replied. 'Great care should be taken in choosing the right number of chairs for an apartment.'

'I don't think it is a matter for the police – not so far,' she said.

'No.'

'It might not be an offence to put chair pieces into bins. It is not theft. In a way, it is the opposite of theft.' She laughed a while at the contrariness of this. She had a large, oval face. Talking about her worries seemed to have calmed her.

'I agree with your views about legal points,' Mount said. He could have done without a mention of the police – even a negative mention 'so far' – but on the whole he enjoyed the conversation. It was neighbourly. It lit up the bit of staircase landing, otherwise dour, though carpeted hotel-quality in crimson. Spontaneously, she treated him as like-minded, part of a community. She had thick fingered boxer's fists and wide feet that would have given solid purchase on the canvas when leading with a punch, left or right. She wore pink rimmed spectacles and watched Mount's face carefully for changes of expression as they spoke. Some of her views reeked, yes, but she willingly discussed them with Mount, as if certain he would go along. From the job point of view, the content of what she said didn't matter, only that she chose to say it, and to him, in full, confiding style. He kept his amiable look on, occasionally increasing it to extremely amiable. There'd been no training on management of one's features, but Mount considered he had an inborn gift. It seemed to work now. For a few minutes they became friends. Acceptance. Everybody in his kind of work longed and schemed for this: integration, a spy's grail. During an utterly fortuitous meeting, she had at once shown him the ins and outs of her thinking: some of it obnoxious, some of it fairly sane. For instance, people *did* generally have more than one or two armchairs in their apartment in case more than one or two people wanted to sit down at the same time, the host or hosts requiring at least one chair for himself or herself or themselves. The logic of this was unassailable.

Back in his own apartment he sat alone in an armchair, though, and tried to do some planning. Of course, Olga had it hopelessly wrong when she said Mount should find it easy to check at Toulmin's office or home that he was all right. The girls couldn't ask at these places for fear of embarrassing Toulmin. Ditto. Mount couldn't ask about Toulmin at these places, either, for fear of embarrassing him, and embarrassing him far more severely than the girls: embarrassing him possibly to death.

Mount could probably safeguard his own anonymity by ringing the Foreign Ministry from a public phone, and asking for Konrad Eisen, Toulmin's real name. But anything incoming on the general lines would go through a switchboard, and who would trust government switchboards in this country as it was at present, or, come to that, government switchboards anywhere at any time? Germany kept an exceptionally strict eye on government employees since the formidable 1933 'Restoration of the Civil Service' law. If Toulmin had been exposed and arrested, the switchboard might have instructions to divert any calls for him. Possibly, someone else would reply and apologize courteously for Konrad Eisen's absence, while trying to find the purpose of Mount's call and his name and address and present location – particularly that, yes very particularly that – and, in any case, keep him chatting.

Instant hang up by Mount would follow, to defeat a trace, and this must be the end of all inquiries at the office, and the end of any nearness by Mount now or ever to that phone booth. But, in fact, he knew he could not risk such a call, in case Eisen-Toulmin *was* still at the Ministry and liable to be pinpointed by it. To ring would be diametrically against all agreed procedures for contact.

So, then, should he get down to the Wilhelmstrasse in the morning or evening or both and try to intercept Eisen, known as Toulmin, between the station and the Foreign Ministry building there, on his way in or out? Irksome. Had he allowed Olga's worries to take an unwarranted hold? They hardly added up to much: a client fails to arrive for a week to a couple of girls, and this gets the alarms going. Did that seem reasonable, even taking proper account of what this country was at present and of Toulmin's congestion? In Mount's view, the whole project had started from panic – SB's strange tremor of regret – and perhaps now drops of it had percolated through to Mount. Maybe; if a man as habitually solid as SB could panic, panic must have something to be said for it occasionally, such as on *this* occasion.

Anyway, Mount decided to carry out some loitering near the Ministry at the right times on three successive days.

He didn't think he would be noticeable. Because of its clutch of famous and historic government buildings the area attracted tourists, and he could merge: the area was known as Diplomatstrasse. They would see the new Reich Chancellery under construction for Hitler at the junction of Voss Strasse and Wilhelmstrasse, and not far-off was the Unter den Linden, one of Berlin's main drags. He hadn't settled what to do if he spotted Toulmin. At least he'd have proved Toulmin existed still. But this wouldn't explain why he had not appeared lately – supposing the girls' anxieties made sense. Should Mount try to speak to him? If they'd turned Toulmin, might this be what they were waiting for, planning for, keeping Toulmin apparently unmarked and able to walk for? Would he have plain clothes attendants nearby, ready to bag any stranger who approached? It could be the simplest of pounces. Mount remained uncertain how to react, hoped he'd make the right instinctive decision at the time. Possibly, he'd get some kind of signal from Toulmin: warning him off, or welcoming him.

In fact, though, Mount's ardent shilly-shallying didn't matter. He foot-leathered around the big buildings and wide streets, staring everywhere, as if seeing it all for the first time. His staring never found Eisen-Toulmin. Accosting wasn't offered.

After the third evening's dud duty, Mount went to the Toledo club, hoping Toulmin might have by now come back to Inge and Olga. Perhaps he had somehow missed him around the Wilhelmstrasse. Perhaps Toulmin had been ill at home or even in hospital. Inge wasn't present in the club. She had several appointments of a charmingly established type every other Tuesday, Olga said – consecutive bookings. They had not seen Toulmin. Mount and Olga drank rum and blackcurrant together at the bar. She seemed to think he might like her to return to the apartment with him. 'Inge does not take her accessories with her for the Tuesday appointments. They are not required. These clients are elderly and physically limited in what they can do. Inge leaves her accessories here behind the bar. I am certainly entitled to borrow them,' she said in a pleasantly inquiring tone.

He'd make sure no further chair breakage occurred. Tomorrow, when she had left after breakfast, he must take the underground again, this time to the eastern suburbs where

Toulmin had a flat in the Lichtenberg district. A loiter here might be more risky – the same sort of possibilities, but stronger. If something bad had happened to him, his home could be under watch, in the hope of catching contacts like Mount. Toulmin, who was Eisen, lived alone after a divorce, or lived alone last time his dossier was adjusted. No children.

Mount had his details on recall: address, home telephone number, real name – Konrad Paul Eisen – former wife's name, political sympathies, career stages to date, present salary, parents, siblings; nothing written. Notes were peril. To offset the need for them, there had been two days in training given to memory exercises and tests. Besides those word-for-word extracts from his 'Psychological Silhouette', he could still recite a big slab of Robert Burton's *Anatomy of Melancholy*, one paragraph of it backwards, starting with 'laughter of occasion ridiculous or cause such no', instead of 'no such cause or ridiculous occasion of laughter'. Oliver Fallows, in the Section, could do the first half of Browning's poem 'Fra Lippo Lippi' – in English, 'Friar Lippo Lippi' – backwards, and would, if you encouraged him, finishing on the title, 'Lippi Lippo Fra', which he thought had a better ring to it than the original.

FOUR

An officer in the field had a lot of autonomy, and Mount decided he needed no authorization from London to burgle Toulmin's place. '*Please, sir, may I spin his drum?*' Serfish. Of course, he hoped a break-in would not be necessary. He'd walk the streets around where Toulmin lived in the hope of seeing him coming or going, just as he had walked the streets around the Foreign Office. But if this search also failed he might have to get inside the apartment somehow.

His training course had spent a week on how to break into properties and do a thorough rummage – so, clearly, they expected you to break into properties and do a thorough rummage some time, times. He'd been issued with very effective 'children', as lock-busting equipment was known. The term came from rhyming slang: children = boys and girls = twirls, slang for skeleton keys. But he guessed that a request now for permission to pop into Toulmin's nest on the quiet would be refused. He'd never convince Stephen Bilson the urgency justified the risk. After all, the real impulse came from Inge and Olga and their anxieties over Toulmin's untreated congestion, apparently made worse by hitting the floor in the furniture mishap with Olga on top of him. SB was better off not knowing this, especially as Mount's report to London on the ruined chair had been an outright lie. Suppose he went ahead and it came to light he'd ignored the ban on forced entry; Mount would most likely get kicked out of the Service. What kind of job could an ex-snoop get? Yellow Press reporter, maybe. He didn't think much of that, though.

Any break-in would involve two different peril types. First, to Mount, personally and physically, and through him to Toulmin. If they'd detected and arrested him, Mount's search would give final proof of Eisen-Toulmin's treachery: a spy suddenly short of whispers had turned up desperately seeking his whisperer. Get both into a Gestapo sack. Second, came the prospect of an appallingly flagrant espionage catastrophe that would fracture Anglo-German relations and put at hazard Hitler's state visit to London, so dear to the king. If SB considered any or either of these likely, he might urgently pull Mount out of Germany. This wouldn't be another panic, but tactics, based on a profit and loss forecast. In that estimate, loss might look much likelier. SB had seen God knew how many troops sent to their death in the war. The experience made him careful with his men's and women's lives. Also, he'd want to safeguard the Hitler visit, if that's what Edward and Wallis desired, and what he might desire for his own purposes, also. The monarch employed him, was his commander in chief. Fealty: SB owed it, existed for it.

Mount didn't feel ready to quit Berlin yet, though. He'd look like someone who did a bunk when things went rough and left his agent to the hunters. Wasn't Mount bound to feel big loyalty to someone he'd taken part with in a thoroughgoing foursome, this in addition to Toulmin's worth as an informed, informer voice? If things went rougher Mount might still have to run, or try to: effect 'instant unscheduled closure of mission and withdrawal', as the official vocab went.

Decoded and de-euphemized, 'unscheduled' meant 'Christ, they're on to us'. And 'withdrawal' meant 'make a run for it'. But he judged galloping retreat not at all necessary so far.

He did recognize another worrying uncertainty. If they knew about Toulmin, how *long* had they known and watched him? As a result, did they also know about Toulmin's trysts at the Steglitz apartment, and about Stanley Charles Naughton? Mount wondered, and knew SB would also wonder. Mount chose not to make him wonder even more by disclosing too much. At any rate, not immediately. Mount thought of the woman on the stairs and the broken chair conversation. Was she really just a woman on the stairs and the broken chair conversation only a broken chair conversation? Did she report back somewhere? And report back what?

But he mustn't let himself get paralysed by such doubts and frets. The training preached carefulness, yes, but also enterprise, resolve, audacity. He began to plan the break-in. It might be unavoidable. There'd be two objectives. One: discover if Toulmin were there, possibly dead. Two: suppose Toulmin weren't in there dead, look for anything that might say what had happened to him: mainly, this meant documents, notebooks, memos, blood and bone fragments on the wallpaper, photographs, letters. He saw complexities:

(1) He must decide the best time of day or night for it.
(2) No window entry was possible because Toulmin didn't live on the ground floor, so Mount would need a reconnaissance to identify the apartment from inside the building, before an actual crack at entering.

At Lichtenberg, Toulmin's place was in one of those famous apartment blocks made of prefabricated concrete slabs, *plattenbauten*. Mount loved the mass-produced look of them. For coolness and lack of frippery, these buildings went even further than the 'New Objectivity' creations in Steglitz. People needed accommodation, and they could get it in Lichtenberg behind such gorgeously unfancy, swiftly installed walls. Plain, utilitarian, grey-buff facades announced their honest purposeful purpose – shelter. This was how architecture should be. It recognized a job had to be done and did it. A crane swung

an arm about for a couple of days a few years ago, dangling
those destined jigsaw rectangles, and suddenly, out of nothing,
homes arrived. Hitler often demanded living room for the
German people, *Lebensraum*. Well, voilà, old cock! Plenty of
living rooms here in neat, two and three storey developments.

Mount had been brought up in Bath when not away at
school. His mother still lived there for some of the year. You
could get sickened by the saucy elegance and swank of all
that smug Georgian stuff in piss-yellow local stone. Beau
Nash, the eighteenth-century Welsh dandy-fop, delighted in
Bath. Naturally he did. Curved streets – why? Flamboyant.
Someone had had a bad attack of geometry: describe an arc
and call it Royal Crescent.

You didn't get any of that malarkey in Lichtenberg. When
they originally took on Toulmin as an agent, Mount and Nicholas
Baillie secretly tailed him home one evening to check he lived
where he said: standard courtesy for new chums, or those
wanting to become chums. Mount fell for the construction style
then, rhapsodized to Baillie about its clever practicality. Nick
objected. He *would*. While doing an ink sketch of the frontage
to mark out what they guessed to be the Eisen or Toulmin
windows, he had sounded off with the stock arty chatter about
concrete's drab impersonality and the inherent slabbiness of
slabs. The buildings looked jaily even without iron bars, he'd
said. Anyone could tell he was stuck with standard, snobby
Cambridge reverence for the pretty lines of King's College.
Of course slabs were slabby. Slabbiness kept winter out.
Personality? Yes, they had personality – dutiful, protective,
unpretentious, good at fitting in.

Mount had memorized Baillie's drawing and could identify what might be the windows of Toulmin's apartment, just
as Toulmin could identify *his* second floor flat in Steglitz,
though Toulmin never had to signal a welcome with lights,
because the rules of contact said Mount must not, repeat NOT,
come calling, or even hang about the district. Visits might
deeply imperil the host. And in usual conditions Mount
wouldn't have visited or even reconnoitred. Conditions,
though, had become very *un*usual, hadn't they? He thought
he might have to break in and do a nose about. The apartment was the only concrete – concrete! – connection he had
with Toulmin now. It gave a focus, of a sort. He didn't know

which sort, only that it seemed more precise than wandering around the Diplomatstrasse pavements near the Foreign Ministry.

But the break-in must be a far-off prospect. It assumed he never saw Toulmin coming or going outside, and never managed a word or two. It also assumed the apartment remained dark at night. In a sense, Mount *did* want a signal from Toulmin's lights. Of course, if the lights came on they wouldn't necessarily prove Toulmin was present, or Toulmin alone. There might be a reception group, devoted to the Fatherland and Lugers, hoping to catch someone searching for him at one of the two most likely spots: his home and the Ministry.

Mount began to list in his head further difficulties in this operation. He resumed the numbering:

> (3) The need to identify Toulmin's apartment from inside the building arose because, when he and Bailey had checked Toulmin's address, they decided it would be too obvious to follow him up stairs and along a corridor as far as his front door. It would have required them to stay impractically close. The fact that he'd gone into the building was enough. If he'd noticed them it could have made him feel not wholly trusted. And, of course, he wasn't, at that early stage, when he hadn't been fully transformed from Konrad Paul Eisen into Samuel Toulmin. But you had to look after an agent's self-esteem and morale, in case you needed to exploit them some time. They thought they'd glimpsed him momentarily at one of the windows just after they'd stopped following, and this gave Baillie the basis for his sketch.
>
> (4) Mount would have to note the door's type – solid wood or ply on a frame.
>
> (5) Note, also, the number and nature of lock, locks. Did they look ticklable by the bunch of children?
>
> (6) He must assess the likelihood or not of getting enough time in a corridor to open the door unobserved by neighbours. But, clearly, it would be a guess, not a proper assessment: no telling when

someone might pop out from one of the other
nearby flats to go to the *bierkeller*, or smash up
a few shops owned by Jews, if any still were.

(7) He'd need to be alert for signs that the apartment
had become a trap, though he couldn't itemize
what those signs might be. If they were in there,
eager for his arrival, they wouldn't put a sentry
on the door outside or a 'Knock and Enter' plaque.
For this kind of situation, training had suggested
trying to detect whether cigarette smoke escaped
under the door and/or through the keyhole. Well,
yes. But did he have nostrils sensitive enough to
smell it, and the time to smell it on a quick, pre-
break-in, research walk through the building?

(8) He ought to observe if there were anyone, or more
than one, keeping an eye on the block and on
everybody who entered – particularly on somebody like Mount, who blatantly wouldn't have an
apartment to go to or call at.

(9) If there were such patrols, that might be the end
of things. They'd nab him, most probably, or at
least glue continuous surveillance to him. Which
would close down all activity. There'd be no break-
in at the apartment and possibly no more safety
at Steglitz. He would have to implement 'instant
unscheduled closure of mission and withdrawal'
from Berlin; in fact, from Germany. If, that is,
they'd permit withdrawal, which, obviously, they
wouldn't. You didn't concoct a trap for someone
so as to let him out of it.

Before entering the block for his look-around, Mount walked
the streets near Toulmin's flat at all times of the day and night
for half a week. He did not concentrate any longer on the go-
to-work and return-from-work hours. That would be illogical.
Hadn't Mount's failed trawls proved Toulmin was absent from
the Foreign Ministry? Now, his trawls at Lichtenberg seemed
to prove Toulmin was absent also from his flat. Mount did
not encounter him about the streets, and no lights shone in
his windows at night, although the curtains were back. He
had to keep in mind that, if things had gone wrong for Toulmin,

they'd be paying attention to this entire area, as well as to the apartment itself, *qui viving* for any of his spy-trade contacts doing a heartfelt search for him. Mount was a spy-trade contact doing a heartfelt search for him. He varied his routes and walked as if he had a destination and an aim. He *did* have a destination and an aim, but he'd rather not be asked what these were, for instance by a trio of intent and bulky lads in an unmarked car. Of course, nearly all cars he saw were unmarked. He eyed each of them. It was the driver and passengers who interested him, not the vehicles as vehicles, especially if the driver and passengers looked intent and bulky and male.

Suppose such a patrolling contingent did show up and stop him and invite conversation, or at least invite answers to questions, what should he say about his reasons for being here? And, if they had spotted him previously, what should he say about his reasons for being here not only now, but regularly for the last few days? Could he say – credibly say – he was thinking of coming to live in this area and wanted to give it a good once-over before making his choice? Yes, he could say that, he hoped credibly. Yes, he would have to say that. He couldn't think of anything else to say. He made himself remember street names, so he could express an interest in dwellings here or there, or register distaste for other streets. It might be an idea to find an estate agent somewhere and get a load of brochures about lettings or sales.

To keep himself reasonably calm and clear-headed about why he had come to Berlin at all, he went over in his head as he walked more of SB's briefing at their private Section meeting. 'Oh, yes,' Bilson had said, 'Russia and Germany might look like inevitable enemies. But such appearances are always adjustable, in the interests of survival. Survival is quite a motivator. Think of Darwin.'

'But which of those two might have fears for their survival?'

'Russia was excluded from that snug little Munich *causerie* from which our Prime Minister has just returned.'

'Russia's interests were not directly involved, were they?' Oh, hell, did that show more naivety, Mount wondered.

Bilson had been patient. 'It depends what we mean by "directly", doesn't it, Marcus? Try to see the Munich chats as Stalin might. He observes Britain, France, Italy, Germany

apparently cosily concordatting. Does Moscow suddenly feel
shut out and menaced by a gang of four?'

'The Munich Agreement was surely defensive – peace for
our time.'

Bilson sighed. 'Sweet, modestly limited phrase, isn't it? But
the defensiveness is as *we* see it. Consider Uncle Joe's view.
Four against one. Not defensive at all. A hunting pack? Mightn't
he want to weaken that quartet by sneaking a separate agreement with one of them – say, Adolf, easily the most dangerous
and unpredictable? There's already the 1926 neutrality agreement between Russia and Germany, isn't there?'

Was there? Toulmin had said so. 'Oh, quite, sir.'

'They might wish to bring it up-to-date. That could look
reasonable enough, legitimate enough, diplomatic enough.'

'And if an agreement *is* being cooked up?' Mount asked.

Bilson's answer seemed oblique. 'Do you ever look at the
left-wing journalist Claud Cockburn's paper, *The Week*?'

Mount said: 'Well, I—'

'You should.'

Caught up in these recollections, Mount had not been
concentrating enough on his walking style as he hiked the
streets around Toulmin's apartment block. His pace had
dropped to a stroll. Someone ambling along like that, with no
apparent purpose, could cause curiosity. He might give the
impression he was looking for someone, something. He *was*
looking for someone, but didn't want to look as though he
was looking for someone. He upped his speed a little. Not
too much. He might need to suggest he had a destination, but
not that he wanted to get to it urgently. That, too, could cause
curiosity in anybody keeping a watch. Perhaps someone would
wonder: why this urgency? Especially if that someone had
orders to spot a visitor who might be making for the Toulmin
apartment. Mount needed moderation – a relaxed, but not too
relaxed, progression: faster than a stroll, but not a sprint. And
if he were reconnoitring for a possible place to live he'd want
to do it in a thoughtful, observant way, not at a gallop.

'Cockburn has some clarity of vision, Marcus,' SB had said.
'Resigned-from-*The-Times* man, distinguished family with an
Admiral who burned down the White House among his fore-
bears, apparently. He's continually lambasting what he calls
"the Cliveden set". That seems to mean the moneyed and, or,

titled group, and their hangers-on, who think Hitler is no bad chap at all and might, on the contrary, be a saviour. Nancy Astor is said to be prominent: Viscountess Astor. Cliveden is the family seat in Bucks.'

'A saviour from what, sir?'

Bilson gazed at him in a kindly, forgiving style, as if he were sure Mount knew the answer to this and, given time, would cough it.

'From Russian communism?' Mount said.

'A similar state of things in France', Bilson replied. 'I hear of governmental and military opinion badly split as to the German threat.'

'Do you think France would not fight, sir?'

'Might not fight. Almost certainly would not fight effectively. Some of the high command are not committed. Some regard an arrangement with Germany, a nominally Christian country, as preferable to what they consider the only possible alternative, the Reds. The Reds would, of course, be welcomed by France's Left – perhaps are already being prepared for. Against that, Centre and Right parties believe an occupation by Germany could be controlled and to a degree would stay civilized.'

'Adolf, "controlled," "civilized?"'

'"To a degree." A hope. Also, by agreement, the occupation might be only partial. Nearly half of France could remain French, possibly under Pétain, despite his age. It would be in the South and run from a provincial town, not from Paris.' Despair seemed to touch Bilson's face again. He would probably remember Pétain as he used to be, the revered Field Marshal leading the French in the war. 'But enough of France,' he said eventually. 'The point is, Marcus, there are distinguished, even lordly, folk in Britain, too, who think the Nazis offer a bulwark against communism.'

On his Lichtenberg walks there were usually plenty of other pedestrians about. Mount could have done with more though, so he could merge and guarantee inconspicuousness. On the other hand, he had to try to study all these people, in case one of them, or two or three of them, seemed focussed on him. That would be trickier if the numbers were higher. And he had to examine the cars and their contents, too. A car did draw in ahead of him and he wondered if someone would step out on to the pavement and speak – speak something like, 'May I see your papers, please?' But it was an elderly woman who left the vehicle and went into one of the buildings. He walked on and passed the car. In a little while he heard it rev up again and soon it passed him, another woman at the wheel.

'Did you see and hear that Eton phalanx at Heston, Marcus?' SB had asked at their conference.

'Eton?'

'Certainly you did. Well, Etonians, but more especially Etonians' mothers and fathers, and grandmothers and grandfathers, might find sweethearting with fascist Hitler reasonably tolerable, even desirable.'

'Possibly.'

'But not – repeat not – if Hitler's into a rosy friendship with the big, brutal, anti-capitalist, revolutionary, sequestrating Commy bear. The Cliveden set and similar wouldn't care for it either. Dread of Russia has dominated upper-crust thinking in Britain since . . . well, take a look at some old copies of *Punch* – the massive, fiery-eyed animal, muzzle dripping blood and fragments of civilized Europe just gobbled up. Bugbear. And, vice versa, Moscow's Commie mates here would love to see Eton and its likes wiped out, as well as the Cliveden set and similar.'

'You mean there'd be a ready supply of young, high-born, well-heeled officers again if Russia were one of the enemies, despite that Oxford Union vote and so on? They'd be glad to join up then, like the boys in that Newbolt cricket poem, or Rupert Brooke "into cleanness leaping"? So, if we can establish a coming together of Germany and Russia you'd advise the government that we should fight Hitler at once – regardless of the holy piece of paper and your previous view – yes, at once, immediately, before he and Stalin become allies and perhaps unbeatable?'

'You read poetry, do you, Marcus?'

'Poets occasionally have something to say.'

'Maybe. There were a few in the war who had something to say. It could be quite sharp, quite penetrating.'

'Owen? Sassoon?'

'Look, my morale took a sickening blow at Heston, Marcus,' SB replied.

'Oh? Nobody could have guessed.'

'But one has to keep buggering on, you know. That way, perhaps we'll win. Only that way. Or, failing all else, there's the visit.'

'The state visit by Hitler? What about it?'

'Oh, yes,' SB replied. 'There could be opportunities there.' Bilson had a long, angular, full-lipped face, extravagantly lined forehead, and wore wire-rimmed, very fragile looking spectacles. Perhaps it was a keep-buggering-on sort of face, with the forehead trenches put there by the French mud ones, and the spectacles helping him gaze, impassively, on horrors, as well as to snipe. Mount possessed no expertise on that, but Baillie might have recognized it. SB stood about 5′ 8″ and was as thin as a jockey. When a marksman, he wouldn't have needed much cover.

'You think war is certain, sir?' Mount said.

'For a time at Heston and afterwards I thought *defeat* was certain. It seemed we'd forgotten how to bite – could only yelp: "*Nev*ille, *Nev*ille, *Nev*ille."'

'Because of the Etonians?'

'Because of what they and the rest of the crowd there symbolized. And I wondered: God, did I contrive this? I'd talked to the PM before he left, you know.'

No, Mount didn't actually *know*, but he would have bet on it.

Now, on his Lichtenberg walk, he had Toulmin's apartment block in sight. There appeared to be a small crowd around the entrance. He didn't like that very much, but kept going.

'Self-blame battered me,' SB had said at their interview. 'You claim not to have noticed, which is kind. But, of course, you did. And then I had a bit of a recovery. Thank heaven, it always happens. We do keep buggering on, don't we? As the first move, I decided to send you to Berlin. I had to correct an error, and at once. Yes, I can see where it came from. When I joined the Service just after the war, its main concern was Russia and Russia's British mates. The powers here feared copycatting of the 1917 Soviet revo. Why I mentioned the tradition of lurid anxiety in *Punch*, though that goes back into the last century. I considered this obsession with Russia to be only that – an obsession, and foolish, narrow, ill-informed. I tried to dispel my colleagues' fixation by argument and, as

far as I could, by pushing Russia to the far edge of my own
thinking. A glib mistake. D'you know, the PM actually asked
me on what basis we decided which information to let him
in on and which we kept back as not relevant? I said,
pompously, "Judgement." And I judged that the Russian
aspects need not be mentioned to him. You must help me
compensate for that idiotic error, Marcus, while we have time,
if we have.'

SB had climbed back from collapse, had he? He'd become
constructive again. Baillie's theory that a stoic's breakdown
would be total and final didn't fit. He hadn't disintegrated like
the abused apartment armchair. No? Mount wondered. This
sudden focus by SB on fantasized secret bargaining between
Berlin and Moscow might, in fact, be a symptom of that total
and final breakdown forecast by Baillie, mightn't it? Was SB's
assessment of things improbable, unsubstantiated, half-
cracked, hurried, desperate? *Please, please, get to Berlin and
dig me out of this hole, Marcus.* Mount hadn't liked hearing
him ask for help. He was SB, a rock.

But Mount would try to dig him out of the hole. Viewing that
group of people near the entrance to Toulmin's apartment block,
Mount found himself recalling cliché shots from thriller films,
when extras clustering around the doors of a building signalled
tragedy inside. Now, he considered getting out of sight. If Toulmin
were the tragedy, it might be foolish to approach. Perhaps there'd
soon be a swarm of police, as well as this swarm of sightseers.
In their thorough way, police would possibly start asking who
knew anything about what had happened, and about whom it
had happened *to*. Stanley Charles Naughton of Steglitz and
London must not appear in police notes, even as someone entirely
unable to help as a witness now. Nobody could tell where that
might lead. Perhaps a passport check? Vamoose, Stanley Charles
Naughton? Walk phoney businesslike, but unhurried, in a
different direction and disappear?

Then, though, the strong needs of the operation took hold,
and perhaps the disciplines of the job. He had come here to
find if Toulmin was OK. Tag on to this group now and he
might discover something, though probably not that he was
OK: crowds gathered because someone was *not* OK, not
because he or she *was*. Spying always involved a lot of tagging
on, attempted merging, attempted blending.

Mount didn't bolt, but approached the gathering. A woman was addressing them. In a while, he thought he caught the word *plattenbauten* and then *Splanemann-Siedlung*. He slowed. He heard: 'Amsterdam.' He realized he was listening to an educational lecturette on this accommodation block, built with the *plattenbauten* – those concrete slabs – and part of the renowned Lichtenberg *Splanemann-Siedlung* development, completed a few years ago. Although very influential, it was not completely original, but part copied from a suburb in Amsterdam. She'd generously admitted the debt. Perhaps there had been no tragedy, after all. A kind of seminar under way? The woman said that the *plattenbauten* here were made from 'locally cast slabs'.

At the end of the woman's briefing, two men did a translation summary, one into English, one into French. Mount decided the crowd must be local-authority housing experts from other parts of Germany and Britain and France, here to see and learn, in case the *Splanemann-Siedlung* example could be followed on their own patches. Several people were making notes. There might be a tour inside. He sidled up to the outer edge of the audience and gave pretty good attention to some costing details, average construction times, and detailed specifications of the slabs' dimensions, weight, tensile and compressive strengths. God, but this was interesting! He'd hook on. He'd blend with them.

He had a copy of Baillie's drawing with him for double-checks and brought this out of his pocket now, folded it vertically and laterally to make a pad, with the sketch inside, and jotted quite a few figures and that phrase, 'locally cast slabs', on the blank reverse. 'The slabs, and therefore the properties, have their own aesthetic,' the woman had concluded. Mount agreed. To hell with Nick Baillie's snobbish comments. She shouldn't have sounded so defensive.

'Excuse me, but I couldn't help seeing just now what you'd written. I think you've put your finger on it there,' a man standing next to Mount said in English – English English. He spoke quietly, so as not to interfere with the French translation, just underway.

'The measurements and so on? They'll slip from my mind otherwise,' Mount said.

'Not those so much, but "locally cast slabs". Important,

conferring a sort of wholeness and homeliness on the project: a means of providing not only flats, but work in the vicinity. Useful, given the unemployment figures in England now. But the words "slab, slabs". Ugly? Something lost in translation there, surely. *Plattenbauten* sounds acceptable. And the French equivalent: "maisons à panneaux". But "slab, slabs" . . . Off-putting, wouldn't you say? Not just unpoetic: anti-poetic. "Panels", better? Or "tablets"? Too Mosaic? "Lozenges"? There's a classical justification for that: isn't lozenges from the Latin, *lausiae,* slabs?'

Mount's Oxford Greats degree was founded on Latin and Greek. 'True.'

'But "locally cast lozenges" not quite right, perhaps.' He was tall, aquiline, very thin, friendly looking. He wore a long off-white raincoat and an off-white silk scarf. For each point he made he nodded his long head sharply once, as if to state: 'We agree on that, yes, no argument needed, surely?' It might be a technique brought over from town council meetings. Some polite aggression would be necessary there. 'Wolverhampton,' he said.

'Tottenham,' Mount replied.

'I'm impressed, so far.'

'Very.'

'I don't think I saw you at the hotel when we assembled last night.'

'I was delayed,' Mount said.

'Mainwaring.'

'Naughton.'

'Clifford.'

'Stanley.' They shook hands dispassionately.

'Yes, impressive but . . . It's odd, isn't it, Stanley, that one wonders how, in the event of war, these buildings would stand up to bombing – ironically, bombing by the very country that taught us how to erect them? Should one ask the lady how strong the *plattenbauten* are – not so much in themselves as individual *plattenbau*, which is unquestioned – but at the join points, where they are put alongside one another and on top of and under one another in the metal framework? Ultimately, although these *plattenbauten* achieve a kind of unity and form a wall, each *plattenbau* remains separate, discrete, a unit, and therefore perhaps liable to become inchoate.'

'It's quite a question.'

'Do you think there'll be a war?'

'There are a lot of factors to be considered in that regard.'

'Well, yes. Which?'

'Many,' Mount replied.

'Some back home obviously think there will be: Winston Churchill, for instance, and Lionel Paterin, the Cabinet Minister. They don't try to conceal their bleak, alarming assessments of things. I've met Paterin, as, perhaps, you have, Stanley.'

'I don't think so.'

'When he was a minister concerned with housing. I found him very sensible, very balanced. He's not one to overdramatize.'

'I've heard of him, naturally,' Mount replied.

'People like Paterin and Churchill as well, they often have information beyond what is generally available, and they feel a duty to pronounce on it.'

'All kinds of competing information these days. It's rather baffling.'

Mainwaring said: 'I ask myself, and possible *you* ask *yourself*, Stanley, might they – I mean, the Germans – *want* us to put up this kind of block because they know it will be easy to knock down in a *blitzkrieg* raid, causing civilian casualties in a "softening up" strategy? Consider a sequence where a couple of *plattenbauten* are pushed out of connection with each other by high explosive. What happens? Aren't these *plattenbauten* by their nature extremely interdependent, although separate? If two *plattenbauten* go askew, isn't the whole structure likely to shift and disintegrate?'

'*Flattenbauten*,' Mount said.

He nodded once and gave a smile-grimace and suppressed retch. 'These *plattenbauten* look and are heavy and strong. Because of their function, they must be. But, in a collapse, the very strength and weight of the *plattenbauten* become a danger to those living in the apartments, surely. When falling they might give an occupant quite a whack, probably fatal. I imagine Luftwaffe officers consulting their maps before an aircraft raid and pointing to the spot in Wolverhampton or Tottenham, London, where *Splanemann-Siedlung* structures are waiting to be smashed. Their location would be known because of information exchanged at sessions like this one today.'

'Would the Germans have gone in for these blocks themselves if aware they could be destroyed easily by bombs? After all, the location of this block and the type of its construction is well known.'

'That, also, is quite a question,' Clifford said. 'I can see it might be thought untactful to raise these matters now. We are guests.'

They all began to move into the building, led by the guide and the two translators. It was announced that a family on the third floor had kindly agreed to open their apartment, number thirty-four, for examination by the visitors. Luck; Mount felt pleased he had joined the group. Sometimes that enterprise, resolve, audacity recommended in training did work. They would enter the selected apartment in relays. On the way up, the guide spoke of the spaciousness of the landings and gentleness of the stair incline, to suit old people. All the apartments on this floor had dark-blue corridor doors. They were numbered: odds on the front of the building, evens to the rear. Mount thought thirty-seven should be Toulmin's, but the doors did not show name labels.

As he entered thirty-four with several of the others, he paused for a moment to let Clifford go ahead and took the chance of a good gaze at the lock, only one. It looked elementary and very susceptible. The door was not solid. He assumed that thirty-seven's would be the same. He assumed, also, that the layout of thirty-seven would match thirty-four's: one big bedroom, one smaller, bathroom-lavatory, kitchen, living room, utility room. He'd get the geography into his head as useful if he had to investigate thirty-seven in full or part darkness. The occupants of thirty-four were a young couple with a baby. He worked in a factory and had arranged his shifts so he could be here this morning. They declared their apartment splendid, ideal. Possibly they'd been picked to say so. Perhaps there was an Iron Cross medal for services in praise of *plattenbauten*.

When it came to questions, Clifford asked through the translator whether there had ever been evidence that any of the *plattenbauten* were not lying as snugly together as they should be, allowing moisture to enter the apartment. And perhaps the fault prevented pictures from hanging flush against the wall owing to a bulge, or, similarly, a looking glass, which might consequently give imperfect reflections, as with comically distorting mirrors in a fairground.

'Not at all,' the couple replied.

Mount said, also through the translator: 'A more general point, if I may. Are the apartment blocks neighbourly, or does the construction's very solidity make residents isolated? Do you know people next door to you and perhaps opposite?' He thought too much fluency in German from him would not be wise.

'Very neighbourly,' the man said. 'The apartment block is compact enough not to become impersonal. We have many friendships.'

'Are apartments occupied exclusively by families, or do some have only one occupant?' Mount said.

'Mostly families,' the guide said. 'That was the main aim of the development.'

Mount made a note: 'Mostly families.'

'But not entirely,' the young mother said. 'For instance, in thirty-seven there is only one man living alone. Or we think so. We have not seen anyone else go into the apartment, except for a furniture delivery. He is very civil, but never talks very much. We have tried to be sociable with him, but unsuccessfully.'

'Is he away sometimes?' Mount said. 'That might explain his behaviour.'

'We know very little of him,' she replied.

'Good questions of yours, if I may say, Stanley,' Clifford remarked as they were leaving. 'Is there a danger these people will become boxed off from one another in their concrete cells? "Very civil, but never talks very much." Can you think of a better description of urban isolation?'

'Will you be recommending against *plattenbauten* building for Wolverhampton, Clifford, because of that and the pictures and mirrors?' Mount replied.

'The whole thing looked so cheap and shoddy. Did you notice the front door?'

'The front door?'

'I always say one can deduce a lot from front doors. Flimsy. Gimcrack. Not much resemblance to wood.'

'No, I didn't notice.'

'Take it from me, front doors can say so much. I wonder if you've ever been to look at number ten Downing Street, the Prime Minister's residence in London. That is a wonderful front door: solid, regularly painted, I'm sure, domestic, yet also internationally significant.'

'I suppose people could buy themselves a proper wooden one, even if they're only renting.'

'They *could*. Of course they could. But that is the point, isn't it? They live in the kind of context, the *Splanemann-Siedlung* all-provided context, where people do *not* bother about the nature of front doors. This is very basic living, with no concern for refinements.'

'Too basic for Wolverhampton?'

'Would they even notice if moisture were getting through imperfect joins in the *plattenbauten*, caused by movement? Or jutting pictures and mirrors? Such moisture or jutting would not, in itself, be important – only as symptoms of a general instability of structure, which might increase dangers during a bombing raid. But perhaps we'll meet at the hotel this evening and talk further on these matters, Stanley.'

'I'd enjoy that, Clifford,' Mount said.

'I feel there is a natural rapport between us, demonstrated in the fact that we both noted as very significant the "locally crafted slabs".'

Even if he had known which hotel Clifford was at, Mount thought he'd have to skip this next meeting with him, despite the deep rapport about slabs. The spy business was like that: you met all kinds of fascinating and dull people, and you treated them the same. They *were* the same: they were equally there to be fooled and possibly milked, and once this necessity passed, they were equally there to be ditched. Instead of rendezvousing with Clifford that evening he would go back to Toulmin's apartment block. As long as he saw no obvious watchdogs, he'd enter thirty-seven. Earlier, he hadn't tried to identify possible surveillance. It would have been useless: too many students of *plattenbauten*, or supposed students of *plattenbauten*, occupied the stairs and landings, the corridors, and apartment thirty-four.

Mount still had no pistol, only his bunch of twirls and a narrow-beam torch, intended to provide concentrated, controllable light and limit the spread of give-away glints. He decided he wouldn't get down on hands and knees to sniff at the bottom of the door for cigarette smoke, or worse. That was potentially farcical and would be hard to explain if someone came into the corridor and stood over him, perhaps sympathetically assuming a fit or heart attack. Non-conclusive, too. The crew waiting might be non-smokers, or had been ordered not to smoke, for fear their prey did the under-door test. Most of these trade tricks were internationally known among secrets people. It might be possible to have a sniff for cigarette odour through the keyhole. Mount believed, anyway, that the couple opposite in thirty-four would have noticed, and mentioned, if strangers had installed themselves at thirty-seven.

It was just before nine p.m. when he returned, and October-dark. He rambled for a while again in the street, staying close to the apartment block now and observing carefully. He saw nothing to trouble him. There were still folk about, yes, going in and out at the apartment building, but ordinary folk carrying on their ordinary lives, as far as he could judge, not waiting for a visitor to Toulmin. Of course, he couldn't be sure. They might be folk skilled at looking like ordinary folk carrying on their ordinary lives, but really folk waiting for a visitor to Toulmin, to the traitor Toulmin. If they were on that kind of pounce duty, though, they'd most likely reappear regularly. It didn't happen while Mount looked, and he looked for half an hour: no encore performances. He'd push on. There was a small entrance foyer to the apartment block. As he stepped towards it, he saw a man descend from the stairs, obviously on his way to the street. Mount knew he must keep going, not veer off abruptly, scared. It could be a giveaway. He must pretend some of that ordinariness.

'Ah,' the man said, 'you are still here?'

For a moment Mount had not recognized the host from thirty-four. The delay was excusable. He appeared much scruffier now. He wore a grubby navy jacket and black canvas cap, a rough navy jersey, greasy looking dark trousers, and was pulling on an aged, long raincoat before going out into the autumn. He had on heavy black boots. Mount guessed these must be work clothes. He was going to the factory he'd spoken about earlier. He'd arranged his shifts, hadn't he, so he could be there when they called this morning?

'Our session with you was very helpful, very instructive, but I wanted half an hour to look at the development on my own,' Mount said.

'Without your English friend who is so concerned about the *plattenbauten*?'

'It's a matter of getting the full picture,' Mount replied.

'You couldn't do that this morning?'

'Ah, but that *was* this morning. I've seen the building by day, and as a matter of fact done a plan of it, but I wanted also the evening perspective. The occupants' activities will be different at this time of day.' A low-powered bulb lit the foyer. Mount pulled the papers out of his pocket again, this time with Baillie's front-elevation sketch visible. 'I have to be able to tell my colleagues at home in Britain exactly what I've observed here. I, and I alone, represent their interests.'

The man looked. 'It's a good drawing.'

'One aspect only.'

'But correct, I think. Here is the apartment we discussed.' He put a finger on thirty-seven's windows.

'Which?' Mount said.

'Number thirty-seven,' he said. He moved his finger. 'Here the bedrooms, the living room, the kitchen, the bathroom.'

'Thirty-seven? Ah, yes, of course, the man you never see.'

'Almost never.'

'Now and then?'

'Yes, now and then.'

'Special occasions!'

'Yes, perhaps so. He had a new chair delivered not long ago, so, obviously, he must open the door and talk to the men. My wife saw this when coming back to the apartment one day. She thought it seemed an expensive chair – metal and wood, laminated.'

'I expect he wants to be comfortable when he sits in there alone.'

'I must go now. I'll lose a quarter of an hour's pay if I'm late,' he said, buttoning his raincoat.

'Night work?'

'Oh, yes.'

'The factory operates non-stop – twenty-four hours?'

'Oh, yes.'

'There are plenty of jobs, are there?'

'Oh, yes, recently.'

Making mortar shells? U-boat fins? Dornier P59 bomber parts? Mount wanted to ask, but didn't. Questions could become too insistent, too professional – or non-professional for a dwellings specialist. 'When I refer to the evening perspective, I want to find what sound levels are like in the building now most people are at home, relaxed and playing their radios and gramophones and so on. This is quite important. Some people in Britain don't like neighbours' din. It's an attitude they've taken from the upper classes, who live in manor houses away from the populace. I'll stroll the corridors.'

'You fear that if the *plattenbauten* have shifted, as your friend suggested, noise might be able to crawl through the gaps and attack?'

'He *was* a worrier, wasn't he?'

'I won't slam the door when I leave now in case the apartment block falls on you because the *plattenbauten* are unstable. Then you wouldn't be able to go back to your country and say how wonderful the *Splanemann-Siedlung* apartments are, owing to your death.'

Mount climbed to the third floor. The corridor was empty. He walked pretty silently, he thought, to thirty-seven. His fourth key turned the lock. The corridor had remained clear. He went in and closed the door quietly behind him. That took a struggle. The training said you always left yourself a ready exit, especially when going on to unknown ground which might contain an enemy – or enemies. And, God, surely it must be a plural, if he was expected. But he could not let the door stand ajar. That would bring attention, because this door's usual and notorious state was shut. He waited.

The training had taught him how to disarm someone when not armed himself, but not how to disarm several when not armed himself. He crouched a bit against the door. This seemed the best countermeasure he could manage if guns surrounded him in here. The training hadn't taught him, either, what a corpse would smell like after a longish time, but he thought it would be fairly bad, and he detected nothing like that now. SB, ex-no-man's-land, might have been able to tell him. There was a cigarette odour, but ingrained, not new. He stood still, bent against the door for a minute, sniffing the darkness, but also trying to sense whether in fact this place seemed to match

thirty-four for layout. He heard what might be footsteps and
the scrape of moved furniture. But he thought these sounds
came from other apartments, not this one, perhaps because
plattenbauten had shifted, leaving holes, or simply because
this was an apartment block with the usual neighbourly noises
when people lived on top of and alongside one another, jam-
packed. If he had really been on an accommodation mission
from Britain he would have made a note. He switched on his
torch. He was in a small hallway, which gave on to a passage
with doors leading off. That did square with thirty-four. All
the doors were closed, so he could safely show light here. It
did not reach a window. He thought the living room would
be straight ahead. He'd try that first. He extinguished the torch
and opened the door.

The curtains were not pulled across the windows. He knew
that already, from viewing outside. A middling sized moon
escaped the clouds once in a while and gave some light. And
a bit of a glimmer came from street lamps a good way below.
The room looked untidy, as if someone left in a big hurry, or
as if a slam-bang search had happened, with no effort made
to restore things. Three drawers in a sideboard had been pulled
open and left like that. A crumpled shirt hung over the back
of an armchair. Pages from several newspapers lay on the
floor near one down-at-heel brown shoe and an empty beer
bottle.

Mount did a full eye-inventory. Two armchairs: brown
leatherette, not laminated wood and metal. Of course not:
Toulmin and the girls had brought that one to Mount's apartment. He saw a burly radiogram in what might be mahogany;
a couple of straight backed wooden chairs, perhaps also
mahogany; beige-brown fitted carpet, newish; three framed
watercolours of rural and river scenes, which seemed to hang
all right, no jutting over wall bulges; the sideboard of some
light wood that Mount couldn't place, out of tone with the
mahogany. Some books and papers lay on it: he'd scan the
books and papers shortly and look in all the sideboard drawers.
Before that, he must get through the other rooms and see
whether they contained anything or anybody, or any body, he
needed to see. By now he felt certain thirty-seven was no
ambush. He hadn't been grabbed, clubbed or shot when at his
most targetable – coming through the front door.

The big bedroom and kitchen seemed as disorderly as the living quarters, maybe worse. The bed had not been made, and clothes were strewn about. On a kitchen unit he saw what appeared to be the leavings of an interrupted breakfast – half a grapefruit, some fragments of bread, a quarter-full coffee mug. A fork lay close to the mug in a small pool of gravy, perhaps from the previous night's meal. But the single bedroom, when he opened that door, was neat and spruce, a kind of ladylike touch, as good as anywhere in thirty-four, and *they'd* been forewarned to get tidy. If the apartment had been searched, wouldn't they have done this room as well? The idea strengthened in him that Toulmin had gone somewhere urgently and fast, not having time to spruce up the rooms he actually used, promising himself it could be put to rights when he returned. But the other explanation for the showpiece small guest bedroom might be that searchers had found whatever they were after elsewhere in the apartment and didn't need to turn that one over. The open drawers in the sideboard looked like evidence of a failed search, but might not be: possibly they'd taken something they'd been hunting from one of them. What, though?

He went back into the living room. To examine the papers and books he would have to use his torch. Had a good education made him regard books and papers as incomparably important: all that devoted labouring over Greek and Latin texts had slanted his mind? At any rate, he did regard them as important. But no matter how thin the torch's ray, it might be noticeable from outside: a sudden stab of white after long-time blackness. He switched on, though. He kept the torch close and stood with his body stopping most of the light from reaching a window. He put the beam momentarily on the papers. They seemed to be mostly family letters, including a wedding invitation. But he saw, also, the receipt for a birch wood and metal laminated armchair. That troubled him, though he couldn't fathom why. It told no real tale. He put the receipt in his pocket. Never mind the reason.

He wanted a better look at the papers and wondered whether he could draw the curtains briefly. He might then even risk switching on the living room's overhead bulb. A reasonable gamble? He came to think so. The curtains were heavy and almost reached the floor. They would let little or no light through. He put the torch out, moved to the side of the window and paused. Closing the curtains would involve standing behind each in turn, concealed from outside, and tugging it to the centre. He must act quickly, because a half curtained window would be conspicuous. Right. And he was just about to start when he instinctively glanced down around the edge of this curtain to check whether anyone outside watched.

On the pavement in the street leading to the apartment block, he saw three men walking at a good lick, perhaps making for this building. It was shadowy despite the overhead lamps, but he thought one of the three might be Toulmin. Although he couldn't make out faces at that distance, the physical shape of this man and a rather jerky way of walking suggested Toulmin. Yes, 'suggested' would be the right, imprecise word. The man walked between the other two. He and one of the pair carried a suitcase. Mount couldn't prolong this view of them. He had to get out of sight fast. He did nothing with the curtain and, stepping backwards, retreated from the window into the darkness of the room. He stood still briefly, trying to work out the meaning of what he'd seen. At least Toulmin – if it *was* Toulmin – could obviously walk all right, in that special, recognizable, undamaged style.

He had on a fur-covered, Russian-style winter hat, which obscured some of his face. But Mount came to feel half sure it *was* Toulmin – and felt fully sure he must get out of thirty-seven in case those three arrived. He reckoned he had about four minutes: two for them to reach the apartment block, and two on the stairs and along the corridor. He hadn't noticed any of them look up at the window. Assume, then, it must be Toulmin. The two men had both stayed half a yard behind him. How to read this? Were they escorts, jailers, or flunkeys? That could be important. Well, of course it could be important, bloody important. If he was a prisoner, a captive with captors, being brought back here for some reason, could Mount leave him to it? That abominable prospect of scampering retreat – of 'save-yourself-do-dear-Marcus' – troubled him again. Poltroonery? Panic? Appalling selfishness? Professionalism?

But the training would undoubtedly say 'bail out and bail out NOW' for this kind of situation. It was one of those 'greater good' moments. Here, that would clearly mean safeguarding the Berlin operation's secrecy and effectiveness. This put considerations for the welfare, even the life, of an agent like Toulmin, more or less nowhere. In any secret project there might come a crisis where someone, or more than one, was dispensable. Meticulously, unemotionally, anti-emotionally, the training had spent three days carefully itemizing emergencies where flinging a former mate and informant into the acid bath would be not only OK, but a bit of a triumph. Compensation for the family should be properly seen to, of course.

Still standing in the centre of the room, Mount went on trying to get his thoughts in order. Why would they bring Toulmin back here, if that's what they were at? Perhaps they wanted something from one of the rooms, something he could point them to. The papers? As Mount had suspected, maybe there had been no search of thirty-seven. Had they caught Toulmin trying to escape? Hence the suitcases and the poor state of the apartment, left in a rush. Had he sensed, or even been tipped off, that they meant to move against him? Toulmin might not be the only whisperer in government employ, nor the only active anti-Hitlerite. For instance, SB had a Most Secret dossier on two brothers called Kordt, well up in the state hierarchy, yet possibly plotting against the regime and Adolf. One of those or someone like them might have got a word out to Toulmin, the word being: 'Vanish!' Wherever the warning originated, did Toulmin make a run at once? And had they anticipated he would and snared him at the airport or railway station?

The papers, again. He hadn't looked at them properly. Might there be something that would incriminate Toulmin? Could they lead to Mount? Should he sweep them all up, jam them into his pockets like the chair receipt, and disappear while he had time? But was this another symptom of his college-boy obsession with ink and papers? Possibly it came from even further back – those regular espionage tales in the lads' magazines, *Hotspur* and *Skipper*, about the theft of what were always called 'vital secret documents', threatening the safety of the realm. And then there was Richard Hannay's search for the crucial notebook in Buchan's *The Thirty-Nine Steps*. Fiction. And fiction putting a strain on credibility. Would an agent in continuous danger like Toulmin write sensitive stuff down and leave it around on a sideboard? Was he a suicidal idiot? Forget the papers. Try another tack.

Suppose Mount didn't, in fact, give in to wise, standard-issue funk – took no undeniably prudent flit. Instead, if he went to meet them in the corridor now, or on the stairs, would Toulmin be able to indicate somehow whether he was OK – a sly wink, a fleeting half-grin, a frown? After all, they would probably encounter other people in the apartment block as they made for thirty-seven. Mount could be simply a resident, entitled to some formal greeting, as far as those two were concerned. Naturally, Mount wouldn't speak or show special recognition, and neither should Toulmin. But he'd realize he was not forsaken. Foreigners sometimes referred to Britain as 'perfidious Albion', meaning faithless. He wondered whether he could prove this false, at least about the Mount subdivision of Albion. Honour still had a place, hadn't it? There'd been no time spent on honour in training, though.

True, the men with Toulmin might be especially alert. To locate and lure any of his contacts could be one reason they'd returned to thirty-seven. Everyone around the place would be regarded as a possible secret pal of Toulmin, his brother spy. And, of course, if those two forced a conversation – didn't allow the encounter to stay silent, as Mount planned – they would at once know him to be British. His German was good, but admittedly not mistakable for German German: Wellington school had insisted he take a 'living language', as well as the classics, and there'd been an excellent German crash course in the Section. But, although the Berlin assignment would help him improve fast, he knew he came nowhere near bilingual yet.

In any case, what if Toulmin somehow signalled he was *not* OK, deeply *un*OK? Mount wouldn't be able to do much about it, except grieve: those two probably armed, and he with just twirls and a torch and some unarmed combat skills. So, then, do a bunk while doing a bunk remained possible? Mount carefully piled up these reasons to justify his own quick flight now – and felt sickened by them. Could he really abandon Toulmin? This was an agent who had taken huge risks for Mount, and, if for Mount, for SB, for the Section, for GB, for the empire. Reward? Write him off. Disgusting. Yes, that 'greater good' gloss was merely 'the end justifies the means' in poor disguise: chuck morality and loyalty for the sake of some possible, undefined advantage. Stephen Bilson might say he believed in the greater good, but Mount would bet that if he and SB's special agent in Berlin, Ahasuerus Fromanteel, so-called, were in this kind of situation, SB would not abandon him. Although Mount had no gun, a sudden physical corridor attack on those two by him – the surprise of it, the shock of it – might enable Toulmin to bolt, and perhaps Mount could somehow hinder, obstruct, any pursuit, or handgun volleys, from those two attendants.

He hung on in the apartment as if semi-paralysed, while trying to deal with these doubts, then decided in a spasm that they were sentimental, goofy and – worst of all – defeatist. When he joined the Service he deliberately picked a career where the greater good was the *only* good, if things went rough. It would be paltry to rat on that now. He had just proposed to himself two ridiculously probable killings in a corridor of this *Splanemann-Siedlung* development – Toulmin's and his own. They'd be inexplicable back in London; *kaput* for the operation. SB would be stunned, not just by the absurd, wanton deaths, but because Mount had flouted the most basic of rules and gone to Toulmin's home, endangering Toulmin and himself, *fatally* endangering Toulmin and himself, and blazoning the Section's stealthy purpose and preposterous incompetence. No, it mustn't be like that.

Pieties and quaint honour duly strangled, Mount edged to the side of the window again. The three men were not in sight outside now. They must have entered the building and be on their way upstairs. Get out, get out, before they reached the third floor corridor. NOW. He left thirty-seven and turned towards the other end of the building. In his saunterings earlier he had seen a secondary set of stairs and an entrance there. To residents he passed in the corridor and on one of the landings he gave a small but bonny smile and nod: tokens of solid, *Splanemann-Siedlung*, communal feeling.

Surrounding the apartment block was a stretch of public space, part grassed and with some trees. He got behind a holly tree and watched the windows of thirty-seven. From here he could see virtually the whole frontage of the block. After a few minutes, lights came on in the apartment. Then Toulmin appeared and drew the curtains of the living room. It was unmistakably Toulmin and, in any case, this association with the apartment decided identity. To Mount, he looked relaxed and still thoroughly undamaged. He seemed to have a lit cigarette sticking up between the fingers of his right hand, away from the curtain material. His head and face were half turned back into the room. He might be chatting to people behind him. He pulled at the curtains with what looked like a sort of leisurely satisfaction, as though delighted to be back in the cosiness of his own place, shitheap or not. A faint line of light was visible above the living-room drawn curtains.

Mount stayed on behind the holly. More or less automatically he'd done a description in his head of the two men with Toulmin, and he memorized it: a tic from training, a ritual, but the men might matter. He went over these impressions now. He'd judge both to be less than thirty and physically powerful and fit, though not in the loose-limbed way male ballet dancers might be powerful and fit. The one to Toulmin's right was about 5′ 10″, wide-shouldered, wide-chested, dark hair cut close. He wore a long trench coat, no hat. What Mount took to be a small cigar had glowed between his lips. The other man would be four or five inches taller; leaner, but not gangling. His hair appeared dark, also, though Mount couldn't make out much of it because he had on a cheese-cutter cap. His overcoat was navy or black and looked like good material, very well cut. He wore the hat slightly to one side – a sort of attempted raciness. It was this taller man who, like Toulmin, carried a suitcase. Mount could make out nothing much of the faces.

After about ten minutes Mount saw these two leave the apartment block. The man with the cap no longer carried a suitcase. Mount felt bludgeoned by choices again. He could follow them and try to discover who they were, where they came from. But he had never been good at tailing, nor at counter-tailing, come to that. 'Too self-centred,' they'd said at training. The two men might have a car, though, parked somewhere away from notice. He couldn't track that. It would be much simpler, easier and quicker to get Toulmin to tell him about them. But this supposed it to be Toulmin in there, alive, and still working for Mount, and, if for Mount, for SB, for the Section, for GB and the empire.

Yes, instead of gumshoeing, Mount might go back to thirty-seven and ask Toulmin what had happened, suppose (1) Toulmin could be asked; (2) Toulmin wanted to answer; and

(3) wanted to answer with the truth. Or, Mount could put an end to this evening's business, go home, and wait there to see if Toulmin called in. If not, Mount should get down to the Wilhelmstrasse tomorrow and perhaps the next day, hoping Toulmin would soon be back at work and interceptable.

To Mount, only the return to thirty-seven now, tonight, seemed right. All the alternatives looked like postponements and evasions; *would* be postponements and evasions. He went back up to the third floor on the stairs he had just come down and was about to use the skeleton key on Toulmin's lock when a middle aged couple came out from apartment thirty-nine, next door, perhaps on their way to a restaurant or to visit friends. They might know Toulmin, at least by sight. Perhaps they'd find it odd – worse than odd – to see a stranger able to open the door. They might suspect a burglary and call the police. Mount kept the key hidden in his hand and knocked gently with his knuckles, like a visitor. Toulmin did not respond. The couple paused behind Mount. 'We think he was certainly there a little while ago,' the man said. 'We heard sounds. Perhaps with company. Voices.'

Did Clifford have it right and some of the *plattenbauten* had slewed, letting noise through?

'Men's voices,' the woman said.

'He has been away, but we believe he came back,' the man said.

'Perhaps he is asleep after a journey,' the woman said. 'But if your business is important and you don't mind waking him, it might be necessary to knock harder on the door.' She came forward and formed fists, then gave the door a patterned beating with them. '*Mein herr!*' she yelled. 'Here is someone to see you.' She turned to Mount. 'I do not know his name. He is very solitary here.' The man also knocked on the door: heavier blows, and less frequent.

The woman from thirty-four opposite came out into the corridor to complain that the din had woken her baby. Mount could hear it screaming. The door to thirty-seven remained shut. 'I wanted to see some other apartments,' Mount explained to her. 'Certainly yours was very impressive, but I need additional information.'

'These apartments are famous,' the man said.

'Indeed, yes,' Mount replied.

'It is what is known as a settlement,' the older woman said. She continued to hammer the door, but in a slower series of blows now.

'He knows about it. He was here with many others this morning, examining,' the woman from thirty-four said.

'I thought I'd do some random calls, to extend my familiarity with the . . . the settlement,' Mount said.

'We are very satisfied with number thirty-nine,' the man said.

'We are proud to be in the vanguard of this type of accommodation,' the older woman said.

The thirty-four woman went back into her apartment to calm the child.

'I'll try an apartment on one of the other floors, I think,' Mount said.

'You could have come to look at ours,' the man said, 'but we have an appointment elsewhere.'

'I think you must be English,' the woman said. 'You speak German, and understand it, very well, but I think English.'

'Are the English interested in this settlement?' the man asked. 'Many countries admire it. Although there is not always full friendliness these days between Germany and England, certain civic problems, such as accommodation, are the same, and we can help each other.'

'Why I'm here,' Mount said.

'Cooperation,' the man replied.

'Vital,' Mount said.

'In a social sense,' the man said.

'In many matters,' the woman said.

'Civilized,' the man said.

'Certainly,' Mount said.

'Doesn't life have to continue, despite political troubles?' the man said.

'I agree,' Mount said.

'Mutual help,' the man said.

'Not to be denied,' Mount said.

'For instance, didn't the Führer kindly attend the wedding of your Diana Mitford and Oswald Mosley, held in Josef Goebbel's own house because some English did not like Oswald Mosley?' the woman said.

'A happy international gesture,' the man said.

'If you wish, you may call on us in the morning, and we

would be glad to show you thirty-nine,' the woman said. 'Certain special features.'

'That would be very kind,' Mount said.

'At eleven o'clock?' the man said.

'Excellent,' Mount replied.

'It is the least we can do to show how much we appreciate our good fortune as residents,' the man said.

Mount went down to the grass patch outside, where he had stood before, and looked up at thirty-seven. Now, he couldn't make out that weak line of light over the living room curtains. He waited a timed five minutes. When he returned to the third floor there was nobody about and the child in thirty-four no longer screamed. He opened the door to thirty-seven, stepped inside and closed it quietly behind him again. The apartment seemed dark throughout. He switched on his torch and opened the door to the living room. 'Toulmin,' he said, in a big whisper. 'It's I, Stanley Charles Naughton.'

At first sight, the room looked more or less as it was before, except for the closed curtains: the pieces of newspaper, the single shoe, and a bottle scattered about the floor, the three sideboard drawers still open. He swung the torch beam slowly, systematically, left to right, right to left, looking for any changes, such as blood on the carpet and a body, from, say, a knifing or efficiently silenced pistols. No. He wondered if the woman from thirty-nine was right, and Toulmin had fallen into a deep sleep following . . . following what? Following whatever he had been doing. Mount entered the big bedroom. Toulmin was not there. The bed remained a mess. Mount looked under it and in a wardrobe. Again nothing. And nothing different in the guest bedroom or anywhere else in the apartment. He returned to the living room and put the torch beam on to the papers and books. Yes, family letters and a wedding invitation, plus official notification of the visit by housing experts. The books were *David Copperfield* in English, and an English-German dictionary.

When Mount returned to Steglitz a couple of hours later he found Toulmin waiting in one of the armchairs. 'Stanley! Good,' he said. 'I came at once. I knew you'd be concerned. I wasn't able to call lately because I've been in Moscow. It was decided very abruptly that we should send a reciprocal mission about the non-aggression pact – to show, and, indeed, to emphasize, Germany's continuing enthusiasm. I was drafted into the support team. I've had bodyguards with me the whole time. They even had to take me home tonight – sort of finally sign me back over to myself. All very secret. We came by car, but they parked it around the corner out of sight.'

Toulmin must have left the building through the main entrance immediately after the escorts had withdrawn. Mount realized he would have been on the way up those rear stairs then from his holly-tree post, hoping to talk to him in thirty-seven. 'We've all been anxious,' Mount said. 'I went over to have a look in your apartment.'

'In case I was dead there?'

'That sort of thing.'

'Thanks for worrying.'

'You're important.'

'A whispering voice.'

'An important whispering voice. And for the greater good.'

'Which is that?'

'You know, don't you?'

'I called in on the girls at the Toledo to tell them I was fine,' Toulmin replied. 'They both had pre-commitments for part of this evening, but they will be with us shortly.' Mount's front doorbell rang. 'And here they are, the loves.'

'They were concerned about your congestion,' Mount replied.

'I bought a fur hat there. Also, I found the very cold Russian air suits me,' Toulmin said. 'I have hardly coughed.'

'I'm glad,' Mount said. He went to the door.

'Hasn't he been a very naughty man, Stanley?' Olga asked. 'He told none of us he would go on a pilgrimage to Santiago de Compostela in Galicia, where it is said the remains of James, son of Zebedee, lie.'

'True,' Mount said.

BOOK TWO

FIVE

MOST SECRET

*To: Major Andreas Valk, Deputy Commandant, Internal
   State Security.
From: Lieutenant V Mair and Lieutenant BL Schiff*

*In accordance with our instructions issued Tuesday, October
11 1938, we went by car to the apartment home of Konrad
Paul Eisen (KPE) in Lichtenberg at 07.30 on October 12
1938. We had been ordered to act as a Designated Protection
Unit. We accompanied Eisen to Templehof-Berlin airport.
We subsequently flew with KPE and other Foreign Service
officials and Protection Units in a chartered aircraft to
Moscow. Our orders listed 4 (four) objectives:*

(1) *Provide bodyguard protection for Eisen.*
(2) *Ensure he did not compromise the mission by
    undisciplined behaviour.*
(3) *Ensure he did not:*
    (a) *defect, or*
    (b) *establish secret connection with any member
        of the host party.*
(4) *As routinely required, note any material (con-
    versation, actions, possessions) relevant to his
    personal dossier.*

*We left the car at a distance from the Lichtenberg apart-
ment block, to avoid attention. We understood KPE had
been pre-informed by telephone he would be in delega-
tion to Moscow and that we as escorts would call at his
home, present our identity documents and exchange the
codewords 'Rudolph' (us) and 'of Austria' (KPE
response), then remain with him throughout the journey
and period in Russia. All formalities were successfully
concluded. We waited unsupervised in his living room*

*while he completed packing in the larger bedroom. He
said he had heard of the Moscow journey only fifteen
minutes before we arrived, while he was having breakfast and preparing to go to his office.*

*We were able, as required at (4) above routinely, to
examine certain items, to add helpful biographical matter
to his Internal State Security File. Papers available in
our plain view are listed below. (This search was incom-
plete. It had to be discontinued on his return to living
room and departure to airport. Factual detail unverified
at this stage (repeat, unverified).)*

> (1) *Parents live Bremen. Regular financial support
> from him. A letter offered 'once more, dear Konrad'
> thanks for sending a 'very welcome addition' to
> 'our pension'. Amount unspecified. In case the
> Bremen address not already on File we noted it.*
>
> (2) *Invitation to brother's marriage, November 19,
> also Bremen. Cheap, write-in-names card on poor
> paper. Brother Luca, fiancée Agnes Rosina Ritzel.*
>
> (3) *Letter from Luca praising romantically her looks
> and temperament, attacking rumours of pregnancy,
> and suggesting possible wedding presents in
> descending order of expense. Top: genuine china
> dinner service with floral pattern. Bottom: flat iron.*
>
> (4) *Receipt for one-day hired van payment, October 3.*
>
> (5) *Untouched questionnaire about apartment life in
> plattenbauten block.*
>
> (6) *Receipt for purchase payment of birch wood and
> metal laminated armchair, October 3. (No such
> chair visible among apartment furniture, but only
> living room viewed at this stage. See, also, later
> entry in report.)*
>
> (7) *Notification of forthcoming organized visit to the
> apartments by international party studying effects
> of plattenbauten construction, Monday, October 17,
> with possible temporary inconvenience for resi-
> dents.*

*We left the vehicle in the official airport car park to
await our return.*

MOSCOW:

(1) Armament
As instructed, DPUs carried no weapons in case of airport searches. On arrival we were met as scheduled by special contact at the hotel and issued with unfired Walther PPK automatic pistols. Transfer of weapons to us difficult owing to marshalling (see (3) below), but efficiently and confidentially carried out. Pistols to be returned at end of visit if not used.

(2) Accommodation
We and others of party allocated to Ravan Hotel not far from Kremlin where negotiations to take place. The Ravan third-quality Russian, but adequate for short stay. Our rooms, second floor: KPE. No. 6, a double; we a 'family room' (No. 8) with communicating door to No. 6, as requested. Searched both rooms for listening devices while talking about non-sensitive topics, such as the flight, sport and Moscow weather. Nothing found. The search to be repeated at least daily.

(3) Marshalling
A 'tourist guide' allocated to each hotel, function to shepherd and monitor delegates. Soviet GUGB – State Security. 'Ivan.' Fluent German. Present at all hotel meals. Joined different table each time. Listened and occasionally talked. Delegates alert to him and spoke only generalities in his presence. Held conversation with KPE at dinner about Martin Luther, holidays in Black Forest, plattenbauten buildings, the American non-Jewish actor, Clark Gable. 'Ivan' organized afternoon visit to Lenin mausoleum, Red Square. Said we should regard this as 'a solemn but joyful occasion' because of Soviet history. Body of Lenin preserved by constant use of chemicals. When leaving tomb, KPE asked 'Ivan' about possible girls, but 'Ivan' said 'inappropriate' and topic not raised again during Moscow stay.

(4) Work timetable
Negotiations all day each day and evenings until dinner, except for Lenin tomb excursion, visit to a Kremlin cathedral, escorted shopping. KPE bought hat. Designated Protection Unit personnel excluded from negotiation

*sessions. On standby in adjoining ante-room – reading
and cards. KPE did not talk about discussions except
description as 'difficult but positive' and 'very wearing
though satisfying' for all German party.*

RETURN:

*October 17. In accordance with our orders we accompa-
nied KPE to his home, as completion of our door-to-door
assignment. We again left the car at a distance.*
    V Mair
    BL Schiff

*This report now necessarily divides into two. Separate,
individual accounts follow.*

*VM writes: we had identified the windows of KPE's apart-
ment from outside on our introductory visit. No curtains
had been drawn when we left for airport. As we approached
the building on foot, bringing KPE back to apartment, I
noticed what appeared to be a man watching us from the
living room. He stood very briefly at side of window, part
concealed by material of furled back curtain. Heavily built,
over 6 feet tall and with thick black or brown hair. It was
dark. He seemed shocked at our arrival. I say this because
he almost at once moved away from the window and out
of sight. He made no sign of greeting. A 'welcome-home'
gesture would have been natural in someone well known
to Eisen. Perhaps he noticed that I had seen him.*

    *Once he'd gone I was not certain someone had actu-
ally been there. I could not tell whether BLS or KPE
had noticed him. Neither gave any sign. I decided it was
in the best interests of the assignment not to ask.*

(1) *In poor light and from a distance I might have
    mistaken the outline of the bunched curtain for
    the physique of a man.*
(2) *Possibly it was important to know the relationship
    of KPE to this man, if someone had in fact been at
    the window. It might put KPE on guard if I showed
    awareness:*

(a) *Our original briefing said KPE lived alone after a divorce. We had been given no information that he might have a lodger, guest or homosexual partner.*

(b) *That is, of course, if KPE knew this man. The fact that apartment was unlit suggested the man might be an intruder, possibly a stranger to KPE.*

We continued. We entered apartment 37. There appeared to be nobody present now. I wondered again if I had been mistaken about the man at the window. The living room looked as we had left it. I told KPE it was a specified duty for us to check the whole apartment, to ensure his safety. I went into all the other rooms with him and did basic searches but found nobody. Most of the apartment was very untidy. Evidently no-one had been in to clean during his absence.

Andreas Valk had already read the report twice. He rested and put it aside for a few minutes now. Obviously, he'd have to bring both of them in for a meeting, Mair and Schiff. And obviously, too, he'd have to congratulate them, though what they'd done, and described towards the end of the report, was well outside what they'd been told to do. You could call it initiative. You could call it insolence. On the whole, Valk thought he'd better call it initiative. Otherwise, he might look grudging, or even envious. He would be warm and sincere with his praise, but unextravagant. These two must not get to think themselves abnormally talented and sharper at the game than he was. If they spotted the flimsiest chance, people like this pair would try to take over.

Naturally, it was in periods of prolonged, unrelieved stress that leadership could falter and, having faltered, never recover. Valk had been at the Somme as a junior officer and in four or five months witnessed several of these sly, *de facto* mutinies. Eventually, he became involved in one himself: a tottering, useless senior man had to be replaced. Possibly the experience made him unduly wary of such dethronings today: that is, his own, Andreas Valk's. He went back to the report:

BLS writes: it surprised me to hear VM say we had been instructed to search the apartment on return. Untrue. I therefore assumed he might have noticed something unusual but did not wish KPE to know this. While they examined the entire apartment I scrutinized the living room looking for what might have disturbed VM. At first, nothing apparent, but could not find among sideboard papers receipt for the birch wood and metal laminated chair. This had unquestionably been present when we first called on Eisen (see paragraph 6 of original inventory of papers). VM and KPE returned, both seeming relaxed. KPE drew curtains, said the journey had tired him and that he would soon make the bed and sleep. We said we sympathized and left.

Outside, I told VM that someone had been in the apartment while we were away. I explained how I knew – that is, the missing receipt. He said he thought he had seen someone at the side of the window watching our approach with KPE. Obviously, this was why he had insisted on a full search of the apartment with KPE. We discussed these unexpected and unexplained matters and agreed that the nature of the assignment had markedly changed. We agreed we must improvise a policy to cope with these new factors. We decided we should pretend to leave the area, in case we were under observation, but circle and return to watch the building from behind some kind of cover, although assignment technically over. We took position a little way off behind a delivery van.

After ten minutes KPE came out from the apartment block and began to walk swiftly away. We decided it would be impossible to follow him unobserved, although we are both trained and expert shadows. He, of course, knew us and our appearance well by this time. We had specifically told him our work with him finished when we saw him home. We would have no explanation if we were spotted behind him. We did not want him alerted. We therefore continued to watch the apartment block in case he returned and to note any other developments.

VM writes: there were a fair number of people about around the apartment building and we could not be sure whether any of them connected with our operation. At one stage we thought a man emerged and stood possibly watching the windows of 37. Then he went back into the building. Soon after this the driver of the parked delivery van we'd chosen to hide behind came out and drove away. We therefore needed different cover and moved to a grassed area with trees in front of the apartment block, where the man had stood earlier. He might be of the same physique as the man glimpsed by the side of the curtains in 37.

We took a position behind a holly tree and continued to watch entrance and windows. The living room curtains of the apartment were drawn now but at one point I thought I saw a very brief gleam at their top edge, as from a moving torch beam, not an overhead room light. I spoke of this to BLS who said he also had seen it. Shortly afterwards a man left the apartment block. He seemed of the same build and height as the figure I believed I'd seen at the side of the window earlier. He wore no hat and his hair was black or brown. I thought he might have a torch on him somewhere. Three points arising:

What linked him with KPE, suppose there was a link?

Had he been in the apartment when I searched it with KPE? Could I have missed him?

Had this man removed the chair receipt for some reason?

We decided the apartment offered nothing more of interest and we followed the man. He travelled on the underground to the Steglitz district. We separated and stayed very distant from him for this journey so as to remain undetected.

BLS writes: I removed my cap, which might be distinctive. At Steglitz our target male entered an apartment building. We found the entrance to a service lane on the other side of the street from which we could watch the apartment building unseen. After a few minutes two girls in their twenties, immodestly dressed, noisy, arrived by taxi. They went into the building. I returned to Lichtenberg by train to bring the car, while VM watched the building. I came back with the vehicle and we remained near the apartments until morning, taking two hour watches each while the other slept.

As a matter of fact, Valk didn't really have anything much against either of this pair, BL Schiff and V Mair. That was the point, though: the 'either' aspect. He found each governable enough on his own, and very capable. Difficulties began when they worked together. Then they could become pushy, uncontrolled, headstrong. They primed one another's egos. Look at the way they wrote of altering 'policy' and referred to 'our operation'. They had no authority to alter policy. It was not *their* operation, but the department's. Valk felt irritated. Jointly, they might turn maverick. Probably psychologists could explain the case. 'Mob Mentality' was well documented. What about 'Chums' Mentality'? Naturally, having noted three or four times how they behaved when linked, he'd finally ordered Schiff and Mair should no longer be teamed. How did the ban get ignored or forgotten, then? Well, there had been exceptional manpower demands lately. Perhaps these made the error almost forgivable.

Error? Error! What error? Wasn't it because they'd been pushy, uncontrolled, headstrong, that they'd come up with these undoubtedly brilliant finds? They had to be hailed as a gifted, improvising twosome. All right, he'd hail. They had to be regarded as a dangerously independent twosome. All right, he'd stay watchful.

More of the report:

VM writes: At 7 a.m. KPE left the apartment building. This was another new factor. We had not known until then that he had gone to this apartment block. He had obviously reached there unfollowed by us on the night before and remained until now. Consequently, there might be some connection between him and the man we had followed. It is possible they use the same apartment. We could not determine this without becoming obvious. It appeared likely that Eisen was on his way to work at the Foreign Office.

BLS writes: The two girls left apartment building at 09.50. We had car's standard equipment surveillance camera ready. (Photographs included with this report.) The girls will be traceable, possibly to a club offering this kind of amenity. We do not know, of course, which

*apartment they had spent the night in, though possibly
with KPE and the other man. Considered it best at this
time not to confront them, nor ask for information from
other residents or the caretaker. Vital they should not
know they were under observation. We asked by radio
telephone that both apartments – Lichtenberg and Steglitz
– be put under continuous surveillance.*

*VM writes: At 10.05 the man we had followed last night
from Lichtenberg to Steglitz left the building.
(Photographs included with this report.) He had what
appeared to be a tourist guide book with him and went
to study Steglitz town hall (famous architecturally for its
nineteenth-century Gothic style). After an hour and a half
he returned to the apartments. The new surveillance team
we had requested arrived and we briefed them and with-
drew at 11.25 hours.*

Of course, Schiff and Mair had supplied a verbal report of
some items immediately, because twenty-four surveillance of
both apartments had to be put in place at once, as well as
permanent tails on both targets. Some backgrounding of the
women was also needed, although they seemed on the face
of it authentic, bar-stool whores, probably with only standard,
surface knowledge of their customers. Leave them untroubled
for now. They might have a use later – an operational use.
On Valk's first readings of the written report, he had marked
several paragraphs for possible follow up and expansion,
including the whore references. Plus:

(1) He wasn't certain he understood the time sequence
of incidents at apartment 37. Clarify.

(2) Why hadn't they radioed for support when the job
suddenly grew complicated and clearly needed
extra personnel? He knew the answer, though he'd
never get it from them: this triumph they typically
and graspingly regarded as theirs only, and they'd
keep it exclusive, no invitation to others. They
respected team spirit: *their* team, and only theirs,
the Schiff and Mair team, the Mair and Schiff
team.

(3) He wanted a much more thorough description
of the outside geography at the apartment block.
Or he'd say he did. Damp down their combined
cockiness.

(4) He wanted a much more thorough description of
the apartment interior. Or he'd say he did. Damp
down their complementary cockiness.

SIX

'Those twins of yours – they've done astonishingly well, wouldn't you say, Andreas?'

'Well, yes, astonishingly, sir.' Valk got something like hearty but unhysterical enthusiasm into his voice. Necessary. Wise.

The Colonel Commandant flipped over several report pages so he could remind himself of the signatures: 'V Mair, BL Schiff. Perhaps a little fancifully, I call them twins because they operate so naturally together. Veritable birds of a feather.' For that last bit, the birds and feathers, he dropped into English momentarily. Knecht, the Colonel Commandant, liked to show his international side. 'Oh, do forgive me,' he said, as if poor Andreas Valk must be floored by the foreign phrase. So, back to German: 'They combine by instinct. Or as if by blood. Remarkable. This report – remarkable! And photos!'

'Yes, remarkable,' Valk said. 'I naturally had them in to give my congratulations and, of course, sir, I said they could rely on you and even those above you to be very impressed by their work.' There *were* people above Knecht, naturally, but he might not care to hear them spoken of so bluntly.

But Knecht said: '*Very* impressed. Did you see them as a pair, Andreas? Excellent. Perceptive. To me they seem very much a unit.'

Valk thought that most probably this vindictive swine knew he had interviewed them separately. 'Well, yes, sir, they *are* in some senses a unit. I felt, though, it was more appropriate to do it one-by-one. That is, I think, the customary way to interview our people, whether to praise or reprove.'

'Oh, yes, I suppose that *is* the rule book. You would know it better than I.'

This, to Valk, sounded as if knowing the rule book was the pinnacle of his abilities. Knecht's tone was carefully polite and damaging. God, to get him some comeuppance! 'I wanted to check certain matters. I thought it more suitable to hear them individually.'

'To catch them out?'

'For clarity.'

'Which certain matters did you want to check?'

'A degree of obscurity here and there in the report.'

'Oh, where? I thought it remarkably graphic.'

'The sequence at thirty-seven, mainly.'

'Plain enough, surely. They take Eisen back. There is some-body in the apartment. He is surprised and gets out, so that, when they arrive, the apartment is unoccupied. They keep watch. Eisen almost immediately goes out to somewhere – somewhere unknown till next morning. The man who'd been at the window then returns to the apartment, most likely by some other entrance to the building so as not to bump into your two. In a while, he also leaves, and they tail him to Steglitz, where Eisen is presumably waiting.'

'Yes, sir.'

'No difficulty or possibility of a clash in their stories, surely? We're so fortunate to have them on the staff. These are men who make our Department strong, and, if our Department, our country. I don't think it's too much to claim.'

'Certainly not,' Valk said. What else could he say? When the Colonel Commandant went off on one of his unfettered word trips – turned all fanciful, as he'd term it – you agreed with him. That is, you agreed with him if you were only the Deputy Commandant, older than the Colonel Commandant, and merely a major, and almost certain to remain a major, like Valk. It would be a kind of irreverence to contradict him – in fact, a blasphemy, bringing very rough reprisals, perhaps, in the way that the Old Testament God said, 'Vengeance is mine. I will repay.' Of course, because Maximilian Knecht, the Colonel Commandant, was Maximilian Knecht, the Colonel Commandant, youngish, and in touch with all sorts

of higher-ups, including even, he said, Himmler himself, he
didn't have to worry that those remarkable, feather-matched
twins might want to climb over him, kick him into oblivion.
Or not yet he didn't.

'We must cherish people of that calibre, Andreas. And I'm
sure they cherish you, too. You, at your level, are so closely
in touch with them and their work. Really down alongside
the lads in the, as it were, engine room, accustomed to the
sweat rag and so on, the sweat rag that is not without its own
nobility. I float here, a little above it all. A Colonel
Commandant's privilege! But also a Colonel Commandant's
loss. I feel the distance from our boys and girls in the field.
"Colonel Commandant" – oh, a very nice title to have on
one's office door. A barrier, too, though; an obstruction to full
and deep contact with the troops.'

They were behind the barrier and obstruction today, in
Knecht's untidy office suite with coffees. 'You – fortunate
you – could be *au fait* with their achievements so soon after
the actual events they describe.' Knecht picked up his copy
of the report and pointed delightedly to part of it. 'The frank
admission of uncertainty about that possible watcher behind
an undrawn curtain in the *plattenbauten* dump! This is scrupu-
lousness. This is self-scrutiny. This is acute observational flair,
Andreas. These are men we can trust. And the tailing skills
and the brilliant caution and discretion.'

Knecht thrilled to an earlier paragraph. 'The request in
Lenin's tomb – my God, in Lenin's holy tomb! – for pointers
towards living floozie flesh that offended dear "Ivan". The
contrast! Dick-twitch in a mausoleum! A humanizing touch.
They acknowledge mausoleums exist, but do not allow this
mausoleum to impose its defunct mausoleum nature upon
them, nor upon their writing about it – the mausoleum.'

'Well, no.'

'And I love the way they speak so confidently, so offhand-
edly, indeed, of changing "policy" because the circumstances
have changed. This is assurance. This is intelligent boldness,
don't you agree?'

'I hadn't really thought of it like that.'

'Oh, yes – intelligent boldness, the term exactly. And it has
become "*our* operation". Did you note that, Andreas? That is,
they are at once willing, unprotestingly willing, to assume

absolute responsibility. They are willing and they are auda-
cious enough. Reading their report as soon as it was ready,
you must have become instantly aware of that almost magical
link between them. Together they are clearly more than double
their solo efficiency and invention. Inspired. Formidable.'

Excitement made him stand up from his desk and walk about
the room, giving fist blows to the air as he went on enumer-
ating the report's gorgeous strengths. Did this bastard Knecht
sense how much Valk loathed and feared those two as a working
combination? Their 'magical' cooperativeness could also be seen
as conspiracy – against him, Valk. Was Knecht's lilting enthusiasm meant to weaken Valk, shred his confidence, rupture his
soul? Had he by some foul and filthy instinct guessed how
much Valk would be offended by that reference to 'policy' and
'our operation'? Didn't he detect their abominable arrogance?

But Valk did feel there was usually a purpose to Knecht's
multilingual, insistent, sky-high jabber. Nobody got to colonel
at his age on flimflam. Although you could easily come to
think he was off his head, or drunk, or drugged, or into prema-
ture, galloping senile decay, he'd suddenly come out with
shafts of perception that seemed even more spot-on than they
really were because of contrast with the lunatic lead up. He
didn't need to argue a case. Surprise bordering on shock did
that job for him. People obeyed from a kind of sudden happy
thankfulness: they'd feared they were led by a rampaging
maniac, but now realized that beneath the purple froth his
brain did manage the occasional passably sane stint.

Knecht returned to his desk, his blue eyes behind heavily
horn-rimmed spectacles still brilliant with wonder at the report's
treasures. 'Tell me, Andreas, how do you see it all?' he said.

'In which regard, sir?'

'The whole canvas.'

'An officer from British secret intelligence has recruited a
Foreign Ministry employee as agent and informant. It's a standard peacetime operation. Perhaps the agent dislikes the
present regime. There are people like that about, even in posi-
tions salaried by the state.'

'To what purpose has he recruited the agent?'

'This to be made clear in due time, sir.'

'In due time. Yes, I see.' He paused, then said in very throw-
away style, 'What, specifically, is Eisen's area of work?'

Of course, Knecht would know this. But he liked to show the processes of his mind. 'He's on the Russian desk,' Valk said.

'So, they are interested in Russia. The British are focussed on our relations with Russia, you think?'

'Not established, Colonel. They may have looked for an agent anywhere in the Ministry, or anywhere in government service.'

'And the choice fell on Eisen by chance, you think?'

'My mind is open at this point.'

'Your admirable, typical caution, Andreas.' The dreary tone said he considered Valk's mind as not just open, but open and catastrophically void, like some empty cardboard box caught by a gale and flung noisily all ways along the esplanade, but the noise hollow, booming evidence of emptiness. Knecht glanced down at the report again. 'And they improvise so well, Schiff and Mair! Decisions taken in, as it were, the field of action. Their assignment was simply to take a functionary from his home to Moscow and bring him back. Mere couriers. Chaperones. Bodyguards. But, suddenly, as they near the end of their duties with Eisen, the face at the window – *possibly* a face at the window. And then the missing chair receipt. And then the unexplained sortie by KPE. Mair and Schiff could have ignored all this. They might have decided their assignment was over and they could go home and relax. But not at all. They see beyond their named task. They sense a new *magnitude*. Yes, *magnitude*. They swiftly get into tune with those fresh factors. And what are these factors? What is that new magnitude?'

'At this stage we don't really—'

'The girls look very pleasant and more or less entirely unscarred, as far as can be seen, don't they?' He had the photographs in front of him. He bent closer to squint hard at them. 'We can be fairly certain, I think, that they spent the night with KPE and friend. KPE is interested in *filles de joie*, as we know from the mausoleum. I believe these two doxies –' in English – 'work out of the Toledo club. Yes. I may have run into the fuller-figured, dark-haired one now and then – Olga? A warmhearted kid, and very conversational during wind-down, yet no badgering for extra gifts or to get the fee higher.'

'We have an identification of the man,' Valk replied.

Knecht rapidly, flamboyantly, put a finger to his lips. 'Don't tell me, don't tell me, Andreas!' he cried. 'I absolutely refuse to listen.'

'You want it kept confidential, even from you, sir?'

'Not that. But let me get there without aid, would you, Andreas? Entirely without aid.' He pulled off his spectacles for a second, as though they might give him unfair help, enable him to see through mysteries. 'Please, do allow me to play the detective! It's a little *bêtise* of mine.'

'But you *are* a detective, sir.'

'All the more reason I should be permitted to speculate, then, and to speculate with virtually no prompting, no information, except, that is, what comes from this photograph – which, incidentally, is very much a snatched job and less than fully clear.' He'd put his glasses back on and stared now at pictures of the man.

'We've done a dossier identification from it,' Valk said.

'And I'm sure you have it right, Andreas. But I want to give the old mental machinery a bit of a run, if you don't mind. This will be an exam – an exam I have to sit and pass or fail! Now then, what do we get from the picture, imperfect as it may be? Of course, we have some assistance in the report: he's described as dark-haired, tall, heavily made. The photograph can confirm that much, I concede. But, Andreas, as a challenge – as, indeed, fun – I think I'd like to come at this test from quite another direction. My own method.'

'Fascinating.'

'I'm going to do it in classical, syllogistic style.'

'Interesting,' Valk said.

'The syllogism. Such a highly disciplined, formally regulated way of getting to the truth – to a conclusion. Aristotle loved a good syllogism.'

Valk said: 'He certainly knew what he was about, though many years ago and abroad.' He made this reaction as inane as he could. He wanted to shout: 'You posturing, pompous piece of horse shit, Knecht.' But that might mean not just that Valk would never get higher than major, but he might get a lot lower.

'First thing required is a premise,' Knecht explained for Valk. 'A starting assumption. What do you think that is here, Major?'

'That this man is a spy.'

'Correct! Where do we go from there?'

'That he's a *British* spy.'

'Correct again! We get ahead, we get ahead. And thereafter?'

'Thereafter, I imagine you—'

'Thereafter I propose this, Andreas – that he almost certainly comes from Stephen Bilson's outfit, the Section, as it's tersely, familiarly, known by those who work in it.'

'Yes?'

'How I can be sure this is a Bilson man? Answer: (a) it is a Foreign operation, and Bilson heads aspects of Foreign, though also with Home responsibilities sometimes, if Foreign and Home are inextricably intertwined, as can happen. And (b) Bilson's focus as a chief of Foreign is at present on Germany and, specifically, Berlin. How can I prove this?'

He held up a finger, and then, as more points were added, further fingers. 'One: the general British political climate makes it likely, and (two) Bilson has been seeing that feeble freak, Chamberlain, privately for some time. Chamberlain will obviously be preoccupied with Germany and the Führer. Bilson is not head of the entire British intelligence service, only of his Section. The meetings with Chamberlain are therefore out of line with normal procedure. This does not appear to be a sexual liaison. There is no evidence that either Chamberlain or Bilson is homosexual or bisexual. Goebbels' people have been looking into that, but without any significant findings to date.

'Finally, (three) Bilson was at Heston to welcome the British Prime Minister back from his meeting with the Führer. This kind of public appearance by Bilson is exceptional. The break with custom might be a sign of something fond between them: he wishes to see Chamberlain safely returned. Or it might be simply that Bilson is interested in anything involving high-level dealings with Germany. Whichever it might be, extreme good luck enabled one of our people to spot him there, at the airport. We keep an eye on a senior member of our London embassy staff, Theodor Kordt, who has shown disapproval of the Führer – flagrantly and continually shown disapproval. For his own reasons, Kordt went to Heston in full morning suit to witness Chamberlain's departure, and also turned up to greet his return. Our tail on him noticed Bilson present, recognized him from dossier research. He was with what appeared to be a bodyguard or apprentice.

'Now, (a) this bodyguard was not photographed, but the description we have of him tallies with the description in the Mair–Schiff report of the man they followed, and with the pictures they took near his apartment at Steglitz. Therefore, (b) I would propose that the bodyguard-apprentice at Heston and the spy associated with Eisen are one and the same and work for Stephen Bilson. Eisen would have a code sobriquet, of course. Bilson likes to take names from old clockmakers. It is a hobby of his to collect ancient clocks, as we know.

'Happily, (c) we have a reasonably up-to-date personnel list for Bilson's Section. It tells us what I presume the surveillance pictures from Mair and Schiff tell us, that the British spy is Marcus Delaware Mount, aged twenty-eight. And so, here we have what I humbly propose – subject to correction, of course – the conclusion of our syllogism, Andreas!'

'Bilson was at the Somme,' Valk replied.

'Yes. As were you, of course, Andreas, but on the other side of no-man's-land. You a platoon commander, Bilson a sniper, until both of you moved up the ranks: he rather more slowly than you, at first. Two medals, which again is a similarity between you. Odd to think he might have blown your head off if you'd stuck it above the trench parapet one day. We must consider the present, though. Now, a different sort of battling.'

'Yes, we also thought Mount,' Valk said.

'There are two other men close to Bilson in the Section – Nicholas Baillie and Oliver Fallows, but they don't fit the photo. Shorter, physically slighter people. Undoubtedly, Mount, I'd say. Mother a widow, houses in Bath Spa and Rome. Marcus brought up in both. Wellington School. Oxford. Greats – Latin, Greek, philosophy, ancient history. A First.'

'He'd know about the syllogisms.'

'Possibly recruited at Oxford,' Knecht said. 'Cambridge gathered in students to spy for Russia, Oxford for the king. One of Mount's tutors was Quentin Impey-Reid, who'd done Intelligence work himself in the war. He might have recommended Mount.'

'We've tried to find—'

'Obviously, we will let this run, Andreas.'

'Run? In which respect, sir?'

'Minimum surveillance. In fact, not much more than token.'

'For which?'

'Both – Eisen and Mount.'

'We have them under continuous watch.'

'Pull back at once. And the Foreign Ministry needs to know

nothing yet. We can do without Ribbentrop's nose into things
at this point.'

'Pull back? Wait?'

'Absolutely.'

Valk said: 'I might have trouble with those two.'

'Which two? Mount and Eisen?'

'No, sir: Mair, Schiff. The pair you justly admire so much
for an array of talents.'

'What trouble?'

'They'll want to wrap things up, soon make the arrests.
It's *their* case. Or it's *become* their case, because of that skill
at improvising you so rightly praised. They'll be afraid some
of our other people might sneak in and steal part of their
credit. Yes, as you say, sir, they've been admirably careful
and unobtrusive so far, but they won't want to hang back
for ever.'

Knecht went into something between a shout and a hiss. 'Oh,
won't they? Won't they? Well, you tell them *I'm* sneaking in,
Andreas.' Knecht was fat faced and stout bodied. Valk found it
hard to think of him sneaking in anywhere. But Knecht said:
'Tell them the Colonel Commandant is sneaking in, and that if
the Colonel Commandant is sneaking in, Heinrich Himmler
will know the Colonel Commandant is sneaking in and has
good cause for sneaking in. Tell them they'll have to deal with
at least me, and possibly Himmler personally, if they move too
soon. Or if they move at all without my specific orders. My
specific orders via you, of course, Andreas. The chain of
command will be respected. Certainly. What are they, after all,
these two? Minor, ditheringly hesitant makeweights.' He stood
again and made as if wiping his behind with their report. '"BLS
writes." "VB writes." Whom do they think they are? Goethe?'

Valk said: 'But, sir, you found their work so—'

'Oh, they did their run-of-the-mill stuff all right. They earn
their "Beta-double-plus" –' this in English and Latin – 'and
I don't begrudge that. But street-level material. Now we have
to consider what these events *really* mean, in their widest
sense, don't we? The magnitude I referred to.'

'Absolutely.'

Knecht threw the report back on to his desk and sat down.
He gazed at the picture of Olga. 'Absolutely sweet, and her
friend can supply charming variants,' he said. 'Both use quite

expensive perfume. These things make all the difference, don't they? I might go and have another chat with them, and so on.'

'The Toledo – a select sort of place.'

'It seems strange now.'

'What, sir?'

'To be in a way linked to Marcus Mount and/or Eisen, through these girls.'

'But you got there first. Of the three of you, I mean.'

'I want no intrusion, no disturbance of the normal state of things,' Knecht said. 'For instance, it troubles me that a woman neighbour of Mount told the police she'd seen two men hanging about outside the Steglitz apartment block for a long period, both bare headed and in long top coats. Part of the time they were on foot, but they also used a car. This woman has been especially vigilant and troubled because more than once pieces of broken chairs have appeared in her refuse bin, not put there by her. She didn't know whether these items had been deposited by an apartment block resident or by somebody from outside, which is why she has watched the street a great deal lately.

'I hope this does not sound boastful or patronizing, Andreas, but it's one of my strengths that I understand the feelings of quite ordinary folk, and I can see why pieces of a chair appearing like this would disturb an elderly woman. It's a circumstance she is not likely to have come upon previously. Repeated bits of broken chair in the wrong bin is outside the normal run of things. What kind of activity or philosophy of life can give rise to broken chairs? It might be explainable if they were old chairs, which had to be replaced. But the woman told the police that this was not the case. The chair pieces had every appearance of very-up-to-dateness. Although these loitering men were not, in fact, carrying pieces of a chair to drop in her bin, nor have any further pieces of broken chair been left there very recently, she found these lurkers frightening just the same. Routinely, all instances of unexplained behaviour are passed on by the city police to us for consideration. Do your people, Mair, Schiff, wear long coats?'

'Is this to do with the missing chair receipt somehow, do you think, sir – the one mentioned in the report? Did the woman say the actual *type* of modern chair?'

'I'd like you to consider what the Führer's *real* view of the Russians is,' Knecht replied.

'Well, as a prospective ally and non-aggression partner he—'

'He hates them. Of course he hates them. He does not trust them. He sees their leadership as heathen, their ballet as pornographic, Stalin a murderous crook, and Dostoevsky a bathhouse paedophile. He will never countenance a pact with the Soviets.' He stopped again. 'No, I withdraw that. He will countenance a pact if that pact seems at the time in Germany's best, immediate interests. *At the time*. I stress that. But he will discard it as soon as it becomes a nuisance.'

'But why, then, is he—?'

'He allows this pantomime of visits and discussions to continue because it suits his long-term aim. Long-term aims are what Führers have to take. It is what makes them Führers, Andreas. They see things very large, very clear, very thematic.'

'Which long-term aim?'

'He would not wish us to interrupt the present diplomatic interchanges between Berlin and Moscow, absurd though they may be.'

'Which long-term aim?'

'Oh, he longs for a treaty with the British. He esteems them. I can understand that – Shakespeare, Milton, the cricketer, Dr WG Grace, the spinning jenny. Hitler believes the world should be divided between them and us.'

'But, sir, they behave like a secret, destructive enemy. They send a spy here. He entices, no doubt pays, Konrad Paul Eisen, a Ministry official to betray us. The spy debauches our women, at least one of whom you have previously conferred yourself upon and might revisit in a friendly manner in person.'

'These are routine moves. All countries who can afford it spy on other countries. We don't want the British to think we're deeply scared our talks with Moscow will be revealed. That would give more importance to the talks than they actually have. It could lead to the British deciding to attack us now, before they might be faced with a double enemy: Germany plus Russia. They have difficult, warlike voices there – Churchill, Lionel Paterin, Vansittart. Lionel Paterin particularly, in his brutal style, has been making very aggressive speeches lately, three or four. He is in their Cabinet *and* Defence Cabinet. This is a man of big influence, and big influence not exercised in our favour.

'The Führer wants his State visit to London next Spring. It would help bring him closer to the romantic king, Edward known as David, and therefore to the British people and their government. A king in a democracy is *only* a king in a democracy, but he has massive pull. That pull is exceptionally massive now he has browbeaten so many high-born figures into accepting his much-travelled Yank woman and letting her live in Buck House, as they call Buckingham Palace in their seemingly self-puncturing way. We will be able to forget Russia. A British–German treaty might soon follow this London jaunt by the Führer, despite the ravings of that drunken lout, Churchill, plus Paterin, Vansittart, Eden, and their noisy, Jew-sponsored clique. A spy hunt and capture here, now, in Berlin? No. The repercussions would make that State visit impossible. Mount and Eisen strung up? How could that help, Andreas? The arrests, trials and toppings would have to be publicized. Not even Goebbels and his Public Enlightenment Ministry could stop that getting out and enlightening. A profound chill would be inevitable between the two countries.'

Knecht jutted his almost Habsburg jaw, signalling determination to fix a grip on the future. His speech remained intelligible despite this jut. 'Therefore, the British and their insider, Mount, should be allowed to continue,' he said. 'Bilson, and perhaps Chamberlain, probably think that if they prove Germany seeks a secret arrangement with Russia, it will show Munich to be valueless. They possibly regret Munich now, in hindsight – the paltry bit of paper. Suppose we jump on Mount and Eisen, or whatever they call him, it will seem, as I've said, that the Berlin–Moscow negotiations are immensely significant and must be kept hidden. It would look as though we rushed to wipe out any possibility of an information leak about our negotiations with Moscow because those negotiations are so vital to us.

'Yes, the contemptible war faction in Britain – Churchill, Lionel Paterin, Vansittart, others – would then find it easier to convince Parliament and the country that now, immediately, is the time to hit us, before we become too powerful, backed by Stalin. Bilson may hope for that, and so might Chamberlain, having lost his belief in Munich. And frankly, Andreas, who could blame him for that? Who would have expected Chamberlain ever to have swallowed the rubbish he was given there? I speak, of course, as between you and me only. Therefore, let the chatter with Moscow continue, as though confidentially. It gives us time and does not endanger the London trip.

'Of course, the Russians know the Führer hopes for a state visit to London, and that he hopes, too, that a lasting alliance with Britain will result. This makes the Moscow–Berlin talks about a non-aggression pact look ridiculous. But Stalin will let them proceed because he needs time to repair the harm he's done at the top of the Red Army. Everyone seeks time. The Moscow–Berlin talks are never going to reach fruition, and Mount and Eisen will have to go on telling Bilson, and therefore Chamberlain, that it's still only an idea, an intent, a fleeting Berlin whim. This would not be enough to convince British public opinion to authorize war.

'Mind you, Andreas, I believe – and others far above believe – that the relief after Munich was so great in Britain, so general, so cross-party, cross-class, cross-newspapers, that it could not now be revisited and rejected, even if our talks with Moscow did get pushed into the open. That would be a gamble, though, and one we do not need to take yet, if at all. Just tell those two labourers in the field, Mair and Schiff, they've done very nicely and it's recognized at distinguished levels, but that matters have now gone beyond chair receipts, and beyond the range and comprehension of industrious nobodies. They should get back into their kennels and await a call for some other dogsbody job. And remove all other surveillance, Andreas. I've told the police to ignore the woman's complaint about men watching the Steglitz apartments.'

SEVEN

M arcus Mount saw the result of this order by Knecht, though, of course, he didn't fully know the thinking behind it. In fact, there had been all sorts of developments over the last thirty-six hours that he hadn't completely understood. But that was true of so much Section business.

Sitting alone now at the Toledo club bar, he went over in his head the core events of the last day and a half. He tabulated them in his mind for clarity. He liked tabulating. It made for tidiness. He'd handled problems by this method since childhood.

He had always greatly liked the look of the Toledo club. It had an instantly obvious degree of what must be termed class, yes, class – that is, compared with some other Berlin clubs, which could be total shitholes. No wonder that cartoonist – Grosz wasn't it? – satirized these dumps in the 1920s, showing customers as bloated, coarse, sottish, lascivious. One of his collections was called something like *The Face of the Ruling Class*. Harsh, though probably accurate. Mount thought Grosz emigrated to America just before Hitler took power; but if he'd stayed he could have still found Berlin clubs like that. Not the Toledo, however. Invariably, Mount felt more or less comfortable as soon as he walked in, and did tonight.

Chiming with the club's name, there were Spanish themes, but muted. Genuine, slightly faded yellow and red posters from last year advertising bull fights in Toledo decorated one wall, plus framed photographs of matadors at work in the ring; and there was one photo of bearded American novelist Ernest Hemingway – a great bullfight fan – beaming and brandishing his famous book about the sport, *Death In The Afternoon*. Mount disliked the title. Mawkish. Flamboyant. People and animals had died in afternoons ever since there *were* people and animals, so why make it special to bullfights? Half a dozen bright-metalled sabres were fixed to another wall of the club, as well as some photographs of fencing bouts. Toledo had a world reputation for steel manufacture, particularly its blades.

The mahogany bar was long and built with a gentle, friendly curve. It invited you to come to it and relax. It spoke to Mount of civilization. Small tables and straight-backed chairs, also mahogany, occupied the central area of the big room, with shadowy booths off, each with a table and leather armchairs. An upright piano stood on a band platform at one end, and next to it a small square for dancing was marked out with thin lines of white paint. The Toledo had order. Floral patterns in subdued colours on dark-red wallpaper gave a feeling of warmth and cosiness, despite the swords. The wall behind the bar was covered by a huge, gleaming mirror that caught all the busy to-and-froing.

Mount thought Toulmin showed taste in settling on the Toledo as right for him, and in setting up a happy arrangement with two of its girls, perhaps more, though Mount knew

only the two. Most of the Berlin clubs familiar to Mount had
poor furniture, little space, dark, bare walls – noisy drinking
shops, nothing better. You wouldn't come across girls of Inge's
and Olga's calibre in that sort of shabby pit, or at any rate
not while they were still young, arses radiantly undropped.
He badly needed to find Inge and Olga tonight.

The last thirty-six hours leading up to this Wednesday-night
call at the club had been full of confusion for Mount: some
very poor stuff, some quite good. Despite all his ins and outs
at the Lichtenberg apartment, he'd failed to reach Toulmin or
discover what had been going on. This was frustrating. All
right, late on that Monday, he'd eventually found Toulmin;
or, more like it, *Toulmin* had found *him*, by turning up at
Steglitz, followed by Inge and Olga. And Toulmin's breakfast
account the next morning of events at Moscow had been brilliantly full, of course, and an entirely unexpected boon. During
Toulmin's unexplained disappearance, Mount had a very
guarded talk with SB from a post-office telephone. 'The business man I hoped to meet to negotiate the deal is absent from
Berlin, I'm afraid.' That kind of dismally uninventive coding.

SB had said: 'Patience. Take advantage of all local resources
to complete these sales, please, Stanley.'

From this, Mount deduced that because of the emergency
his work had been raised to a full, official, operational status:
'take advantage of all local resources' meant the British
embassy. SB had sounded badly concerned. Now, Mount could
use the embassy's services and, if necessary, consult the
Service's permanent resident there – Head of Passport Control,
as he was listed, a standard cover. And, via the embassy, Mount
had sent a detailed memorandum of the Toulmin report to SB
yesterday, though only after a disturbing snag or two caused
a few hours' delay. With the report also went, of course, a
reassurance for SB that Toulmin had turned up and was safe.

Toulmin had left for work immediately after breakfast
yesterday, and Mount decided to do the obvious: get to the
embassy, a.m. if possible, and send a summary of the Russia
stuff. It was smack-on relevant to SB's thinking. The core of
the proposals discussed in Moscow, according to Toulmin, would
stipulate that neither Russia nor Germany would join a grouping
of powers threatening the other. The treaty should last ten years,
with a possible extension for another five. The futures of Poland,

Czechoslovakia and the Baltic states – Finland, Estonia, Latvia, Lithuania – were considered. Secret 'rearrangements' for these territories would be negotiated, meaning that in a carve up Germany and Russia would have properly defined 'spheres of influence' and each would respect these. Russia was given an assurance that Germany didn't want Bessarabia.

But first, before dispatching this, Mount had given the girls some breakfast, too. Didn't they deserve proper hospitality? Money alone might have made things seem only businesslike and cold. Neither the girls nor Mount would have liked that. Mount didn't mind paying them Toulmin's share. He felt this fell within the reasonable duties of a host. He was sure that, in the same way, if he and the girls spent time with Toulmin in the Lichtenberg apartment, *he* would have taken care of the fees – possibly using money given him by Mount for work as an agent. It was that kind of civilized social concord.

He tabulated recollections now: (1) CHAIRS.

When the girls had gone, Mount was about to set out to the embassy, but met his elderly woman neighbour again on the stairs. She said: 'In one way, I'm happy to say, matters have greatly improved. Now, I don't see any more broken chair parts in my bin.'

'Bad times do pass if only one is strong.'

'But, forgive me, I speak selfishly. Are there, perhaps, pieces of chair in *your* bin?'

'Not at all.'

'Good.'

'It was a temporary, very untypical matter.'

'However, I've noticed two men of a furtive nature watching the apartments from near the service lane opposite outside. Have *you* noticed such men?'

'"Of a furtive nature"?'

'Shifty. Intent.'

'Are they there now?' he said.

'This morning they are in a car. I have reported them to the police. They might be connected to the business with the chair pieces. Is it a plot of some kind? This is a question that must be asked. What is the connection between these men and the dismembered chairs? They were not carrying anything of the sort when I saw them, but it is surely a worry that they should lurk like this. We are not used to such situations in this part of Steglitz – ruined furniture and loiterers. The police were surprised to hear of the chair fragments in such an area.'

'Yes, I'm sure. What did they say?'

'That they might look into it. One of them told me he would examine the log of past incidents in Steglitz over a period of years and see if any of them concerned broken chairs. They haven't called on me yet.'

'Ah.'

'But perhaps they will. I said the matter had to be regarded as urgent.'

'Well, yes.' God, he might have to get rid of all the birch and metal laminated chairs in case the police did come and began to ask tenants as a matter of urgency about these fragments. They would see the resemblance between the chairs in Mount's apartment and the bits described by his neighbour. Then, all sorts of questions might start.

He had turned back on the stairs and struck his forehead a slight palm blow to signify forgetfulness. 'Excuse me, I must return to my apartment. I've left the Berlin guide book behind. I'm going to look at Steglitz town hall today. It's been recommended to me as of great architectural interest. Although I come frequently to the apartment here, you know, somehow I've never gone to see the town hall. It's remiss of me. The book has notes.'

'You are British, I think. In your country, perhaps, they don't have town halls of this type, this grandeur. Very handsome. Nineteenth-century neo-Gothic.'

'That period is often underrated.'

Mount had gone back to his apartment and found the book. It would do as a prop. But, really, he'd wanted to check on the street outside. He glanced from the window and saw a parked Mercedes. It was near an old, aggressively simple election poster, stuck to one of the service lane walls. Mount had noticed it on his first stay in Steglitz years ago. Rather weathered now, it would presumably have been for the presidential contest of 1932: a Hitler mugshot on a black background with his surname in big, white, plain sans serif capital letters underneath. It didn't work for him then, but the next year, 1933, he'd made it to Chancellor and dictatorship.

He tabulated: (2) SURVEILLANCE recollections.

The watching car meant an embassy trip at present could be foolish, a give-away – if there was anything left to give away. Postpone it, he'd decided. The town hall called. 'Get diversionary, Marcus Mount,' it said. When he went out, he saw there were two men in the car: one, very tall, at the wheel; the other, shorter, had the passenger seat. They showed indifference to him. To be expected. They'd have been trained in acting out boredom, as Mount himself had been: 'Today, lads and lasses, you learn deadpan: don't alert a target by revealing interest.' And there'd been tips on how to swivel your eyes without swivelling your head, and on how, laboriously, to assemble nonchalance.

But Mount naturally wondered whether these might be the two who had arrived at Lichtenberg with Toulmin – his escort, warders, bodyguards – although the taller man no longer wore the aslant cap. If so, they must somehow have tailed Mount to his flat on Monday night, starting at the *plattenbauten* hive, along the Lichtenberg streets, on the U-Bahn, then through part of Steglitz. Hell, he'd failed to spot them. Had they witnessed from some concealed nook all the comings and goings at Toulmin's apartment block; perhaps watched him while he watched the windows of thirty-seven?

The idea that he'd been viewed while unaware scared Mount. Well, naturally. A spy was supposed to view others unaware of him, not get viewed unaware. The situation shunted him back into long-term anxieties about his competence, and, therefore, his and others' safety. At training school, Mount had been weak at tailing and at dodging tails. They said he had 'a severe, though correctable, deficiency in whereabouts awareness', owing to self-absorption. This they'd described as a serious fault in an intelligence operative, and one he'd better get rid of. They'd made self-absorption sound sort of dreamy and frothy, like a romantic movement poet. In several of the surprise exercises an instructor would get up close and culpably unnoticed to Mount when he was walking or tubing to work in London. What could have been the muzzle of a pistol would jab at his kidneys. Actually, it was only a ratty, stiff finger masquerading for the occasion, and for the wake-up sermon, as the muzzle of a pistol. 'Were you thinking of cunt, cunt?' an instructor had asked after the fourth of these lapses. 'You could be dead, sonny boy. Do attend to your deficiency in whereabouts awareness. It's time you noticed that whereabouts are everywhere, which is why they're called whereabouts.'

Mount would have had to admit that sometimes he *was* thinking of cunt, especially on the tube where there was so much of it to incite interest, clothed but still thinkable about. He *didn't* admit it, partly because the instructor who'd mock-pistol poked him on that occasion was a woman. To Mount, it would have seemed indelicate, even though she'd clearly been the one to bring cunt into things. These days, women appeared in many jobs that previously had been more or less reserved for men. And some spoke like men – perhaps felt especially qualified to refer to cunt.

He hadn't been able to see much of Toulmin's companions' features at Lichtenberg, but, after his quick gaze at the Mercedes, he thought the taller man had a jagged, bony profile, a sharp, Mr Punch chin and a prominent nose. His mate looked plumpish, sallow, round-faced, thick necked. He'd do well under a hook-on Santa Claus beard or touting for customers outside a nude show. In the car, he'd been smoking a small cigar.

Mount had continued towards the town hall, flourishing the booklet in his swinging left hand. He hadn't looked back. It might have shown he knew about them. When he arrived, he walked slowly around the building twice, by turns gazing and studying the notes in his guide. He aped awe, a neo-Gothic worshipper close to ecstasy. But was it credible that anyone could think this bristlingly ugly, pretentious, lumpy creation deserved a visit, unless you wanted to go in and pay your rates or complain about holes in the roads? Mount liked a building's appearance to match its purpose, but this one seemed made to browbeat, to nauseate, to repel.

He had the impression that both men from the car had come on foot with him, but he never saw them, although his devotions around the town hall now allowed him to look about in all directions. Mount might himself be poor at the tailing and counter-tailing game, but he could recognize its skills in others. These two seemed to have most of the tricks, invisibility included, despite the Mr Punch chin and the tree-trunk neck. No deficiency in whereabouts awareness had hampered Mount here. His nerves saw to that. Awareness he had by the tun and ton. Training school had said his deficiency in whereabouts awareness was correctable. He'd corrected it.

But he still failed to locate the stalkers, suppose they *were* stalkers. And if he did suppose it, the meaning was harsh: they

knew of his association with Toulmin – may even have seen
Toulmin leave the building earlier that day, making for the
Foreign Ministry. And possibly they'd also observed Inge and
Olga arrive or depart or both, though perhaps the watchers could
not be sure which apartment they'd visited. Mount might have
several lives dependent on him. The training would say it didn't
matter much as long as they were foreign lives, 'collateral lives',
but, in his sloppy way, he couldn't go along with that.

He'd spent about an hour at the town hall, then returned to
his apartment. The Mercedes had still been there, though
empty by then. He'd watched it from the window – concealed
again, he hoped, by the drawn back curtain, as at thirty-seven.
And after a while the two men had reappeared, walking, from
the direction of the town hall, and climbed into the car. Furtive?
Shifty? Mount would have said 'purposeful', 'unshowy'. What
had they thought of the architecture?

Not long after this, two other men had arrived in a blue
Opel Olympia. They left their vehicle and got into the back
of the Mercedes. Furtive? Shifty? Mount would have said
'urgent', 'alert'. The two men in the front turned and the four
of them seemed to chat. Mount thought it must be a briefing
session for the Olympia relief team, a changing of the guard.
His ostentatiously reverent visit to the town hall would be
described and his attempt to semaphore innocence with the
tourist book. *He* would be described. Perhaps Toulmin and
the girls would be described. Yes, Mount had lives dependent
on him.

Soon, the Olympia crew returned to their own car and the
Mercedes drove off. Mount had moved away from the window.
The two in the Mercedes, and those two who'd taken over
from them, plainly believed he didn't realize they were there,
or the sentry job would have been split: one to watch the front
of the building, one the back – though, of course, there might
be another unit at the back, not seen by Mount or the woman
on the stairs.

Perhaps these watchers at the front had heard of Mount's
whereabouts awareness deficiency and couldn't know it had
just been cauterized. And perhaps he *might* have been unaware
of them, but for his neighbour on the stairs again with her
anxious adjectives and refusal to rest easy. He'd still felt he
must get to the embassy as soon as he could.

Now, at the Toledo, Mount tabulated recollections: (3)
MOSCOW.

One of the other main disclosures from Toulmin at breakfast
yesterday morning had been that there were signs of a growing
importance of Molotov, while Litvinov sank – Molotov a much
tougher proposition for Britain, of course, and probably
much closer to Uncle Joe. In Toulmin's view, Germany and
Russia were each terrified of the other. Hitler was scared of the
Red Army. That was partly why he wanted Czechoslovakia,
though he'd postponed the actual assault. Toulmin could sense
that Hitler was worried a Russian attack could come that way
and reach east Germany in a flash. But, Toulmin also got the
impression from some Moscow gossip that Stalin probably knew
what a mess the Red Army was in – since he'd purged more
than half the generals. 'He doesn't want conflict with Germany,
not at present, because the Russian military is nowhere near up
to scratch.' Stalin, it became plain, trusted nobody, especially
not his friends and potential allies. 'Apparently, he listens only
to Nikolai Yezhov, the "poison Dwarf", head of their
Organizational Bureau and so on,' Toulmin had said. 'Yezhov
tells him there are enemies everywhere, determined to destroy
the Soviet Union. Many were inside Russia and had to be elim-
inated. So, the Terror. But some were other nations and must
be treated as likely, dangerous aggressors. For the moment
Yezhov is powerful, perhaps third after Molotov and Stalin.
Yezhov nourishes Stalin's phobias.' According to Toulmin, both
countries sought friendship, as protection. Or appeared to.

Mount tabulated recollections: (4) SURVEILLANCE
(continued).

It had been crucial to get this material to Stephen Bilson
as soon as possible. So, Mount had decided he'd exit from
the rear and somehow get to the embassy, if the Olympia pair
looked likely to remain in the car for a while. He returned to
the edge of the window and looked down. The men were still
together in the Opel. Good.

The next time Mount peered out, an hour or two later, the
man in the passenger seat had a wireless handset up to his
ear. Mount decided to wait and watch. After a few minutes,
the man put away the handset and spoke to the driver. Their
conversation was brief, but seemed animated, and then Mount
heard the Olympia's engine start. The car pulled out from its

parking spot, turned right at the end of the street, like the Mercedes, and disappeared.

Again Mount waited. Perhaps they would circle, and then vary their parking position on return, hoping to be less obvious. They couldn't have gone for keeps, could they? What was happening? Did it make sense to relax their vigil, maybe abandon it? Everyone knew that surveillance had to be continuous or it became useless. When you resumed after a break you might be starting surveillance on a totally changed situation. There could have been quick, secret departures, quick, secret arrivals, though you did not know it. Perhaps the woman's complaint to the police had been passed on and the Opel couple told they were too noticeable there. Perhaps the men had detected the woman watching and decided they'd switch.

Or . . . or. Mount did wonder if they'd just had the order to withdraw, withdraw permanently. Why, though? He knew this might be hope rather than a wise guess. A trap? Was it an inducement to go out again, and perhaps lead to somewhere more significant than the gorgeous Steglitz town hall – such as, for instance, the British embassy?

He had waited in the apartment for another couple of hours yesterday. Neither of the cars reappeared, and he'd seen nobody on foot patrol. He felt increasingly baffled that the watch might have been lifted. If the original pair had followed him here from Lichtenberg it must mean, mustn't it, that they suspected a shady bond between a Foreign Ministry official, full of important secrets, and this stranger – supposing, that is, they hadn't identified the stranger? How had they connected him with Toulmin on Monday night? They clearly had, hadn't they, and seeing Toulmin leave the building on Tuesday morning would have confirmed the connection for them. Yet they, or their chiefs, had closed the operation. Madness? Impossible?

Mount tabulated recollections: (5) BRITISH EMBASSY.

He'd made himself a soup and cheese meal, then had yet another look down at the street: still nothing and nobody hanging about. He went from the apartment and, very watchful, set out for the embassy. For the present, he shelved his worry about the chairs. He did some unnecessary changes on the U-Bahn to check for gumshoes, classic anti-tail drills. No. He'd been sure he had no tail. He'd become sure that, if he did have a tail, he would have located it, them. Yes, he'd learned something permanently useful: Mount, stay awake and aware.

At the embassy in Wilhelmstrasse, Bernard Kale-Walker, Head of Passport Control, Germany, as it were, had helped him draft then encode the telegram to SB. It would be decrypted and on his desk at the Section by the end of the day. 'High-grade material,' he'd said about the dispatch. 'High-grade and alarming. What comes next?'

Well, I'll give things a day and a half in case of develop-ments, and then, if there aren't any, tomorrow night I must get to the Toledo club and warn two commercial girls there that they might have recently qualified for a state police dossier. I'll have to concoct some non-espionage tale as to why this should be. Perhaps I'll take one or both back to the apartment so I can give the yarn in privacy.

Mount had thought this, but didn't say it. It would have involved telling Kale-Walker he'd unknowingly, stupidly, allowed himself to be tailed from Lichtenberg to Steglitz on Monday night, and that Inge and Olga visited the apartment now and then for a bit of an orgy. These topics Mount preferred to keep quiet about. It might also suggest he was putting an operation at risk for inanely big-hearted reasons. 'I'll lie low for a day or so, see if there are any developments,' he said.

'What sort of developments?' Kale-Walker had asked.

'Occasionally it can be wise to do nothing.'

'"Masterly inactivity." Who said that?'

'Me, if I'd thought of it.'

Perhaps the German security people had become keen on masterly inactivity, too, and so the Olympia had been called home yesterday afternoon. For a reason Mount could not see, did they want for now to avoid a public espionage fracas in Berlin? Politics? Would they allow the link between him and Toulmin to continue? Mount had decided not to make it a priority to warn Toulmin. Another journey to Lichtenberg would be needed, or a wait around the Foreign Ministry once more, or an attempt at a booth phone call. And he couldn't tell what results any of these might have.

Even if he did get a warning to him, what could Toulmin do? Would either he or Mount be allowed to flee Germany? That was very different from being tolerated inside the country as a clever tactic of some sort, possibly supervised at a distance

– at liberty, it seemed, but on a long lead. After all, Toulmin would rate as a traitor, and Mount was a spy. Could Germany possibly let them do a flit? Quite a question, that, and the answer depressing. Possible exits might be arranged, though: a small plane lands at night on a remote, improvised airstrip; a submarine surfaces to meet a rubber dinghy off some secluded beach? Possibly, it would come to something like that. But either would take a deal of setting up, with Kale-Walker most probably in charge, as Service chief in Germany. For now, Mount shelved the notions.

Kale-Walker – square built, blunt faced, hard voiced, grey-eyed – had been messing about with passports, or not, in Berlin for five or six years: an exceptionally long spell in such a sensitive post. SB admired what he called his 'management abilities, rough-house aura, and polished instincts', though Mount didn't know how Kale-Walker had applied the qualities in those five or six years. At Mount's Oxford college, Kale-Walker had been a scholar with two rugby Blues as a scrum-half, and then a don. But he'd moved over to this other trade a few years before Mount arrived as an undergraduate. 'Your Russian stuff from the agent – I think it fits with what I've been picking up,' Kale-Walker had said.

'On which front?'

'Czecho.'

'Munich won't stop him from going in when it suits?'

'Munich means nothing, as you must know. I'm not sure our people understand the full, mystic dimensions of the problem. Hitler believes he has a mission, a destiny. He thinks he's the greatest German ever and that, therefore, Germans in what's been Czechoslovakia since 1919 expect him to free them. He accepts they are entitled to. As he sees it, he has no option. *Noblesse oblige.* Only he can do it. He's a saviour picked by Fate. Same with Austria.

'It's not Munich that's holding him back from a march into Czechoslovakia. It's the military. His generals tell him an attack there would start a European war, with France, Britain and Russia allied against him. They talk to him about belligerent politicians in Britain – Paterin, of course, Churchill, Vansittart. They believe the German army would be under-supplied and smashed by an international coalition. Beck – General Ludwig Beck – has written a secret analysis for Hitler, warning of

certain disaster if he acts too soon. I've managed to get sight
of that. Beck favours a Czecho invasion, but not yet. I've given
SB the contents, of course. It's backed by the views of others
in the High Command. Some are vehemently anti-Hitler. As
you'd expect, he constantly fears assassination, maybe by high
rank, disaffected service men. He wears a lightweight bullet
proof vest at all times and protective metal in every hat. He'd
have to be shot in the face. As an ex-sniper, SB probably
would have worked that out for himself. But I've mentioned
it to him.'

'In case he's involved in security for the state visit, you mean?'

'That kind of thing. And snipers are trained always to go
for the top man available. Double shot at him. Don't waste a
bullet on somebody lesser. And don't get cocky and think you
can do it in one. A rapid pair. Knock the leader over and it
brings chaos. SB probably *will* be involved in security for the
visit, although he's nominally the overseas chief. Chamberlain
trusts him.'

'To do what?'

'But, despite all the risks, *kismet* still calls the Führer,' Kale-
Walker replied. 'Perhaps he thinks he can keep Russia out of
any alliance against him by a pact – or by the long pretence
of seeking a pact. That would tie in with what you sent from
your man.'

'Entirely. Brilliant of you to have got access to the Beck
analysis. May I ask how?'

'Of course you may ask,' he said.

Mount waited.

'I have it in mind to get rid of the Steglitz apartment
fairly soon,' Kale-Walker said. 'We've been there too long.
These places can become noticeable. And I hear you had
trouble with some of the furniture. Do you spot anything
else untoward?'

'It's ideal.'

'Well, perhaps. Neighbours all right? Any nosiness, intru-
siveness?'

'We keep ourselves to ourselves.' Mount stood up to leave.
'I'll be in touch again,' he said.

'I'm not here for a week. I have to go with the map-makers
to Dresden.'

'We need a new map of Dresden?'

'The war, if it comes, will mean heavy air-bombardment of important towns.'

'But Dresden is just one big baroque china shop, isn't it?'

'Was, until a couple of centuries ago. Meissen next door does the porcelain business now. We need to take a look at the Dresden changes. Key rail-junction? There'll be all kinds of targets.'

Mount had done what he told Kale-Walker he would do – remain in the apartment and wait for the rest of Tuesday, and most of Wednesday, in case of 'developments'. None. Toulmin did not arrive, nor Inge nor Olga. As far as Mount could tell, nobody watched the apartment, front or back. Again he postponed any decision on the chairs. Or, rather, he postponed any decision to get rid of them. It would be very hurtful if any, or all, or some, of those three visited and found the chairs had all been removed, including the one they'd so kindly brought. Olga had thought the four chairs vital to the apartment's ambience. No chairs at all – or different chairs, hastily bought – would upset her and the other two.

Mount had caught up on some reading: a Christopher Isherwood novel set mostly in present day Berlin, *Mr Norris Changes Trains*; and a story called *Venusberg*, the second sparse book by an emerging, old Etonian novelist called Anthony Powell, about a British foreign correspondent sent to some Baltic city. Mount thought both tales illustrated pretty well the rackety state of Europe since the October revolution and the war. No wonder there were plenty of jobs in the Service.

Mount, still in the Toledo bar, tabulated recollections, bringing him firmly up to the present: (6) TOLEDO (this evening, earlier).

Tonight – also as he'd told Kale-Walker – he'd gone to the Toledo to look for Inge and Olga and warn them, with the possibility that Toulmin might be there, too. The club soothed him, after all the uncertainties of Monday and Tuesday. SB probably wouldn't have thought much of the Toledo, though. He was used to the stately comforts and sedate Englishness of the Athenaeum, a different kind of club, not one where anybody could walk in off the street. Mount had walked in off the street to the Toledo. The Athenaeum wouldn't have let Mount in as a member, of course: too young, too insignificant and lightweight. Clubmen ran Britain. You couldn't say clubmen ran Germany, not even Toledo clubmen.

The place was pleasantly busy. He couldn't see the girls or Toulmin, so he stood at the bar and ordered a beer. There were other girls here. The club clearly had a rule that they must not come and pester customers. They stood in a group at the far end of the bar, chattering, laughing, doing an occasional pirouette to exercise their muscles and show all aspects. The mirror took up almost the whole wall behind the bar, so he could look at the girls from two angles. An elderly man in a tuxedo began to play some leisurely tunes on the piano. A couple stood and sedately slow foxtrotted. Mount found himself thinking of the Toledo for a moment as genteel. He approached the girl nearest to him: a thin, quite tall, eye-bright, small-featured blonde. They joined the other couple. He thought he'd be able to get a better view into some of the dimly lit booths from the dance square, in case Inge and Olga were there. The girl moved fluently, and at a respectable distance from him.

She gazed, smiling, into his face. 'Ah, but you are looking for someone else,' she said.

'Yes, sorry. Some friends.'

'I'm quite new here, but I'm told people often make friends in the Toledo and then come back later looking for them.'

'This is the mark of a good club,' Mount said. 'Which club did you go to before?'

'There are many clubs in Berlin.'

'Few as good as the Toledo.'

'What does "good" mean?' she replied.

'Of exceptional quality.'

'But what gives it that quality? I think you and I would have different views about that. After all, you don't work here, do you?'

'I feel at ease in the Toledo.'

'Why? Because of the bullfight posters? It is not really available to me, you see.'

'What?'

'To feel at ease. A customer can feel at ease. For us it is not so simple.'

'You will get to know people, I expect.'

'The other girls?'

'In general.'

'In this work you don't get to know people very well.'

'There are some who come here regularly,' Mount said. He felt as if everything he said jarred.

'Yes, I expect some men do. I don't know whether we ever get to know them, though. Yesterday somebody was here looking for people he knew. People he *said* he knew.'

'You didn't believe him?'

'It's an easy thing to say – that you know people.'

They were silent for a while. The music ended. Mount and the girl went to the bar. She asked for champagne, as he had expected her to. He said he'd also have champagne, to make sure she was really drinking what he'd paid for. He watched to see they were served from the same bottle. They were. He didn't know much about champagne, but it seemed OK. The Toledo must really be quite a club. He said: 'Do you know the people whom the man yesterday was looking for?'

'You are English, are you?' she said. 'I couldn't tell at first. Your German is excellent.'

'But?'

'But it's German spoken by an Englishman. And your appearance – English.'

'English in what way?'

'As if you own an empire.'

'We *do*.'

'Is that a nice feeling?'

'I've never thought about it very much.'

'Because it seemed natural to have an empire?'

'Yes, like that.'

'Will you always have it, do you think?'

'Empires do come and go, decline and fall.'

'I've heard of that book,' she said.

'Which?'

'*Decline and Fall*, by your Evelyn Waugh.' She sounded the g.

Mount said: 'There's also *The Decline and Fall of the Roman Empire* by our Edward Gibbon.'

'And that might happen to *your* empire?'

'Perhaps.'

'If there is a world war two?'

'No, we would win that.'

'I think world war two will not take place,' she said.

'Who knows?'

'I expect you're trying to find the same people as the man who came in yesterday was trying to find,' she replied.

'Was he also English, then?'

'No, very German.'

'What does that mean?'

'No accent. And he asked questions about the people he was searching for as if I must answer.'

'Did you tell him?'

'I am not happy to be asked questions in that manner.'

'I'll be careful. Do people who own an empire also ask questions in that manner?'

'But you haven't asked any questions about these people. You're too clever. You'll wait for me to tell you about them. This is how you got your empire – in a roundabout way, not just by fighting.'

'We lost part of an empire by fighting. The others fought better.'

'You should have behaved in a roundabout way. Then America would still be yours, and you would control the world and Hollywood. But you had a foolish king at that time, didn't you? His family came from Hanover. They should have stayed there. I am Annette.'

'Stanley. Which people do you think I'm searching for?'

'Olga. Inge.'

'And the man yesterday asked about those two? Did he find them?'

'They weren't here. They must have had appointments elsewhere.'

'Have you seen them recently?'

'I've only been here a little while. Now, you're asking questions in the way he did.'

'And that doesn't work?'

The barman gave them refills.

'Why are you in Berlin, Stanley?'

'Business.'

'Which?'

'Property.'

'Do you own property in Germany?'

'You mean, do I have a personal empire in Germany?'

'Your English money is strong. Have you bought property

with it in Germany because houses and apartments are cheap
for you?'

'I am here to study some of your admirable property on
behalf of local government, in case they should want to copy
it in England. The *plattenbauten*. And the town hall at Steglitz.'

'Perhaps I believe this.'

'Many countries are interested in *plattenbauten*. Town halls
as well. A colleague called Clifford, also visiting Berlin, is
even more interested in *plattenbauten* than I am.'

'You are an employee?'

'Certainly.'

'You, yourself, do not own *plattenbauten* developments
here, and will not own them in England?'

'Nor town halls.'

'Why are Inge and Olga special?' she replied.

'Have you seen them lately?'

'Once, they say, Olga went with a member of the security
police. I think more than once. She can be very boastful about
this, I gather.'

'The Gestapo? Was it this man from the Gestapo who came
searching for her?'

'Is that important for you? Also, some of the girls say Olga
and Inge know a man from the Foreign Ministry – know him
very well. I think he must be in a high post. He has plenty
of money.'

'And was *he* the one who came searching for them, Annette?'

'No. But often he'll come in and meet them here, I understand. I don't know which he prefers. Olga is very adept, the
girls tell me. They seem to like to be three. That is not unusual.
Or perhaps they meet some other man later.' She became irritated. 'We would all like to be so successful. It's not pleasant
to be with someone who wants to find somebody else.'

'It's a business matter.'

'To do with *plattenbauten* or town halls, I expect. Or are
you to do with that other kind of business?'

'Which?'

'I'm not sure. How could I be sure? Security perhaps?
Secrets.'

'Secrets? But *plattenbauten* are known about internationally. My colleague, Clifford, is exceptionally well acquainted
with them.'

'Steglitz town hall is a monstrous mess.' The music had begun again. 'Now I must go and be ready to dance with another partner.' She went back to the group of girls. Mount couldn't make out what had made her lose interest in him. Was it because he had crudely translated her words 'security police' into 'Gestapo' twice? Not roundabout enough? Or was it because he had told her he did not own properties and was, therefore, only an 'employee'? Of course, he *was* only an employee, though not in the property game. And she'd half sensed that. He'd thought of asking Annette back to the apartment when her stint at the club finished, but that might offend Inge and Olga if they arrived there with Toulmin, and it would put the numbers out. Probably Toulmin himself wouldn't mind any addition.

EIGHT

Andreas Valk thought the first full security meeting for the Führer's likely trip to London a truly joyous gathering. It had the feel, the rich scent, of victory. Invitations to make a state visit were rare. Yet the British authorities had virtually pleaded with the Führer to come, and to share all the pomp and grandeur of the occasion with their king. Wisely, they had realized that Edward VIII would spectacularly benefit from very publicly associating with – and hosting – the Führer. They sought a fusion of the traditional and the new, the historically founded and the dynamically creative.

By contrast, that loud, posturing, Italian oaf, Benito Mussolini, would never be asked: impossible to rely on decorum from him when with royalty. For the Führer to be welcomed into Buckingham Palace to stay several nights as a guest meant, didn't it, that he, and therefore the Fatherland, were both recognized as noble parts of the great, advanced, civilized, community of Western nations? For today's meeting, Valk wore what he called his 'Vienna suit': dark blue, fine material, tasteful cut, acquired with very little difficulty during the recent trouble-free incorporation of Austria into Germany.

The Führer, an Austrian-German himself, had for years longed to bring back into the Fatherland this country lost in the peace settlement.

'Edward the Eighth' – Valk liked the actual spoken sound of this noble rank, in either German or English. Time had produced that number eight: a fine continuity for the name, appearing, reappearing, off and on through hundreds of years since Edward the Confessor in the eleventh century. But this didn't mean the title 'Führer' lacked substance merely because no number was suffixed. The opposite could be argued. This title had not been handed down, but was indisputably, conscientiously, earned and unique to one man. *My Struggle!* That 'my' so significant, so exact and individual, so powerful, yet so poignant, in the title of his famed autobiography.

Of course, other countries' monarchs might have numbers after their names, some higher than eight. In France there'd even been a Louis XVIII. But Valk found a special, admirable resonance and solidity in the current British sovereignty score. If he'd abdicated in 1936, as he very nearly did, there would be a George VI on the throne now. Valk thought this somehow lacked resonance, not just because six was less than eight. The appeal to the ear of 'George the Sixth' somehow fell short of 'Edward the Eighth'.

Valk could be considerably influenced by words. For instance, he very carefully picked 'joyous' to describe his reaction to the present planning conference for the triumphant visit. This was not only because the special gathering pointed to magnificent, justified progress for the Führer and Germany. No, something else: although the subject discussed was security, and, therefore, certainly serious, it delighted him to find that the general atmosphere here today had a remarkably relaxed tone. 'Festive.' This was another word he associated with the proceedings. Yes, the tone reminded him of the pleasant, exuberant cheerfulness of a festival. It was as though the coming splendour of celebrations in London had already begun to show aspects of itself here, as spring flowers would signal the glorious approach of summer. He felt pleased that he had somehow anticipated the pleasantness of the mood and put on the excellent 'Vienna suit' to harmonize.

So, 'joyous', 'festive' – these seemed to Valk exactly suitable terms for the initial planning session. The Führer would call on a supremely friendly king and country, their enduring, happy relationship brilliantly endorsed and enshrined at Munich. Security preparations should amount to not much more than a formality. If the visit remained a real prospect, Valk would go over to London soon with a couple of staff to check well ahead on safety provisions; but he expected the British to have given full, effective consideration to this side of things. It would be merely a rubber-stamping duty for him and his small team. A sniper, or snipers, in some high building overlooking the procession route would be the obvious main danger. Anyone could realize this and provide against it. Of course, Bilson himself had been a sniper, was familiar with their work methods and tricks, so he would know how to guard against the danger.

Valk had been rereading some British history. For his own intellectual satisfaction he wanted to set the Führer's visit in a context. And he'd like to have available some general, informed conversation when working with the British security people. Naturally – and depressingly – the most important recent history must be the war. He and Bilson both knew plenty about this. Valk sometimes wondered if that appalling experience had affected his mind. Possibly Bilson wondered the same about himself. The constantly updated dossier kept on him by Knecht and Valk didn't mention any such weakness, though. And Valk hoped his own career dossier had nothing of the kind, either. He could imagine the sort of seemingly considerate but dismissive commentary Knecht might write: *a capable officer, despite the obvious lasting effects of bombardment trauma. He strives very creditably to fight the consequent neurosis/psychosis, and only rarely can evidence of mental damage be detected, in a zombie blankness of the face and sad, alarming slump of his shoulders.*

These matters of the mind were very vague and elusive. Anyway, he thought it might be best to steer away from the Somme and other battles as an area of discussion if he met Bilson, as he almost certainly would. Valk would concentrate on less controversial and more favourable topics: say, the eighteenth-century British acceptance of the Hanoverian line of monarchs, leading, ultimately, to Edward VIII; or Waterloo – 'choc sanglant', as Hugo called it – a 'bloody clash' in which Napoleon was destroyed by Britain and Prussia as the warrior allies they should always be, Prussia having since become part of a united Germany.

Valk saw that, in an admittedly minor way compared with the Führer's, his own reputation and status could be given a leg-up by this London commission. Although it might in some senses be only a formality, the job was ultimately and unquestionably about the safety and life of Adolf Hitler in person. *In person!* Responsibilities did not come much more demanding but inspiring than that. At this preliminary stage he would have the Führer's well-being entirely in his care. What an accolade, to be trusted with such work! Perhaps, after all, Knecht did *not* regard him as crippled by 'zombie blankness' and a disintegrating physique.

Valk intended taking two of his people to deal with fringe matters, but the main effort, suggestions, observations, scrutiny must come from him. He'd selected Mair and Schiff as support. They'd been more or less idle since their escort role in Moscow, followed by those busy, headstrong, utterly non-agendad activities around the apartments at Lichtenberg and Steglitz. The kind of banal tasks he'd give these two in London would help remind them they were minor figures in the wider international scene.

And they needed that reminder – continually. Valk considered it would be stupid and naive to leave them unsupervised in Berlin if he went to London. They were an ambitious, envious, conniving pair, and Valk had to be on hand and watchful to guard his career. During the war, hadn't he seen many a senior officer undermined by supposed colleagues? Subordinates manufactured hatreds, ganged up, schemed. Often they'd spent more venomous energy on these conspiracies than in fighting the enemy. Perhaps this explained Germany's defeat.

He knew Mair and Schiff resented being so arbitrarily pulled off the Steglitz surveillance. As they saw it, their counter-espionage initiative and skills had been treated with indifference, even contempt. They blamed Valk. Although he'd told them the withdrawal order came from Knecht, possibly even from Knecht's pal Himmler, they probably didn't believe him. They didn't want to. Valk was the one they dealt with – who'd told them the operation was closed down, and who radioed the relief pair in the Opel to quit at once. So, he got their totally idiotic, rank-and-file rage. And, left unhobbled in Berlin, they might apply that dirty rage in tactics to weaken, even destroy, his authority and standing.

Knecht required certain extra inquiries to be made in London, and Valk would drop these also on to Mair and Schiff. This work would be extremely confidential, and Knecht believed Valk's main, and very open, duties in Britain, checking safety measures, would provide cover for this other, sensitive and secret investigation. Knecht wanted detailed, full information on the extramarital sexual life of one of the newly formed, so-called British 'Defence Cabinet': Lionel Paterin. This Defence Cabinet had membership from the general British Cabinet, like Paterin, as well as leaders of the three armed Services, the Prime Minister, armament manufacturers, transport experts, Winston Churchill. It might be that Himmler or Goebbels wanted the information on Paterin and had told Knecht to get it – who then told Valk to get it, who would tell Mair and Schiff to get it. Several times recently Paterin had made abusive public comments about the Reich and its Chancellor. He deserved to be targeted. The name of the woman was known: Mrs Elizabeth Gane-Torr, adulterous wife of a successful businessman. It shouldn't be a difficult job.

Goebbels possibly believed such revelations would have a propaganda value if relations with Britain, so rosy and positive after Munich, nevertheless began to darken. He'd want to show to Germans and, in fact, to the world that, even at the very top, the British political system was ridden with degeneracy. This might help boost morale in the Reich's armed forces and among the general population. The war, if it came, would look like a cleansing operation against a sinful, self-indulgent British empire. But, although he certainly approved of this campaign to discredit Lionel Paterin, the nosing required to secure such evidence seemed to Valk grubby, ignoble. Mair and Schiff could do it. This, also, would remind them of their grade – lowly, talented, muckrakers. In addition, Valk might instruct them to find what they could about the would-be secret, unlisted private meetings between Chamberlain, the Prime Minister, and Stephen Bilson. That was the same kind of furtive, undignified snooping, just right for Mair and Schiff.

Security considerations for the Führer's possible state visit split fairly simply into two areas: outdoors and in. Of these,

the second seemed almost negligible. Staff in Buckingham
Palace would have been vetted when given their jobs. And
the audience at the Guildhall, where the Führer was due to
speak on the final evening of the visit about 'Our New Europe',
should be well-known business and commercial chiefs, most
of them full of respect and admiration for him and his achievements. That 'our' in the title of the Führer's talk made Valk
think. Did it mean *Germany*'s new Europe, which would be
quite an ambitious statement, though probably not contrary
to the Führer's bold thinking? Or did he have in mind the new
Europe of all countries in the continent, plus Britain? Knecht
would probably say it was the second.

Out of doors security might be more difficult. Knecht,
chairing today's meeting, said the Führer would wish to use
an open car for the inaugural procession of the visit. Pavement
crowds must be able to see him properly. The very purpose
of the visit would be compromised, if not. Half hidden away
in a closed vehicle – a mere face at the window, momentarily
glimpsed – he would appear furtive, cowardly, unmesmeric.
Hardly the Führer's style! The king would, of course, have a
place alongside him in the car, and it was crucial they should
be clearly on view together, in wholehearted friendship.
Pictures of them sharing this wonderful, wholesome matiness
would go around the world on cinema newsreels and in the
Press – and, moreover, thrill much of the world. They would
look like equals, which might be acceptable to the Führer, for
the short space of his time in London.

At this stage it was unclear whether the British might intend
one of the gilded royal coaches and team of horses should be
used in that first procession. Occasionally, at, say, race meetings, the royal family did appear in an open coach. 'Perhaps
the basic drawback, though, is that *all* these coaches are rather
ornate and grandiose,' Knecht said. 'This is their essence, their
meaning. They are part of, symbols of, a different regime from
ours. Although such regimes have undoubted attractions and
strengths – and, indeed, an engaging, authentic, though juve-
nile, showmanship – we do not conduct things in that fashion.
A coach, thoroughbred horses, and a driver and postilions in
quaint garb would set the Führer too far apart from the citi-
zenry. That, too, might diminish the impact of the visit.

'Most likely he would prefer the normality of a motor car.

Consider: he is the Führer because the people made him Führer. He is *of* them and *by* them. If he speaks from a platform it is *to* them. That is plainly so in Germany. And now he will desire this kind of natural, easy, two-way relationship with the British, as well. When he raises his right arm in solemn salute it is as if he would bless the people, like a priest or the Pope, and as if he wishes to embrace the people and draw them to his sacred cause. I think we must plan as for an open motor-vehicle. Of course, such openness does entail risk. It is our task to counter and contain that risk, to neutralize it. This, after all, is the kind of undertaking we came into being for, exist for, and – need I say it? – we shall succeed.'

A large screen hung from the ceiling at one end of the room. Knecht had projector slides for parts of the likely route. He presented a series of them now. 'The British king, also, wishes to be thought of as close to his people, and so the procession is likely to take in certain areas away from the well-known London thoroughfares – areas of inexpensive housing, shops and businesses. Here, for instance, is North Lambeth.' Knecht pointed with a cane. 'I can divide my concerns into three categories. One: organized so-called 'political' demonstrations against the visit. Two: a street level assault on the vehicle carrying the Führer and the king, perhaps with a firearm, possibly by someone mentally disturbed and/or Jewish. And three: an organized attack by sharpshooter, sniper rifle, from an upper window in domestic premises or a business property.'

But Knecht spoke lightly of these 'concerns', as if he had absolute confidence they could be comfortably dealt with. Valk thought it demonstrated complete trust in him and his London mission. This illustrated what he had meant by describing the atmosphere as joyous and festive. Although a proper awareness of difficulties and dangers existed, the readiness to cope with them was magnificently evident, along with an absolute belief in the officers, such as Valk, who would counter those difficulties and dangers.

Of course, he felt to some degree patronized by Knecht, the jumped up, self-adoring, pomaded twerp. *Get over to London and do a bit of a survey for me, would you, Andreas? I think you'll manage that quite well.* This was a man ten years younger, of negligible combat experience, if any, who had probably been helped to his present rank by influential friends. He belonged to a new brand of leader, chosen not for ability, but from cronyism and perhaps the youthfulness of his arse, though the Führer had better not get to hear promotion could depend on that: remember his disgust when the head of the army, Colonel General von Fritsch, was accused of homosexuality – wrongly, as it turned out.

But, at least Knecht could recognize the tested flair Valk would bring to this assignment and have full faith in it. He depended on Valk, and he knew he did. That would be regardless of 'bombardment trauma', suppose Knecht really did think Valk displayed this. Knecht had not only put the Führer's basic security in his hands, but also chosen him for the delicate job of collecting any spice and filth findable about the British Cabinet minister Lionel Paterin. Valk would pass that task on, yes, but it would still be nominally his; as a great scientist might have his name, and only his, given to a wonderful discovery, though laboratory technicians had helped with the rudimentary stuff. Naturally, Knecht, that despicable career-monger, might claim it to be *his*, however.

'To take demonstrations first, then,' Knecht said. 'In the preposterously lax interests of what the British call "Freedom to protest" and "Freedom of speech", their governments are wantonly tolerant of choreographed street dissent. Wantonly. They haven't had a revolution for nearly three hundred years and so don't fear the mob, or not enough. Occasionally, they'll suffer a minor uprising with some deaths, as at what they call Peterloo, Manchester in 1819, but such riotousness is regarded as contrary to the national character and therefore swiftly forgettable and, these days, pardonable.

'Such street disturbances aimed at the Führer will not be suppressed by the British authorities. In one sense, they are actually encouraged by people like Churchill and Paterin, bellicose, unreasonable, inflamed, half-mad voices. And, although they may involve shouting, chanting, placards and banners, they probably offer no security threat. If they take place, they will be policed, though policed with a lighter hand than we might consider appropriate – appropriate or sane. Water cannon, staves or firearms are rarely used to disable these agitators. They could be a nuisance, yes, but not beyond that. It will obviously be unfortunate if the political value of

the visit is reduced by Press and newsreel coverage of such
uncivil excesses. Raucous yelling and screaming would impair
the theme wanted by our Führer and the king – a declaration
of lasting accord between the two nations and their heads of
state.'
     Knecht went into English: '"Adolf Go Home." "No Nazis
Here."' He returned to German: 'These might be the sort of
unkind, even insolent, banner messages on show. Press photographs of them will not be helpful. We must accept this, I'm
afraid. In public, the Führer will act as if unperturbed by this
disgusting coarseness, perhaps even as if unaware of it.
     'It is very possible, though, that the presence of the king
will make hostile behaviour of that sort unlikely. He is understandably very popular in Britain. People admire the skill,
humanity and loving loyalty with which he was able to keep
the crown as well as his consort, despite virulent opposition
from many deeply negative, though formidable, figures. And,
of course, the Führer is known to have encouraged the king
not to capitulate, to defy bourgeois religiosity, and, therefore,
will rightly share some of the monarch's popularity. The king
also won good opinions from his subjects by sympathizing
on the spot, and in such a sincere fashion, with the unem-
ployed of South Wales in 1936 during the continuing British
economic depression. People may feel it would be ungrateful,
even subversive, to show crude antipathy towards his, and a
distinguished guest's, celebratory parade. Those wishing to
cause turmoil might realize they would be savagely and entirely
justifiably set-upon by supporters of the king in the crowd,
and this will deter.'
     Valk saw he would need to investigate the kind of organi-
zations who might put people on to the streets with orders to
ruin the procession and its magnificently constructive aims.
Reds probably flourished in Britain; the country was so pathet-
ically broad-minded. The government there even allowed
publication of a blatantly Communist newspaper, *The Daily
Worker*, its title copied from a similar rag in the United States.
Wholesalers wouldn't distribute the British *Daily Worker*, but
readers were actually permitted to take bundles of copies to
the newsagents themselves, without the least action by the
police, and to support the paper with a £1 levy.
     As well as the Communists, the Jews might send groups

to demonstrate against the Führer. Some Communists would actually *be* Jews, of course: an especially undesirable mix. Would the churches put anti-state-visit teams on the streets? The colleges and universities? And perhaps old soldiers' associations would object to friendliness with Germany.

Knecht said: 'I come next to street-level possible assaults. We and the British will have ample bodyguards close to the main vehicle, which would travel at brisk walking pace only. They will easily be able to deal with any approach of this kind. Also, troops will line the route.'

Knecht seemed to become less bouncy. 'Finally, upper-floor windows. These may be the chief source of danger. Several commercial buildings will offer a clear targeting sight of the Führer in the comparatively slow-moving open car below. The rectangular form of the vehicle will, as it were, frame him. A trained sniper could get off several shots in the time it would be in his view.' Knecht pointed with the cane again. 'For instance, this tall property here – a books depository or warehouse where volumes are stored before distribution to the shops. The car would probably have to slow even more to negotiate this grassy island just outside. It's probable that staff in such a building would wish to be on the street to enjoy the procession with the crowd. This might mean a marksman could stealthily make his way to a high floor unobserved and find a suitable spot. It will be very important that the upper floors in these buildings are patrolled, and that householders are told to stay away from bedroom windows while the parade passes their homes in case they are mistaken for possible assassins, leading to unpredictable and perhaps severe results. Shooting of an allegedly harmless civilian would be another factor operating against the amicable purpose of the procession. The British Press would make a considerable fuss about something like that, even the serious papers.'

After Knecht ended his analysis, a medical brigadier outlined the range of first-aid equipment, analgesic syringes, and non-alcoholic energy drinks he would have ready at all times close to the Führer, and indicated on a projector slide the quickest routes to any one of three major hospitals, the choice to be made according to (a) the location where an attack took place and (b) the most serious of the injuries. He listed the respective hospitals' specializations – eyes, chest, general head and face, limbs, abdomen. All three hospitals would be on special standby during the initial parade. He would ask the British to position ambulances at various places near the parade's path. He and other doctors and a nurse would be in two cars following the vehicle containing the Führer and the king. 'I am confident we would do the best possible,' he said.

Then, to close the meeting, a short, portly protective clothing expert spoke. Valk felt the proceedings could no longer be termed joyous or festive. He wished he had left before these contributions. It would be vital, the expert said, for the Führer to wear a hat at all times when outside, and especially during the opening parade. All his head wear was steel-lined: a vital safeguard against gunfire from above. His skull would be totally enclosed within the slightly curving shields. Also, peaks of military caps and rims of other hats would be reinforced. 'Now, it's true,' he said, 'that the weight of the metal can be irksome. But all security advice should stress to the Führer the importance of these hats, regardless of minor discomfort. There will be five different styles of armoured hats available: three military caps, a bowler and a trilby. The British wear bowlers and civilian dress for certain functions, and the Führer must be properly equipped in case he has to take part.'

The expert passed a military cap and a bowler around the table so people could examine them, perhaps knock their knuckles against the steel plates in the lining for reassurance, and compare the weight to that of an ordinary hat. Valk thought them no heavier than an army helmet. The Führer had also been a soldier and would realize this.

The expert said: 'Our Führer did not in the least object to measurements of his skull being taken so the carapaces could be individually fashioned and, in fact, remained good-humoured throughout, speaking of the fitments as his "jolly casques". Unsnug steel plates can be abrasive to the scalp, even drawing blood. This might visibly run down on to cheeks and collar: clearly something to be avoided when with a monarch, and liable to cause unkind, scarcely hidden amusement among those watching.

'Also, if these additions to headgear fit badly, a hat might become distorted and very unsightly, with hard edges of the shield obtrusively prominent. Messrs. Krupps have supplied the metal and carried out its shaping for the crown of the hats and the peaks and rims in their own foundry without charge, as a willing donation towards the Führer's safety. These reinforcement pieces are then sewn in by the Führer's tailor, using small, imperceptible stitches and cotton to match and blend in with a hat's colour: khaki, navy blue or grey.'

The expert was not altogether content with the kind of bulletproof vest the Führer wore these days. It was light and, admittedly, imperceptible. But he wondered whether comfort and chicness had taken precedence over purpose. He passed some vests around now – the lighter model, and the one the expert would prefer: bulkier, stiffer, and needing a stouter leather harness. He claimed it would stop bigger bullets, even fired from very near. Also, it was less flammable. When the hats and vests had been returned to him, he took off his jacket and shirt and swiftly strapped on the heavier vest over his singlet. It provided cover from just below the neck to the navel. Keeping the vest on, he re-dressed and placed the bowler on his head, then walked a few paces back and forth at the side of the conference table so all could see the effect. Valk thought he did look notably fatter than his previous fatness, and forlorn or ludicrous under the bowler.

'Impressive,' Knecht said. He promised to pass the recommendations higher about the hats and the vests, so that they would reach the Führer.

With candour and, for a moment, some fear and helplessness in his voice, the expert said: 'Of course, the more we improve the protection to the crucial upper half of the Führer's body, the more we realize there is one part of the area that cannot be protected. I speak of the Führer's face. People will understandably crowd to see that face. It is the face of an icon and must not remain hidden or shrouded. The masses draw inspiration and resolve from that face. The peaks or rims of hats may partly curtail exposure, and I fear this is the most we can achieve, given the absolute need for a large degree of openness. The overall objective of all the protective clothing is to diminish and diminish and diminish the amount of target area available to a would-be assassin, whether close-to or a distant sniper. For a public figure, the face will always remain vulnerable, though. We cannot give the Führer a visor. The people would not permit it. Neither would he. And he will not allow a double to appear for him. Perhaps justifiably, he believes that no credible double could conceivably exist.'

Valk found it hard to visualize the Führer in a bowler, but that could be a compliment to him. As the expert finished his unsettling contribution, someone mock-fired a rifle at his chest and then fell theatrically to the floor, legs and arms threshing at first, but gradually subsiding, as if a bullet had been repelled by the thick vest and come back like a boomerang and killed the marksman. Valk didn't mind a little humour, even when dark. He felt that almost the whole of the second part of the session today had comical elements, although the objective was supremely serious. It was the spelling out with such thoroughness the details of physical protection that at moments gave a farcical twist to things, the plodding, dogged, specificness. Others must have felt the same, and so the ludicrous fooling just now.

The meeting ended, and most of the participants dispersed. Knecht remained at the head of the table, tidying his papers and smiling to himself. Valk approached and sat opposite. 'Things went very well, sir,' he said. 'A little sombre occasionally, but very necessary topics. They have to be dealt with.'

'What we have to ask, Andreas, haven't we, is whether it's all total bollocks?'

'Whether what is, sir?'

'You like to think things are as they seem, don't you?'

'Which things?'

'Luckily, I've happened to get sight lately of a confidential memo from von Ribbentrop to the Führer,' Knecht replied.

'I don't understand. You came by a private message from the Foreign Minister to Hitler? How could that be? What kind of luck, exactly?'

'It's not a comfortable or comforting document.'

'In which respect, sir?'

'This is what I mean when I say you like to think things are as they seem.'

'Well, up to a point.'

'"Up to a point, Lord Copper." There's a new English novel where an underling tactfully questions something said by His Lordship, but really means: "That's out-and-out rubbish."'

'*Scoop*. Evelyn Waugh. Amusing, as is his earlier work. *Decline and Fall*. The British sense of humour. Mostly based on class. Terse. "Brevity is the soul of wit."'

'There is a girl at a club I go to sometimes who is familiar with that book,' Knecht said. 'The memo gives Ribbentrop's view of the British.'

'He's always been keen on friendship with them, hasn't he?'

'We sit here chewing over details about transport, street protests, tall buildings, hospitals, energy drinks for the London pilgrimage, but to what purpose, Andreas?'

'For contingencies. Perhaps none of the safety provisions will be needed. They must be in place, though. This is a rule one learned at the front.'

'Ah, the front,' Knecht said. 'One learned rules at the front, did one?' His voice assumed false awe and diffidence. From behind the lumpy spectacles, he stared pseudo-respectfully at Valk. It was like a child asking its grandfather to describe his war feats. The blubber rolls between his jaw bones and neck seemed to glow with excitement as he waited for the answer.

'If one meant to stay alive, one learned the rules,' Valk said.

'Which in your case, one did?'

'One meant to stay alive and, yes, one did,' Valk said.

'Thanks to the rules?'

'That's to say, rules we made for ourselves. Not the brass's rules. They would get you killed. Remember that pair of troops in an English poem? They speak quite fondly of their general. But . . . Yes, but. . . . "But he did for them both with his plan of attack."'

'The British will fight,' Knecht said.

'Certainly. As we discovered at the front, the British will fight, did fight.'

'Will fight and win?'

'They fought and won then, yes – with American help.'

'That help might be on offer again.'

'Some would say the United States has become much more isolationist, uninterested in Europe, sir. Times are different.'

'Maybe. But, regardless of the American position, Ribbentrop thinks Britain will fight again. It's evident from his memorandum that he regrets having to write this. As you say, he's fond of the British. So, his view about their readiness to oppose us seems more believable. He's tried to think otherwise, but observation and logic will not allow it. He refers to threatening speeches by Winston Churchill, former holder of many government offices, and similar from Lionel

Paterin, a member of the Cabinet and Defence Cabinet.' Knecht swung his gaze slowly around the big conference room, like a searchlight seeking enemy aircraft to pinpoint for the guns. 'Why are we wasting our time here, then, making preparations for a state visit that might never happen?'

'*Might* never happen, yes. Surely, sir, we have always recognized that. But it also *might* happen.'

'Ribbentrop believes that if Britain and her friends come to consider themselves stronger than Germany, they will strike. He says – regretfully, very regretfully – that Britain must always be regarded as Germany's prime enemy.'

'But Munich. I don't believe world war two will—'

'What I said: you like to believe things are as they seem, Munich included.'

'The winter is coming. Countries don't start wars in the winter.'

'Countries start wars when they think they can win,' Knecht said. 'We have people in our Ministries telling the British on the quiet that, really, Germany is weak at present – that the supposed arms build-up here doesn't amount to much, but it might do in a year's time. So, don't wait. Attack now. That's their message to Britain. They detest the Führer and all he stands for, especially the urgent requirements of *Lebensraum*.

'You've heard of the Kordt brothers, Erich and Theodor? It sounds like a music-hall act. But both are considerable diplomatic figures. A mystery how they hold their jobs. In fact, I don't know how they are still free and, or alive. They talk to London, saying Germany's readiness for war is a sham, and saying also that the Soviet–German agreement is imminent, so Britain should act, before we and Russia are an unstoppable force.'

'Eisen, back from Moscow, will have views on the possibility of an agreement.'

'Oh, yes, of course, and from Eisen, or whatever they know him as – some clockmaking alias, I expect – the report will go to Mount. And from Mount to Bilson and the British government via, as ever, Mr Passport Control at the British embassy.'

'Bernard Kale-Walker.'

'Part of the scenery. But, incidentally, not, at the moment, part of the Berlin scenery. He's in Dresden with a team.'

'To what purpose?'

'A mapping purpose. A bombing purpose.'

'Dresden?'

'Symbolic. All that pretty architecture. Wipe it out and think of the damage to morale. Also, lots of converging railway lines. Kale-Walker and his exploration are another reason I think the war is nearer than some like to believe. I admit it's possible. Eisen will tell Mount and London not to worry about a Soviet–German agreement because it will never happen. However, the Kordt brothers urge the opposite to Vansittart – Sir Robert Vansittart, British Foreign Office bigwig. No chum of ours. And the Kordt brothers perhaps have more clout and credibility than Eisen. Meanwhile, Kale-Walker pops down to Dresden to select a few targets for the future. And how far ahead is that future? You'll know the term "pre-emptive", Andreas.'

'Of course.'

'Attack a possible enemy first, to stop the enemy attacking you.'

'Get one's retaliation in first,' Valk said.

'Where does this leave the pomp and circumstance state visit?'

NINE

Toulmin turned up alone at Mount's apartment. It was early evening. Mount had the curtains open, the lights showing. Mount thought it reasonably safe: surveillance seemed to be finished. Toulmin, wearing one of his very presentable, dark-grey office suits and a strikingly white shirt, brought what Mount immediately recognized as terrific insider stuff: at the least strong rumour or gossip, and possibly gospel. 'The Hitler visit to London, spring 1939,' Toulmin said. 'Still not a certainty, but preparations move forward fast and in considerable detail.'

'Well, they're probably both very keen, the king and Adolf. They see great gains for their reputations in that kind of show.'

'There's some bad interdepartmental strife.'

'Between?'

'The Foreign Ministry – including Ribbentrop himself, apparently – and the security gang. It's about who'll run things, if it takes place.'

'And who *will*?'

'Three people are to go over ahead to check safety arrangements,' Toulmin said.

'I'd expect that.'

'A Major Valk in charge,' Toulmin said. 'That's the name on the grapevine here. I'd heard of him previously.'

'Andreas Valk. Old trooper.'

'Responsible to Knecht. More grapevine. Everyone recognizes that name, of course.'

'Colonel Maximilian Knecht,' Mount replied. 'Young star.'

'Then we have to ask whom Knecht is responsible to.'

'And what answer do we get?'

'Himmler?'

'Quite likely,' Mount said.

'Goebbels?'

'Goebbels? He's Public Enlightenment and Propaganda, surely. No security powers.'

'Possibly not.'

But Toulmin sounded as if this didn't quite meet the point.

'What, there's something else?' Mount said.

'There's something else.'

'Something to interest Goebbels?'

'They have additional orders from Knecht. Or they come *through* Knecht. Who knows from where above?'

'Yes, who does know?'

'Not me, so far. Failure there. Possibly, as I say, from Himmler, possibly Goebbels, or possibly from Himmler at the request of Goebbels. There's all kinds of guesswork at the Ministry. It's not something the Russian desk would normally hear about, but the rumours are everywhere in the Ministry. Important to know whom you're getting into a fight with.'

'And these "additional orders" direct Valk and his team to—?'

'They direct Valk and his team to diversify.'

'Into what?'

'Naturally, they'll do the safety checks, and do them properly. This is the Führer's skin. Valk is thorough and very loyal.

But they're also to dig for any sexual dirt about a member of
the British Defence Cabinet, Lionel Paterin. A sort of on-the-
side, on-the-sly, vice patrol. There's a married woman, Mrs
Elizabeth Gane-Torr. Or Liz. A couple of Valk's people will
go to London ahead of him, or may have already gone.'

'Paterin would be against the visit, I should think. He's
become very strong on anti-appeasement – a powerful member
of Churchill's group.' They sat in two of the armchairs. Mount
had made Bloody Marys. 'Ah, I see why you think Goebbels,'
Mount said. 'The findings for propaganda use, in case ordinary negotiations fail.'

'I'd think so. My people don't like it.'

'Your people?'

'Speaking loosely. The Foreign Ministry.'

'Because it's not cricket?'

'Cricket?'

'Because this extra operation is sordid?'

'There's always been a hate between the Ministry and the
secret state police.'

'Almost all Ministries in almost all countries have a hate for
their country's secret service,' Mount said, 'because the country's
secret service might start poking into their privacies, allegedly
in the interests of the country's greater good. I've got used to
the hostility.'

'Diplomacy against thuggery. This plan to smear Paterin makes
it head-on. Remember, Stanley, it's *von* Ribbentrop. He has some
family cachet behind him. Yes, he's a prime warmonger, but he
also believes in a bit of protocol and refinement.'

Of course, Mount knew it to be a basic of all secret service
practice that if your officers were welcomed into another
country for a specific job, you snatched the chance to look
into extra, adjacent but unrelated topics on the quiet. That
kind of natural, opportunistic deceit wasn't uniquely German.
Britain would do it. France would. Every developed nation
did it – 'developed' meaning, here, able to afford a sophisti-
cated espionage outfit and amoral, adept and ruthless enough
to use it. Spies spied. They spied wholesale. They did not
recognize boundaries. Or they recognized them, but only as
obstacles to be climbed over, got round, or tunnelled under.
If boundaries worked there'd *be* no spies.

Toulmin said: 'Suppose diplomacy wobbles, Joe Goebbels

might want to show Britain as depraved, with drunks and adulterous lechers in prominent, important roles – Winston
Churchill the loud, blood-up, brandy-drunk; Paterin, the
wandering cock adulterer. Goebbels would love to batter
British morale with that kind of attack and lift German morale
at the same time by showing a possible enemy as depraved, easy
to dispose of. Paterin is significant as Paterin, isn't he – not just
for being close to the Prime Minister? He was a business chief
before Parliament and the Cabinet – or cabinets: he's in the standard one, and the special Defence group. He's member of a very
select, male-only – *distinguished*-male-only – politically influential London club.'

'Most of the mighty males *are* members of a politically
influential club,' Mount said. He stood, crossed to the sideboard and mixed some more drinks. 'Not only Churchill can
put away the alcohol,' he said. Toulmin took the glass. He
looked relaxed but formidable in the armchair. 'You're a bit
of a genius, you know, Sam,' Mount said. 'Information speeds
to you, sticks to you. You're a natural.'

Mount felt damn pleased he'd decided not to destroy the
four chairs because of that woman's call to the police. It could
have been really hurtful and bewildering for Toulmin – arriving
at the apartment, understandably excited and proud because
of what he'd discovered, then finding the chairs gone, or in
fragments waiting to be gone. And he'd realize, of course,
that this change in furnishing had been caused by him – or,
rather, him and Olga in considerable concert. He might feel
shame, but also anger that Mount should behave so immod-
erately. Mount's explanation would have sounded like panic,
just that. This could taint a relationship between an officer
and his agent. Mount knew he'd have despised himself.
Toulmin might have despised him, also. Mount simply had to
hope the continuing life – so far – of the chairs would bring
no trouble. Mount wondered whether Paterin and Liz broke
chairs. 'Did you keep an eye for tails on your way here?' he
said.

'As always. Nothing.'

Mount didn't like this blandness about possible gumshoes.
It reminded Mount of himself. 'There've been some scares. I
thought I might have been followed myself from your place
the other night.' Mount sat down again.

Toulmin twitched a bit in his chair. He obviously saw at
once the new hazards. A slice of the blandness disappeared.
'That would be bad,' he said. 'You didn't mention it.'

So true! Mount wasn't going to admit he hadn't known
until later and had needed a prompt from the woman on the
stairs. It would make him look bloody careless and incompetent. As the training school had said, he *was* careless and
incompetent when it came to tailing and counter-tailing. Best
Toulmin did not know this, though. His life might depend on
Mount's carefulness and competence. No . . . No might: his
life *did* depend on Mount's carefulness and competence. You
had to do everything to maintain an agent's trust in your abilities. He'd possibly drop you otherwise. You'd become a
liability. Admittedly, inviting Toulmin in with the light and
curtains signal could bring him danger. Was Mount sure
surveillance had been pulled off? In any case, though, the
contact with Toulmin had to be kept, somehow, and used.
Mount must try to balance things – risk against progress.

'It could have been alarmist to speak too soon,' he said.
'I'm always on guard against excessive haste. And I'm still
not sure I *was* followed. There doesn't seem to be anyone
about. I'm relieved you confirm it.'

'They'd have a link between you and me.'

'But I'm Stanley Charles Naughton and harmless.'

'If they swallow it.'

'Stay watchful.'

'I never come direct. Some doubling back. Tactics.'

'Good. Perhaps it was nothing.'

'Who?' Toulmin said.

'If anyone, possibly the people who went to Russia with you.'

'State security boys. So, definitely not good.'

'Which? I ought to dossier them.'

'Viktor Mair, BL Schiff. They work for Valk, who works
for Knecht, who works for Himmler. Mair and Schiff go to
London, as well as Valk. I don't know how that will function,
if at all. They don't think much of Valk. Too old. Too knocked
about mentally by the war. He was at the Somme. *Began* at
the Somme. Then the rest of it until November '18.'

'My boss got a Distinguished Conduct Medal there. Later,
the Military Cross. Maybe it affects people differently. He
seems all right.'

'Valk might seem all right. It could be only that these two don't like him, and so want to find a reason. They're devious.'

'Our job's devious, Sam, and often sordid. They don't have the sole title. Calling you Sam is devious, when your name's something else.'

'They did some standard trickery the other night, on our return from Russia,' Toulmin replied. 'One of them accompanied me on a tour of the apartment as a supposed safety drill. It gave the other time to go through papers in my room. Personal letters, mostly. A lot of my family will be in their records now. I'm not a bit happy about that. Not a bit.'

Toulmin's face took on despair and fear. Mount had never seen anything like this happen to him before. It was a sudden, deep change. Toulmin spoke of worries sometimes, but they didn't normally register in his features. It was as if he regarded it as a duty to stay calm and look able to cope. For instance, the possibility Mount had been followed troubled him because it would suggest that 'link' he spoke of, between the two of them. His body had suffered the little convulsion, but you couldn't have read anxiety in his face or voice. Concern for his family seemed stronger than any concern he felt for himself. He loathed the regime and those running it, and had resolved to try to help bring it and them down. He was committed. He'd take what came. But he obviously dreaded any pointers towards his relatives. *They* shouldn't have to take what came. *They* hadn't committed themselves.

For a couple of moments, the usual impassiveness left him. His mouth tightened, and his breathing grew laboured. Perhaps he felt guilty for leaving papers around. But if they had him nailed, they'd possibly go after his kin anyway, and it wouldn't take long to find them, with or without the papers.

In a little while, Toulmin began to recover. He was plump, bordering on fat, less than middle-height, roman nosed, heavy cheeked, and it was as if he pulled it all back into customary shape now, like reassembling a torn-up photograph. During the bad moments, his head had slumped forward. He put that right. 'Also, they may have taken a receipt for the chair,' he said. 'I don't understand why.'

'No, I lifted that. It seemed special, somehow. Cherishable. You can have it back.'

'Yes, special,' Toulmin said. 'They look so good, the four chairs. Exactly right; a proper complement.'

'Olga said the same.'

'The way chairs are placed gives a room its character.'

'Her opinion, too.'

There was something half barmy and obsessive about the way these chairs had taken on such importance, but Mount thought he could see how it happened. A spy had no binding connection with anything or anybody in the country where he or she operated. Maybe this deep falseness and professional lack of true involvement could lead in some cases to a need for a bit of token reality. It might be subconscious. Had Mount given that kind of status to the chair, chairs? The spy came and went. That's what spies were for. *I spy with my little eye.* My little eye, and only my little eye, established any join with this or that domain. The stay might be long, but that did not affect the non-rootedness. The spy was trained and paid to watch and efficiently pretend to belong, but never *to* belong, only to watch and collect and reveal. Perhaps the donated chair, and the recent general history of armchairs in this apartment, had acquired a sort of totem significance for Mount. The furniture symbolized so much that was good and spiritually refreshing; particularly, of course, the chair Toulmin and the girls had thoughtfully bought to replace the one he and Olga co-shattered during a very good frenzy. They'd ruined it, but absolutely unintentionally, as anyone observing could testify, such as Mount and Inge.

Mount considered it moot – or, in fact, a damn bit less than moot – whether the chair should have been able to cope with the double, active load. What kind of stress tests were applied by manufacturers? These chairs had a modernistic look and might therefore be bought by young, healthy, vigorous people. Had the makers taken due account of this and of the demands, and gorgeous sudden, hop-aboard urges, of sex? What point laminating if the essential structure of the chair was faulty? That would be like polishing up the exterior of a car when the engine's big end had gone.

Anyway, in his eyes, the other three of the set now possessed some of that gifted chair's fine, communal aura. And, even if they weren't so brilliantly symbolic, Mount might have been put off dismantling them by the amount of sheer work involved.

Four chairs were a lot to tear apart. After that would come
the extremely awkward task of disposal. Things had altered.
He felt he couldn't do a secret share-out around the bins again.
His neighbour might become badly depressed and nervy if it
all restarted, and with more pieces than before. He wanted to
avoid cruelty. It would be grossly heartless to play dumb again
if meeting her accidentally. '*More pieces, you say? Oh, dear,
dear.*' No, impossible.

This meant the river, and two, possibly three, taxi journeys
with the items in a suitcase. And he could hardly have asked
a taxi to wait. The driver, looking on, was sure to wonder
why someone took a trip, or trips, to chuck chair fragments
from a suitcase into the Spree. Mount would have had to pay
him off, then try to find another cab to take him home, or
trek to an U-Bahn station; and subsequently, perhaps, repeat
the chore more than once. This kind of rigmarole didn't seem
necessary, did it? Necessary? It didn't even seem sane. And,
obviously, it wouldn't be possible at all if he *was* being
watched.

For God's sake – he had a First in *literae humaniores* from
one of the world's finest universities and was here to gauge
the likelihood of a second world war involving Germany,
Britain, Russia, France, Italy and a clutch of smaller countries, plus, possibly, the United States: say just over half the
world. He'd been asked to spot signs of Armageddon. Carting
laminated chair pieces about because some woman went para-
noid couldn't be appropriate or worthwhile for him. Plus,
Mount felt it would be a disgrace and a kind of betrayal to
watch the wooden pieces float away towards the Baltic in the
dark river, while the metal parts, flung far out, sank.

But he did mean to stay keyed up for any sign of police
activity in the building over the next days and weeks, and, if
it came to the push, he'd quickly move the four chairs into
the bedrooms and close the doors. Most likely the police
wouldn't have a search warrant – not for such a weird inquiry.
A look at the living room should be enough to prove the chair
fragments didn't come from there, although they did. That is,
if it was *only* ordinary police, not more powerful and dangerous
people. Each bedroom had a straight backed chair for hanging
clothes on or for sitting in front of the dressing-table mirror.
He'd bring them out as replacements into the living room. It

might look under-furnished, but he was a sole occupant, and the room did have a settee, normally, as well as the armchairs, the drinks sideboard, plus a large mahogany table and the tall radiogram.

'Knecht will have resident people in London,' Mount said. 'Their Passport Controller at the embassy is probably a spy. He or she will almost certainly be able to brief Valk and the other two about Lionel Paterin and, probably, the woman. There'll be the beginnings of a dossier on Paterin already, or more. That would be routine for any British Cabinet minister, and especially any Cabinet minister who also serves on the Defence Cabinet, and who also sounds off against Adolf, and who is also giving it to a hyphenated married woman. It's not a difficult operation for Andreas Valk. Child's play, after the Somme.'

'But, as you say, sordid.'

'It's spying, Sam. It's the pursuit of knowledge. Sometimes that pursuit can seem a degree dubious. Consider Faustus. Knowledge comes in all categories, if you're lucky.'

'So do you have a Passport Controller at your Berlin embassy?'

'Passports definitely have to be controlled in any embassy.' Another point against breaking up the chairs: Bernard Kale-Walker, of Passport Control and so on in Berlin's British embassy, intended getting rid of the Steglitz place soon, and changes in the inventory would become obvious. Clearly, questions must arise if four wood and metal laminated armchairs had gone missing, or if, as a precaution, Mount bought four armchairs with his own money of blatantly different style to replace them. Kale-Walker had already mentioned problems at the apartment following Mount's brazenly dishonest report to London that a chair had collapsed under him personally while sitting on it alone. Mount would regard it as very painful to be kicked out of the service because of an armchair. Something like that could be damaging on a CV, even if the new job you were after had nothing to do with furniture. And Fallows and Baillie were sure to find it a wonderful joke. '*On a point of order, Mr Chairman, what have you done with the chairs?*'

'We both might have to be pulled out of Berlin – in fact, out of Germany – very quickly,' Mount said.

'I understand that,' Toulmin said.

'It will be a properly organized trip.'

'By Passport Control? I ought to be at my brother Luca's wedding on Saturday November nineteenth.'

'Well, yes, I can see you ought. But you might not be.'

'I worry that none of them might be, including Luca.'

They had an Ernst Lubitsch season at the cinema now, and a couple of evenings later Mount went to see *Die Flamme,* probably the last film he made in Germany before hopping to Hollywood for keeps in the early 1920s. He'd done a fair job with *Angel* last year, starring Dietrich and her eyebrows. Mount considered it remarkable that Lubitsch's Jewishness didn't rule out this present Berlin tribute. Mount thought *Die Flamme* rated as a quaint historical exhibit, not much more than that. It featured a tart aiming to get off the game, as most tarts probably did, though he'd never heard Inge or Olga say so. Somewhere behind him in the stalls a woman blubbed wholeheartedly, occasionally comforted – or it could be snarled at? – via a whispered few words from a male companion, perhaps her pimp. A mawkish picture, but he stayed till the end. He didn't have much else to do.

He'd decided to sit on Toulmin's report of the possible smear operation against Lionel Paterin. Mount had found it hard to judge the credibility of this. Interdepartmental hates often produced slanted or outright phoney accusations. You could get a kind of looking glass war, a distorted looking glass. He'd like to consult Bernard Kale-Walker on how to deal with this material when he came back from his mapping jaunt; particularly how the telegram should be worded, if sent at all. Kale-Walker was good on wording. Mount considered himself not too bad with words, but his skills remained those of a classics scholar. That is, he automatically went for plain exactitude. He must try to kill the habit. Something different might be required at times – wise vagueness, a bit of polite ambiguity, diplomatic euphemism. It would be a delicate job to announce that one of the Prime Minister's colleagues might be targeted as an adulterer, even though there'd possibly always been plenty of tales in circulation about him, and about half the men of his kind of wealth, position, and opportunity.

Spying called for a big range of skills. Kale-Walker was

away there in Dresden dutifully helping possible bombers in
the future to hit with fine precision. When he came back to
Berlin, Mount wanted him just as dutifully to phrase some
information so that it lacked fine precision, but put the theme
across, anyway.

As Mount approached the apartment block on his return he
thought he saw someone, a man, hanging about not far from
the main entrance. Yes, he *thought*. But perhaps he'd become
stupidly oversensitive to possible watchers and stalkers after
being tracked from Toulmin's place the other night – that is,
if he *had* been tracked. This kind of doubt took a hold on him
now. He knew he should have been deeply troubled and deeply
alert. But he wondered if he was taking fright at nothing much
at all – or nothing much at all to do with him. When Mount
came nearer, the man who had seemed to be loitering there
no longer seemed to be loitering there. He'd gone. Mount
couldn't tell where. *Had* he been loitering, then, or simply on
his way in or out and hesitating briefly for some reason? In
the training there'd been several sessions on what was called
'the psychology of seeing'. These dealt with mistakes of
perception and their causes. He recalled seven of them:

(1) Fear could produce a wrong and perhaps threat-
    ening interpretation of some circumstances. The
    sessions hadn't actually termed this 'galloping
    panic', but that's what was meant.

(2) Hope and optimism could make you see what you
    wanted to see.

(3) Drink and/or drugs, and especially drink *and* drugs
    together, could enhance hope and optimism and
    make you see what you wanted to see.

(4) The wish to offset results of a previous mistake
    might lead you to imagine circumstances where
    you could compensate for the previous mistake,
    perhaps annul its effects.

(5) Events seeming similar to some earlier events
    could prompt you to fabricate resemblances
    beyond the actual, without being aware of it. A
    sort of *déjà vu* with knobs on.

(6) Modesty might tell you your attempts to remain
    unrevealed as a spy could not succeed, and that

what you now saw proved you had been exposed,
as you'd always expected to be. This self-deflation
might lead to error.

(7) Arrogance might make you feel you were so brilliant that you needed obvious enemies so you could
hoodwink, outmanoeuvre and defeat them, as you'd
always expected you would. This self-inflation
might lead to error.

Mount thought that (4) certainly pointed towards his failure
to notice tails between Lichtenberg and Steglitz the other
night, and, consequently, a determination to spot any sort of
surveillance now. There might also be a touch of (1) in his
reaction, and possibly (6). Definitely not (7). Nor (3). He'd
had time to do one of his descriptive paragraphs: age 30–40;
build, slight to thin; height, just under six feet; hair, dark,
plentiful; hatless; dark hip-length pea jacket, black or navy
trousers, black lace-up shoes; face, hairless, lean, small-nosed,
no spectacles. Mount believed it was someone he had never
seen before, and categorically not either of the two men who
had brought Toulmin back from Russia and appeared later in
the parked Mercedes. Nor did he look like one of the Opel
pair.

In his apartment, Mount moved the armchairs into the
bedrooms and brought out the two straight-backed replacements. He would have liked to go to the window and look
down to the street for a possible re-sighting. That could be
difficult, though. The curtains had not been drawn and the
lights were on. He'd be obvious, and obviously troubled. Even
if he kept to the side and tried for cover from the furled-back
curtain, he'd probably be seen. If this was someone who'd
come because of the woman's telephone call to the police,
Mount didn't want to appear jumpy. That could make this
watcher more interested and inquisitive.

He went to the radiogram and put a Mozart record on. It
came with the apartment, plus some Wagner and Beethoven.
To those records he'd added some of his own, lighter, jazzier,
some danceable to. Then he sat on the settee and got himself
pretty relaxed with the help of the non-blare music. He thought
the Beethoven and Wagner would be less easy to relax to. The
Mozart avoided din, but was still loud enough for anyone in

the corridor and near his apartment door to hear it and deduce it was music for somebody very relaxed.

When a knock on the door came he did not answer at once, as if so intent on the flibbertigibbet tune he couldn't register any other sound. But, at the second knock, he called out in German, and relaxed German, 'Who is it? I'll be with you in just a moment, rest assured.' He left the music playing and walked to the door. Through the judas hole he saw the man who had been waiting around outside. The man gave a massive wink to the judas hole – involving not just an eye, but all one side of his face and his hairline, possibly his shoulders – then several more winks. Because the Judas hole offered only one-way vision, he would not know at what point someone inside was watching him, and he'd obviously hate to waste all that effort. 'Mr Stanley Charles Naughton, I believe, or maybe not,' he said.

The accent was educated Berlin. 'Can I help you?' Mount said, without opening the door.

'*I* can help *you*.'

'In which respect?'

'Oh, yes, it would be a privilege.'

'Has someone sent you? Why would you imagine I need help?'

'In my type of *métier* it's very insecure, dawdling and talking in a passageway like this,' he replied.

'Why do you have to dawdle and talk in the passageway like that when in your type of *métier*?'

'Because the door's shut.'

'Who are you?'

'We don't answer that type of question, do we, in our type of *métier* while dawdling in a passageway like this?'

'You know *my* name, spoke my name, although in our type of *métier* while dawdling in the passageway like that.'

'I spoke *a* name.'

'Is there *a* name for you?'

'There is, of course, but it's not to be spoken while dawdling in the passageway like this when in our type of *métier*.'

'Why not?'

'Open up, Marcus, would you, there's a dear, and switch off that footling, cultivated splurge. There's one thing I'd never do. Never. I expect you'd like to know what it is.'

'No, I don't think so.'

'I would never use one of my clever keys on your door. Not while you're inside. That would be deeply uncivilized. An Englishman's home in a German building is his *pied à terre*. I hate confrontations, and I'm sure you do, too.'

'No,' Mount said, 'I don't mind them.'

'Someone listening to that kind of music – I'd say it indicates a desolation of spirit, and all should tread thoughtfully, considerately in its presence.'

The Section had two principal agents in Berlin. Toulmin was the minor of these. The other, coded as another ancient clockmaker, Ahasuerus Fromanteel, generally spoke exclusively to Stephen Bilson. This relationship gave Fromanteel top rank by association. There'd be a dossier on him and pictures at Section, but SB kept them in his safe. Mount had never met or seen Fromanteel, but thought he was meeting and seeing him now through the judas hole and getting massively, possibly fruitily, winked at by him through the judas hole, though the judas hole only just allowed enough vision to get the whole scope of the wink. It could have been mistaken for the beginnings of a fit, or reaction to being struck in a fleshy spot by shrapnel. The photographs SB had probably wouldn't include one of Fromanteel in full wink.

'Ahasuerus?' Mount said.

'People call me Has or just A.'

'Which people?'

'You're right. It's not people in a wide sense. Only SB and Bernard Kale-Walker.'

'And now, me.' Mount opened the door. 'Come in, Has.' Now that Mount could view him fully, properly and non-winking, he thought the smallness of Fromanteel's nose gave him an impish, merry look, as small noses on men often did. This could be a tremendous plus for an agent. There seemed nothing sinister or even serious about him. Such a nose seemed to suggest he had so much natural vivacity, cheerfulness and fun inside his frame that he didn't need to oxygenate things through bigger nostrils. Possibly, he could have done with being a little shorter and plumper to bear out this impression. However jolly and reassuring he might look, though, Mount realized that for Fromanteel to approach someone from the Section who was not SB must mean he brought a message

he considered paramountly important. Mount sensed that it
might be a warning of some sort. Fromanteel would do the
badinage and joke stuff, as if to suit his appearance. But that's
not what the visit meant. Mount began to wonder about an
exit from Germany for himself and Toulmin.

Fromanteel shut the door behind him and then squinted out
through the judas hole in a bit of spoof high security. Mount
said: 'You may find it a little sparse as regards chairs, but I've
been practising ju-jitsu falls and cleared some of them away.
I expect SB stays here when over to see you. You'd know the
address. But, obviously, there'd be more chairs when SB was
in residence. His ju-jitsu is too good to need upgrading.'

'A pleasant part of Berlin with a fine history,' Fromanteel
said. 'Kale-Walker did well to find this nest. He's away lining
up Dresden for a pasting. Myself, though, I don't think world
war two will take place.'

'Well, not today. D'you know a play by Jean Giraudoux
called *The Trojan War Will Not Happen*? Giraudoux invents
all kinds of situations that should logically preserve peace.
But the doomy prophetess, Cassandra, says war's fated to
come. And despite the changed circumstances, it does.
Giraudoux – a student and teacher at Munich university for
a while, incidentally.'

'And, as a matter of fact, quite a *noble* history to this area,'
Fromanteel replied. 'If you go back to the twelfth century,
there was a Knight Henricus of Steglitz.'

Mount dragged a couple of the armchairs back from his
bedroom.

'Do you like music with your ju-jitsu?' Fromanteel said.

Mount switched off the Mozart.

'These are very fine chairs, elegant, laminated, yet clearly
strong,' Fromanteel said. 'As a matter of fact, while I was
waiting for you to return, one of your neighbours – a lady
not particularly young and of some bulk – approached and
asked me if I had come about the chairs.'

'About the chairs? She thought you made chair covers?'

'Then she corrected herself and said, "Not the chairs, exactly.
Pieces of chairs."'

'Pieces of chairs? Strange.'

'She seemed to think I might be plain clothes police
answering a call from her.'

'About chair pieces? Do you think she might be not quite OK in the head?'

'I see you know about this.'

'Weird. A drink?'

'I don't when on duty, and in this kind of *métier* I am always on duty.'

'You should complain to the authorities.'

'Which?'

'Your work requirements sound like exploitation,' Mount said.

'I acknowledge it's very much against the rule book for me to come here.'

'Sometimes the rules have to be stretched.'

'I wanted you to know about Colonel Maximilian Knecht. Hardly something that could be said over the telephone, is it?'

'I suppose you'd have this number even though it's restricted.'

'I know Berlin pretty well,' Fromanteel replied.

'Well, yes.'

'I mean, not just the history going back to Henricus. More modern things. It's a pursuit of mine. More than a hobby. Oh, yes, much more.'

'My tipple's a Bloody Mary,' Mount said. 'What will it be for you?'

'Water. A half glass. No more, please. There's a kind of fun in temperateness. One is teasing, subjugating the body.'

Mount mixed his drink at the sideboard and drew Fromanteel the water. They sat in the armchairs. 'Which part of Berlin do *you* live in?' Mount said.

'Knecht has some difficulties,' Fromanteel replied.

'It's a big job.'

'Some extra, wholly unforeseeable difficulties. I felt it necessary to brief you at once. I expect you'll ask, "What kind of difficulties?"'

'Not if you're going to tell me anyway.'

'At the present stage, this is scarcely going to be open information.'

'How did you get it? You have a tipster inside Knecht's office? Inside Gestapo headquarters? That's almost unbelievable.'

'I've always been delighted with the code name SB found for me, you know – "Ahasuerus Fromanteel".' Enthusiasm and gratitude put a happy lilt into his voice. 'Ahasuerus and his son, John Fromanteel, brought a new accuracy, a new reliability, to the measurement of time. This was rather an improvement on going out to look at where the sun was, so they could make a guess – say when preparing something and not wanting the meat overcooked, yet not bloody, either.

'Of course, as soon as the clocks had measured the time, it was gone. It became the past, and of no more interest, as it were, to the clocks. In the half second it took to say, "It's four o'clock," it wasn't four o'clock because time had progressed. But the clocks themselves remained, ready to take on anything new that came their way, and what came their way, since they were clocks, was, naturally, more time. The clocks, in their unimpassioned, calibrated, windupable manner, handled that magical progress from the nowness of what the hands showed, and, immediately afterwards, the move of that nowness into thenness. This is why the Fromanteel sobriquet suits me perfectly. I like to think of myself as able to encompass with precision and resolve the momentary, the present, so vital in our *métier*; but also to set the momentary, the present, in its uncontainable endlessly approaching and disappearing context.'

'I'm pretty sure SB had that kind of thing in mind when he picked "Ahasuerus Fromanteel" for you. In fact, I think I can remember him mentioning it. He's a smart one. He actually spoke of your flair for it.'

'Which?'

'Not in those actual words, obviously, but I can see now this was what he meant.'

'What?'

'The "uncontainable endlessly approaching and disappearing context". He stated you were just the one for that. SB has at least one Ahasuerus clock in his collection, so he was not talking idly.'

'I don't believe it would be fair to say Hitler is narrow or negative about sex,' Fromanteel replied. 'Ask his girlfriend, Eva Braun. She has a giggle when visiting politicians pose for photographs with Adolf on a certain sofa, because she's thinking what also happens on it – though, clearly, it will have been given a good de-juicing before the important guests sit.

And then there are some of Eva's friends – real sleep-arounds, yet tolerated at Berchtesgaden, getting satisfaction with waiters and guards. Or Goebbel's lech antics with almost any woman under ninety-five. What Hitler can't put up with, though, is public scandal. They've had some bad instances of that, haven't they? He considers they lower the party's tone. And that's so precious to him. He wants the Nazi name to be an admired name worldwide, synonymous with civilization – robust civilization, but civilization. He recognizes there has to be sex, or how do you go on producing the master race? Not complicated, fractious or perverse, though.'

There had been an abrupt change of tone. Mount felt the real reason for the visit would show soon. 'Tone is crucial to a political party.'

'I wonder if you know the Toledo.'

'It's a club, isn't it?'

'Knecht goes there now and then. This would be to divert himself after an especially trying day, I expect. To have a couple of what the British call, I believe, "sundowners".' Fromanteel did the term in English.

'There are clubs in London with the same purpose, though many are all-male.'

'Such as the Athenaeum and Boodle's? That might be a different kind of club. I'd say it's unlikely you've ever met Knecht's wife.'

'Well, no, I don't believe I've run across her. But, then, I don't know Knecht, either.'

'What I hear about Knecht's wife is she's no great hulk of a thing.'

'I'm without reports on her at all, big or small,' Mount said. 'Kale-Walker might have something. Many women prize slimness.'

'And yet she can do damage.'

'Anger will often startlingly empower quite slight-seeming women.'

'Anger *was* a factor. Remarkable you should spot that. It's from reading the classics, I expect. Plenty of angry women there, I suppose.'

'Clytemnestra murders her husband Agamemnon in a right temper. And Maia gets very cross with her son Hermes for rustling Apollo's cattle.'

'Apollo's a god, isn't he? Utterly off colour, surely, to steal a god's cows. No wonder his mother was irritated. But, as to the other, I don't know whether it will get into the Press. That's why I thought I'd better come round and talk to you. If you read something like this in a newspaper without any background information on events it might make you wonder whether matters will continue as previously, or if you should adapt.'

'Thanks, Has. It was a misunderstanding when I kept you out in the corridor. You shouldn't have had to undertake all that winking.'

'This is what I had in mind when I spoke of "context",' Fromanteel replied. 'The incident took place last night, but I have to put it into one.'

'Into a context?'

'There is the occurrence itself, but also the past to that occurrence, the what we may call harbinger, and the future to come *after* that occurrence. This is context. Mind you, they've done a very good repair job. You wouldn't know just from looking that there'd even been an occurrence.'

'At the club you mentioned?'

'The Toledo.'

'Did Knecht's wife go to the club and do some damage, although she's not heavily built?' Mount said. 'Was Knecht there having a sundowner?'

'That's the point, isn't it?'

'Which?'

'Most believe he was off with a girl somewhere.'

'Which most?'

'In the club at the time.'

'She went there because she thought he didn't have just the sundowners he might be entitled to, did she?'

'I don't know whether he brought something home,' Fromanteel said.

'Brought something home?'

'The word is that the girls there are extremely hygienic, with the management supervising and very rigorous. But error can, in a manner of speaking, slip in.'

'Had she heard things about him, and went to the club to check?'

'They met on a fast promotion course years ago in the secret state police. It was a lovely, dazzling, famed romance, I'm told. Two spirited, talented young people, top of their classes, brought together not just by their respective beauty and *joie de vivre*, but by a shared affinity for their approaching . . . well, *métier*. Many have said they were both brilliantly right for the secret police, born to it. This seemed a relationship made in heaven.'

'Lovely.'

'After some time, she left to have the children. But it goes without saying that she knows about prising information and is useful at other skills, too. They were surprised in the club that someone so petite could not just pick up a bar table, but raise it in two hands above her head and fling it. A few argued that, in fact, her petiteness could be an advantage, because she wouldn't have to lift the table so very high to get it above her head. I don't know. This might be illogical. The Toledo has a huge mirror behind the bar, virtually all one wall, enabling men customers to get varying views of the girls. Well, so much glass – that's asking for trouble, isn't it? But all credit to them, they got it replaced inside twenty four hours. One girl was slightly hurt by flying splinters. Named Annette. The lower arm. Not the face, though, which could have hurt her career.

'There's a view that it was unfair for Charlotte Knecht to take action against the club when the real objective was her husband. However, people are not happy about criticizing Knecht, because of his police position. Apparently, he's often in touch with at least Heinrich Himmler. This mirror is very much part of the Toledo's character. People may forget the name of the club, but they will say, "Oh, you know, that busy little place where you can see the girls' faces and arses at more or less the same time owing to a reflection." It became very much a priority to restore that service. As you would expect, the police came. That's why I thought I must talk to you, regardless of the usual prohibition. You'll understand.'

'No,' Mount said.

'Two questions. One, will Adolf hear about it? Two, if he does, will Knecht keep his job? Poxing is no way to produce a master race. Hitler might take a broad, permissive attitude to one of his most gifted colonels going to a whore. Normal male high-jinks. You'd agree, I think. But the Toledo fracas, the rumour of uncleanness, the hurled table, the fractured glass, the injury to another whore – all this might pile up and become unforgivable. Knecht could be damned by that disturbance at the Toledo.'

Mount said: '*The mirror cracked from side to side*, "*The curse is come upon me*," cried, Colonel Maximilian Knecht.'

'That's your Tennyson, isn't it?'

'Prolific.'

'We have to remember, don't we, that Knecht is nominally in charge of a possible mission in Britain to accumulate usable murk about Lionel Paterin. But how valid would any such work of his be in that regard if Knecht can be shown by the British propaganda apparatus to be sexually tainted himself? "The pot calling the kettle smutty."' Fromanteel went into English for these few words. 'Even if I hadn't come to visit you now, news of that Toledo turmoil and its reasons would have reached you eventually, I think. And you'd have transmitted it via Bernard Kale-Walker. Anyway, rest easy, London has been informed.' He paused and blushed slightly. 'Oh, I'm sorry, I shouldn't have said "eventually". It makes you sound slow, dismally out of touch, immature.'

'Yes, I thought so.'

'You'd have cottoned on to the implications and wondered. I thought it vital to brief you face-to-face.'

'Knecht might be disciplined? Moved out of his post?'

'This is why I'm here. You see it now, do you?'

'No.'

'Explanation: it was, on the face of it, Knecht's orders that you and Toulmin should be allowed to continue your operation here without interference.'

'How the hell did you discover he'd ordered that?'

'I gather they had you under surveillance, but this was suddenly stopped.'

'How the hell did you discover he'd ordered that?'

'It's not in the wider policy interest to hinder you. They want a continuing trickle of information about the possibility or non-possibility of a Soviet-German agreement to go to London. They'd like to maintain the idea that things are happening between Moscow and Berlin, though nothing substantive yet. Their aim is to promote uncertainty, and to fend off any decisive response by Britain. German rearmament can proceed. Those cardboard tanks scattered around the country to fool reconnaissance aircraft with the appearance of strength can then be replaced by real ones. Germany needs the time as much as Britain does, and perhaps more.'

'So, following the Toledo incident, there—'

'Following the Toledo incident there will be no change in the tolerance they offer you and Toulmin. The news from the club and the likely repercussions might put you off-balance, made your work seize up, they will think. Even if Knecht is kicked out, the policy will remain. As I suggested, Knecht works for Himmler, and Himmler works for Adolf. Knecht was their messenger boy, that's all. Their mouthpiece. He told Valk to let you run free and to call off the gumshoes because he'd been told to tell Valk to let you run free and to call off the gumshoes. The overall thinking hasn't altered.'

'The context.'

'The time factor. I thought you should be informed at once that you will have no immediate trouble should Knecht get pushed. You must not panic. But neither will you and Toulmin be any safer in reality than before Knecht got pushed. I don't know the Dresden area very well. Do you think there might be reasonably remote flat ground somewhere nearby for a make-do airstrip? Perhaps Bernard will tack on a little survey of the environs with this in mind. Quite often in our kind of *métier*, there's the main task, but also a side issue to be dealt with, isn't there?'

'As just discussed.'

'Quite,' Fromanteel said.

So there *had* been a Fromanteel warning, though nothing outright or absolute. In this operation, absolutes were rare. When Fromanteel had gone, Mount swapped the chairs back, then got into the shower and gave himself a good check over. What was that war poem by Rosenberg about a 'cosmopolitan' rat moving between both sides on the battlefield? You could get cosmopolitan lice, too – the pubic kind.

BOOK THREE

TEN

Perhaps, then, it was coming to an end with Liz. Lionel Paterin allowed himself to think so now: allowed himself to think so *at last*. For weeks, for more than a month, he had resisted – had refused to let himself think so, because, of course, he realized the idea would flatten him, drop him into sadness and a terrible sense of loss.

But no . . . no . . . This was a stupidly false account of what had happened in his head, and he knew it. He couldn't really have 'refused to let himself think so'. Thoughts would not be kept walled-off like that. They'd jump over the wall, slither over the wall, get round the wall. Somehow, they'd sneak in. You might *think* you'd been thinking about other things, and you might in fact have been thinking about other things, but the thoughts you thought you had banished would suddenly force their way back, because these were the most pressing, most important thoughts. They had a claim, a solid right. Paterin trained originally as a lawyer, and his mind still led him into that kind of ruthlessly precise and plodding language sometimes. One of the important thoughts he'd tried to smother, but couldn't, declared it would soon be over with Liz.

It wasn't right, either, to say the 'idea' would do him deep damage, flatten him, drop him into sadness. Ideas were wool, ideas were fleeting. The damage came from his decision *at last* to acknowledge to himself what was happening to them: *at last* to recognize the gap that had lately opened up between them, and which stayed there, and which he sensed would continue to stay there and very likely get worse. He believed he understood how this had happened. She suspected she was being watched, suspected *they* were being watched. And that possibly had speeded up her decision to finish it. But only speeded it up. The actual reason went deeper than that, much. 'Well, I don't think there's anyone around spying on us now,' he said.

'Perhaps they're not horsey. And, even if they are, how

would they get themselves fixed up with mounts out here?' Elizabeth had a divorced friend – a 'horsey' friend – who ran stables and could generally provide them with nags if Paterin telephoned. They usually managed a couple of hours on Tuesday and Friday afternoons. Generally, when they went riding together she was at her happiest and most relaxed. And that brought him happiness, too. Now, though, he could spot no pleasure in her face, no contentment at being with him on this stretch of open ground with nobody else about.

Her fair hair was cut short, a part return to the Eton-crop style of the twenties, but bits of it stuck out from under the sides of her riding helmet. She had an oval, usually cheery and friendly, delicate-featured face. Today, though, he read determination there. He didn't like it because he guessed that any determination around was to do with cutting him adrift. Normally, there'd be a bright touch of mischief in her dark-blue eyes. He didn't find it there now, though. Oh, hell, had he brought these peepers, peekers, pryers, these trackers, these intruders on to their love by his special public prominence lately? Of course he had. This horrified him, enraged him, brought him a bucketful of guilt. He'd made himself very noticeable lately with the anti-appeasement speeches. Perhaps he'd also made himself – and herself – targets. And so they were shadowed. He felt almost certain of it. Liz felt totally certain of it.

He recalled a Robert Browning poem, 'The Last Ride Together'. It sounded like a double entendre. He could remember some of its lines, clumsy and prosaic like so much of Browning, but they seemed right for today:

> Take back the hope you gave, – I claim
> Only a memory of the same,
> – And this beside, if you will not blame,
> Your leave for one more last ride with me.

God, 'of the same'! It sounded like a business letter. Anything for a rhyme. They cantered a while. He drew alongside her, and they stopped.

'It doesn't trouble you all that much, does it?' she said, spoken like an accusation. 'These snoopers.'

'I'll try to discover what it's about.'

'Couldn't you have started earlier?'

Yes, possibly he could have. 'I—'

'You didn't accept it was happening, did you?'

'I couldn't understand why it should be. I still can't.'

'I can think of half a dozen, none of them very nice, Lionel. And I expect you can, too, really.'

Near the Highgate flat they used, and once in town when they were waiting at a cab rank, he thought he'd noticed a pair of men close to the kind of description she'd reported to him: both in their twenties, one about 6´ 3˝, dark-haired, bony profile, pointed, Mr Punch chin; the other shorter, plump faced, squarely built, also dark-haired but close cropped. Until then, in the taxi queue, yes, he'd wondered whether she was imagining, and whether he was imagining, too. It wouldn't have been like her to make such a mistake, but he'd wondered. Now, though, he'd admit that she, and perhaps both of them, might have this secret, off-and-on company. Did it trouble him 'all that much'? How much was all that much, his fiddly, fine-point brain asked. He couldn't quantify, but it certainly did trouble him. It baffled him. Who were they? More important, who sent them?

'You're an important figure,' she said.

'I've had some luck.'

'No, you deserve it – and know you do.'

He saw that behind this piffling chatter lay the true cause of distance between them. She'd come to regard him as caught up in a bigger world than hers: the Cabinet world, the Defence world, the Government world, the international politics world, the war or peace world. Perhaps that made it seem he had a place among great events and great people. Did Liz feel left behind, excluded? She wasn't the sort to tolerate that, or not for long. She wouldn't at all object to the kind of theme he'd been preaching lately, questioning the appeasement policy. She thought it was the right theme. What offended her, he thought, was the way this mission seemed to have taken him over, blocked her out.

'Would she put people on to you, on to us?' she said.

'My wife? Detectives?'

She said nothing for a moment, leaned forward in the saddle and stroked the animal's neck. 'No. All right, I can see that's unlikely. A Minister's wife hiring sleuths to track her hubby,

prove his adultery? Suppose it became public knowledge, and
it very easily might. The disgrace – for her as much as for
you.'

'Exactly,' Paterin said.

'Could it be the Press tailing us, then?'

'A pair of reporters?'

'Wouldn't it be news – well-known Cabinet minister's affair
with the wife of company chairman? Now, *extremely* well-
known. Hold the front page!'

'The Press doesn't poke into private lives – not where there's
potential scandal touching important people. Think how long
it took to get Mrs Simpson into the British Press, and then
only when she and the relationship had been made more or
less respectable through the marriage and title of consort.'

'Wasn't that silence a special arrangement with editors?'

'The Press knows how to be discreet, and not just for
royalty.'

She frowned and did some more thinking, some more
pawing of the horse. 'Well, possibly you're a potential security lapse because of me,' she said. 'They could blackmail
you.'

'You mean the watchers are foreign spies?'

'Why not?'

'Because we wouldn't be of interest to them. And because
the spies of all sides have plenty of real work to do at present.'
He knew though, of course, that he and she *would* be of interest
to an espionage operation. They rated as real work for them.
Wouldn't Hitler's propaganda wizard, Josef Goebbels, judge
it useful to have on file a few compromising facts about a
government bigwig, especially a bigwig involved in Defence,
and inclined to speak of the Reich as a dangerous, duplicitous
enemy? This was the kind of mucky tactic he specialized in,
wasn't it? True, relations between Britain and Germany looked
serene after Munich. But not everyone believed that would
last. Goebbels, or someone else high in the German hierarchy,
might not believe it, and decide to prepare a muck fusillade
in case. Paterin had heard that a specialist German team were
in London to examine the processional route for the Hitler
visit and discuss all-round protection measures. Suppose, as
an extra, these people were told to find what they could about
a noisy Cabinet minister's extramarital life. Paterin knew the

rumours of his link with Liz were around in London. They
might well have reached Berlin.

'I feel what I've never felt before about us – dirtied,' she
said.

'If it happened – some sort of exposure – but it won't –
but if it did, they'd be the dirtied ones.'

'How? By contact with us? There are too many ifs and buts
in your answer, Lionel.' She had small children and wouldn't
think of divorce, at least for the present. Possibly she'd begun
to believe he wouldn't either because of that large scale, pres-
sured life he seemed immersed in.

They took a woodland path in single file on their way back
towards the stables, Paterin ahead. He loathed being in front
now: it was as though he wanted to lead peaceably, compli-
antly back to the stables, where they would say goodbye for
good. They'd come in separate cars. How could he convince
Elizabeth he needed her more than he needed these people
who might change the world, and who adored spouting their
brilliant plans from platforms? He'd say his public piece, make
his uncompromising speeches, because he felt he had to. It
was his role, as he saw it, his job. But this shouldn't come
between her and him.

While they were still in the wood, Paterin saw a couple of
men coming towards them on foot. They wore walking boots
and hard-weather coats and trousers. One of them had a haver-
sack on his back. They stared towards him and Liz. Paterin
turned to alert her. He watched her face as she gazed past him
at the men. Paterin made out no recognition in her eyes. He
himself had already decided these were not the two he had
glimpsed at Highgate and the taxi rank. The ages might be
right, but not the physiques. Neither looked over six feet,
neither was heavily built.

'I told Nicholas here that we'd probably meet you on this
path,' one of them said: an educated, cocky voice. 'I'm Fallows.
Oliver Fallows. This is Nicholas Baillie. We carry identity, if
you think that's necessary. We have a security role. Generally,
we do overseas, but there *is* a strong foreign aspect to this,
and it's one of our colleagues in another country who has
drawn our attention to it. This is a passably discreet spot for
a conversation, if you have a minute. The stables won't be
expecting you back quite yet.'

'Which security role?' Liz said. She and Paterin had stopped their horses.

'Oh, yes,' Fallows said.

'Very much to do with your well-being,' Baillie said.

'What is this?' she said. 'Have you been to the stables asking questions? Absolute cheek.'

'Routine, nothing more, believe me,' Fallows said. 'And tactfully phrased.'

'Routine, how?' she said.

'Oh, yes,' Fallows said.

'This is a damned intrusion,' she said.

'Nicholas has some photographs he'd like you to look at, Mrs Gane-Torr. You and Mr Paterin, naturally,' Fallows said.

'I think we should ignore these people and ride on, Lionel,' she said. 'They use our names like . . . like threats. Yes, like blackmail.'

'It's largely a matter of helping us, that's a fact,' Fallows said. 'We'd be grateful. In return, we can offer advice.'

'What advice? Presumptuous. How could we be in need of your advice?' she said.

'Nick Baillie is an expert on basic precautions,' Fallows said. 'He can give you help, and will, quite readily. It's not my specialism, but even I can see that to come riding here at pretty much the same time and on the same days of the week is not . . . well, sage.'

'We realize that to carry out an ambush like this might strike you as distasteful,' Baillie said. 'Oliver gabbles pleasantly, trying to make it all sound of not much consequence, even amusing, but, of course, we wouldn't be here if it were of not much consequence. And wouldn't have bothered on previous days to watch you in and out of the stables. You'd be quite likely to deduce that, in my view.'

'What photographs?' Paterin said.

'Lionel, do we really have to?' she said.

'These are intelligence Service personnel, Liz,' he said.

'Yes, I think I'd have guessed that without being told.'

'We feel like serfs talking up to you like this on your hunters,' Fallows said.

Paterin slid off the horse. She hesitated, but in a moment stood with him. The horses nudged with their noses at the undergrowth and nibbled some greenery. It sounded blissfully, comfortingly rural. It wasn't.

'These are what we term "snatched" photographs,' Baillie said. 'That is, they were secretly taken – well, we hope secretly – and in some cases when the subjects were moving about. Actually, we think the back of your head is in one of them, Mrs Gane-Torr, waiting for a taxi. Focus and light are not always perfect, and bits of architecture or car or other pedestrians might get in the way. And you'll be looking at them in pale, declining winter-afternoon sunshine shaded by trees. But we'd be glad if you'd let us know whether you've seen these men before.' He took the knapsack from his back, opened it and produced six pictures. He handed three each to Paterin and Elizabeth.

'Nick's good on the amateur psychology, as well as precautions,' Fallows said. 'He'll most probably be able to read your reactions in your faces.'

Paterin and Liz each examined their allocated three, then did an exchange. 'Who are they?' she said.

'You've seen them now and then, have you?' Baillie said.

'Certainly,' she said.

'Yes,' Paterin said.

'And it *is* the back of your head, Mrs Gane-Torr, is it?'

'It underlines the fact that you were present,' Fallows said.

'You know I was present,' she said.

'We're taught to get confirmation whenever confirmation is possible,' Fallows said. 'We have to convince others.'

'They are called Schiff and Mair,' Baillie said. 'They're Jerry intelligence hacks in Britain for a short while under the leadership of a Major Valk. Their main task is to ensure that the route for a state visit by Hitler in the spring is safe and suitable. But one of our colleagues in Germany tells us there's a secondary, confidential objective to their visit.'

'My God, to build a dossier on Lionel and me?' she said.

'This is how it appears,' Fallows said.

'A dossier they might publish,' she said.

'Only if things went bad between Britain and Germany,' Baillie said.

'But that's almost bound to happen, isn't it?' she said.

'We have Munich,' Fallows said. 'Concluded with great skill by the Prime Minister and regarded by many as a triumph.

Some folk believe, absolutely, that world war two will not take place.'

Paterin said: 'You think the Munich agreement is going to fall apart – get kicked apart by Adolf? Is that the feeling in your . . . your office . . . your department? You have information to suggest this?'

'We needed to confirm,' Fallows replied.

'Confirm what?' Liz said.

'That they had this additional, undisclosed duty while here,' Baillie said.

'Information must always be tested,' Fallows said.

'I want to leave now,' Liz said. 'It's getting dark.' She remounted.

'What will happen?' Paterin said.

'Can you vary days and times when you ride here?' Fallows replied. 'Likewise the place in Highgate.'

'But what will happen about these men?' Paterin said.

'Schiff and Mair?' Fallows said. 'And possibly Valk?'

'Yes,' Paterin said.

'Well, we know about them now,' Baillie said. 'I mean, know definitely.'

'Yes, you do now,' Paterin said.

'This is what I meant by "tested" – information must always be tested, where, of course, it is possible to test it,' Fallows replied. 'Knowing your habits, we could quite easily arrange this test. But, if we can so easily arrange this test, it is as well to recognize that others might be aware of your habits, also. This is why I referred earlier to precautions.'

'Yes,' Baillie said, 'we know about them definitely now.'

'But we can assure you that whatever happens to them it will not take place here, in this wood, or anywhere near the stables,' Fallows said. 'This area is special to you. Others may have observed that. I don't mean Nicholas and myself, or Mair and Schiff. Stable staff. Ramblers. Poachers. Gamekeepers. If something happened to them in this vicinity, inquiries might be directed towards you, Mrs Gane-Torr and Mr Paterin, as regulars to this ground. This we don't want, do we?'

'What do you mean, "if something happened"?' she said.

'Yes, if something happened – now we have the confirmation from both of you,' Fallows said. 'We would stress, though, that it would be better to vary time and place for your outings and so on.'

Mrs Gane-Torr and Paterin remounted and rode away.

Fallows called out: 'Don't worry about us. No, really. We'll find our own way back, thanks. We're trained in outdoor survival. Many's the hedgehog I've cooked in clay for supper in the forest over a fire of twigs.'

ELEVEN

E ven before he'd arrived in London, a week or so ago, Andreas Valk had known that two middle- or low-rank officers from British Intelligence had been deputed to look after him and ultimately drive him over the processional route proposed for the start of the state visit. Valk was pretty familiar with the route already, from marked street-maps sent by the British to Berlin for examination and comment; perhaps for amendment. But that was on paper only. He needed physically to see and slowly travel the few kilometres, noting the type of buildings, road widths, spots where the cavalcade might have to cut its already low pace – say a roundabout or sharp bend – this drop in speed certain to make targeting easier. According to the maps submitted by London, the route at no time passed beneath a bridge or through a tunnel, and he would like to confirm this now with these two British attendants in the Daimler.

Valk had sent Mair and Schiff off on their special inquiries. He'd kept the first week or so of his own London stay fairly blank, in case he was invited to private meetings with Stephen Bilson, head of the Section dealing with state visit security, or even with the overall head of the British Secret Intelligence Service himself. After all, Valk had come to London on a very significant and sensitive duty, involving not only the life and safety of Adolf Hitler, but quite possibly of the British king, also, who would be in the same vehicle, perhaps with his consort. However, the British adored secrecy – everyone knew this – though they would probably call it discretion or unob-trusiveness. Valk didn't hear from Bilson or the SIS overlord. Britain's top spies liked to believe their identities, their faces, were not known outside a privileged clique, and a run-of-the-mill German major could not expect to be invited into such company. They'd probably be shocked to see the fatness and graphicness of their personal dossiers in the Confidential Records and Profiles room in Berlin.

Valk thought it would have been interesting to meet Stephen Bilson, "SB" as he was called by the underlings he eventually sent with the Daimler. Strange: Valk and Bilson, two enemy veterans of the war, and actually at the Somme simultaneously, according to Bilson's dossier, but now jointly helping manage this wonderful, positive, radiantly friendly project. Valk greatly wished to believe that this proved optimism about the world might be possible, and even intelligent. Was the natural, irresistible evolution from evil towards good, and not the miserable reverse? The dossier pictures of Bilson covered a long period. Official British army portraits and groups showed him from his time as a private soldier, then through various ranks, non-commissioned and commissioned, until he finished as a lieutenant-colonel.

In the earliest photographs he usually displayed a small, slightly deferential, stupid smile. He looked the kind of soldier who would believe the words of a demented song of the time that Valk had often heard British prisoners chant, and even soldiers across no-man's-land in the enemy trenches. It said troops ought to pack up their troubles in their old kitbags and smile – 'old', Valk thought, meaning not so much old as familiar and consoling. This ditty declared the whole secret of winning the war was smiles. 'What's the use of worrying?' the song asked. 'It never was worthwhile.' As long as you had a Lucifer – that is, a match – to light your fag – a cigarette – you should smoke and smile, smile, smile. That slang use of Lucifer aimed to reduce the vileness of Satan and hell by turning them into a simple, brief bit of flame to get a smoke going. But at the Somme, British troops – German troops, too – wondered a bit whether there really was much to smile about, even if they had a dry match for their cigarettes. It was hard to think then that devilishness and evil could be made of no account by singing and smiling. Occasionally, though, Valk would think: they won the war, so perhaps smiling *was* a secret weapon. More likely, the Americans helped them do it. Maybe the Americans believed in smiles, too.

It was hard to credit that the rather baffled looking SB in the early photographs could be an expert head-smashing, chest-smashing sniper. Of course, this word, 'sniper', and the talent it described, worried Valk now, and sometimes worrying could be very worthwhile and extremely necessary, regardless of the song. You couldn't pack up your troubles in your old kitbag and forget them if one of the troubles – possible troubles – was an accomplished sniper like SB, who might still have the skills. Some of the buildings on the route were made for such skills, and for the cold, predatory ruthlessness SB must have had just over twenty years ago.

Strong information came that the Prime Minister and SB met confidentially quite often since Munich. What did that indicate? Although it might be routine for Chamberlain to see the overall chief of the Intelligence Service now and then, SB was head only of a Section, though admittedly a Section that took in a lot of functions, at home and overseas. Occasionally, as Valk understood it, Lionel Paterin, member of the Defence Cabinet, would be included in these meetings. His obvious closeness to the Prime Minister might be what interested those above Knecht in the affair with businessman's wife, Elizabeth Gane-Torr.

Maybe it was odd that Paterin and the Prime Minister should be close now. Paterin, after all, more or less called for an immediate war; Chamberlain had travelled and worked unflaggingly for peace. Perhaps, though, Chamberlain had been forced to change. How would it be if he had come to believe what many in Britain seemed to believe – Winston Churchill, for instance, and Eden and Vansittart and Paterin – that Munich added up to nothing at all, really? Did the British Prime Minister want to get corrected on what he saw now as a pathetic error? Bilson possibly looked to him like someone who could do that job by destruction of the man who, in Chamberlain's revised view, had fooled him. Had he decided Munich was null, but that, nevertheless, if the violent removal of the Führer could be arranged, it might mean the second world war would not take place?

Possibly Bilson had advised the Prime Minister to go to Munich and accept whatever deal he could, so as to get time to rearm. Did Bilson think now that he owed Chamberlain a show of regret for counselling so badly, and that to put a pair of bullets into the Führer could be the way to do it? Snipers, he knew, were taught always to get off a couple of rounds, and not, out of vanity, to rely on one. Conceivably, without any explicit prompting or pleading from Chamberlain, Bilson could secretly conclude he had a duty to kill Adolf Hitler in a style Bilson had been outstanding at.

To Valk, this appeared a disgusting notion, of course. To Stephen Bilson, though, it might seem natural, inescapable, a duty touched with what the French called *gloire*. And who could have a better chance of carrying out that duty? Evidently, Bilson had been given responsibility for security during the visit, although theoretically his Section's sphere was in foreign assignments only. He had the power to arrange matters to suit his purpose perfectly on the procession day. And, most likely, he'd have his own covert method for drawing a weapon and ammunition. Or the armourer might connive. Well, naturally the armourer would. Bilson gave the orders, and this, after all, was a secret intelligence Service, its customary and approved business clandestine and autonomous. It would be a very unusual intelligence outfit if one of the bosses couldn't pick up a gun and ammunition on the quiet when the urge took him.

Today, the two expected members of Bilson's Section came to the embassy in central London to pick Valk up in the big car. Valk, Mair and Schiff had been given rooms at number seven Carlton House Terrace, over the Mall from St. James's park, a very select area of the capital. The embassy now took in the spacious properties, numbers seven, eight and nine of the Terrace, number seven mainly for military attachés. When Valk last came to London he'd stayed at a nearby hotel, but number seven had since been incorporated into the embassy complex and also accommodated special visitors. Could there be any mission more special than preservation of the Führer? As Valk would have expected in an embassy, protocol was excellent and his rooms could be described as virtually a suite, whereas the others occupied boxy little hutches in a different wing. These arrangements seemed to Valk brilliantly suitable.

The embassy had a fine history. It used to be called the Prussia House. Valk liked that. The name brought solidity and renown. In a front garden was the headstone of the grave of a previous ambassador's Alsatian dog, Giro. An inscription read: 'Giro, a true companion.' Inside the main building framed photographs on a wall gave scenes from the funeral of that ambassador, Leopold von Hoesch. He'd died while still ambassador a few years ago, and the pictures showed Grenadier Guardsmen carrying the coffin, while embassy staff thrust out their right arms in salute.

Valk found these photographs excellent. They showed respect. Valk understood that a full nineteen-gun artillery salute had accompanied the funeral. He discounted absolutely tales alleging that, as well as his regard for Giro, von Hoesch had been fond of Guardsmen, findable off-duty and short of money in pubs, and that their funeral role was an affectionate farewell. A cruel and idiotic slander: the coffin party must have been arranged by highly placed officials, and in such gestures Britain had wisely and honourably recognized emergence of the new Germany. That dignified ceremony, the corpse borne by soldiers from one of Britain's elite regiments, surely looked forward to another, even greater, ceremony: the state visit procession, though not to do with death, but with a magnificent, positive, promising future. No, not to do with death, not death. His task? To ensure the procession told the world of that magnificent, positive, promising future, not of a death by clever sniper-fire smashing the Führer's face.

Or would bad injury be worse? What if the sniper's accuracy had faded with time, and the Führer were hit, but not killed – became a permanent cripple, or mentally a cabbage? That cabbage was only a figure of speech, but, momentarily, to his embarrassment and shame, Valk had a vision of a pale-green, actual cabbage with a small black moustache fixed to its leaves. True, America's Roosevelt functioned from a wheelchair after polio. But Valk found it terrible to think of Hitler as flagrantly infirm in any way: the well-known uncontrollable farting need not be apparent to any but those close. Impossible to imagine a Führer who drooled, or whose features had been reconstructed, after a fashion, on the operating theatre, though with the best will in the world; and the best will in the world could be more or less guaranteed in these circumstances.

Valk had been told in advance who would accompany him in the Daimler over the proposed processional route. He had their names as Oliver Fallows and Nicholas Baillie. According to Claus Weigel, the names were authentic. He had good dossiers on both. Weigel ran Passport Control in the embassy, and Valk naturally expected him to be up to scratch on the British intelligence Service.

Oliver Fallows

Born April 7 1912, Calcutta, India. Father, Sir Alaric Milton Fallows, colonial administrator. OF educated Pelton preparatory school Buckinghamshire; Lancing College; Oxford (Christ Church). Second class honours English Literature, 1933. Helped edit Cherwell student newspaper. Entered journalism 1934, Daily Express. *Recruited intelligence Service probably July or August 1935 following journalistic assignment on British military preparedness. During assignment interviewed Brigadier L.H. Q. Eldridge, known scout for Service.*

Training:
Intake ZP6, August 1935–February 1937 at National Command Establishment, Cosford, near Birmingham: stayed standard 18 months. Good or very good grades for physical fitness; psychological balance; unarmed combat; surveillance techniques; driving; diving; memory; political understanding. Poor or only fair ratings for foreign language aptitude; handgun marksmanship; coherent lying; social ease and acceptability.

Assignments:
- *1937: France. Assessment of government morale. Paired for this project with Marcus Mount (see Mount dossier: he presently stationed Steglitz, Berlin, as Stanley Charles Naughton).*
- *1937: Copenhagen. Possible involvement in execution/murder of Paul Farb, German Intelligence officer surveying Danish border defences. Unproven. No action taken against him. Believe Danish authorities obstructed proper investigation of Farb death.*
- *1938: Security for Führer's possible visit in spring 1939.*

Miscellaneous:
Unmarried. Sexual taste not known.
Parents retired to Orpington, Kent, and Bolzano, Italy.

Observations:
Affects a light-hearted, sometimes subversive, undisciplined attitude, but can also be extremely focused and decisive (see Denmark reference, above).

The dossier photographs showed Fallows as square shouldered, fair-haired, pug-faced, composed-looking – composed to the point of arrogance, in Valk's opinion. But you could say that much about the bulk of men who came from his sort of background and education. Most likely they were taught insolence at school, instead of woodwork.

Nicholas Baillie

Born August 15 1911, London. Father, Theodore Barry Baillie, retired stockbroker; career interrupted by war service (lieutenant commander, Royal Navy at demobilization). He and wife live Guildford, Surrey. NB educated at Lawrence-Cooper-Silver preparatory school, Sussex; Harrow School; Cambridge (Trinity). First class honours and various prizes, Modern Languages: French, German, Italian. Teacher at Rugby School 1931–36. Believed recruited to intelligence Service by a pupil's father met at school sports day. (Probably AK North – deputy provost Section 2 of the Service. His sons, Toby and Hugh, both at Rugby during Baillie's time there.)

Training:
Intake OV 11 at National Command Establishment, relocated to Norton, Gleadless, Sheffield, Yorkshire, November 1936–June 1937, accelerated to match exceptional ability in all parts of course. Awarded scroll and medal as top trainee of intake.

Assignments:
• 1937: Assistant Passport Control, Rome.
• 1937: Passport Control, Madrid.

- *1938: Investigation of alleged suborned King's Courier. Courier's death, January 1938, recorded as suicide (rope).*
- *1938: Possible combined operation with Marcus Mount to recruit Berlin agent(s).*
- *1938: Security for Führer's possible visit in spring 1939.*

Miscellaneous:
Unmarried. Hetero.

Observations:
Close interest in psychology and architecture. Probably marked for rapid promotion in Section.

In the dossier photograph, Baillie appeared of medium build and height, with dark or brown hair.

Of course, as Valk would have expected, these two had heard about Knecht's wife at the Toledo – the screaming and cursing and ruination of the big mirror. As they drove slowly along the proposed route for the Führer's visit, Baillie and Fallows pretended to feel sympathy for Knecht, as might most men confronted by a report on any hysterical woman, possibly made exceptionally hysterical by her husband's wanderings. Really, though, Valk saw they considered it a splendid joke, especially Fallows. He said: 'We received quite a good account of the episode, Major, but you would probably know it in much better detail.'

'No,' Valk said. 'I'm not very interested in events of that sort.'

'There've been others?' Baillie said.

'As we have it,' Fallows said, 'Charlotte, Knecht's wife, age thirty-eight, the same as Knecht, wearing a three-quarter length, navy-blue woollen coat, matching scarf against the weather, flat heeled black or navy shoes, and black leather cloche-style hat, arrives at the club a little after midnight and stands for a moment just inside the door, surveying the crowd of customers and girls, obviously looking for someone – most probably her husband, Colonel Maximilian Knecht, who is not a regular at the Toledo, but drops in from time to time, seeking relaxation and so on. His is a demanding job and, most probably, he feels entitled to be, as it were, offered diversion and companionship now and then. Of course, Major, it is the *nature* of this diversion and companionship which perhaps invites some controversy. One has to try to imagine how the wife might regard things; oh, yes, that is only reasonable.

'We understand that her husband was not, in fact, present. Possibly some wives would have retreated at this point, maybe to continue the search elsewhere. But not Charlotte, mother of two. As you'll know, Major, she had security police training when younger, and the qualities instilled then have not faded: resolve, directness, audacity. Clearly, these are admirable characteristics for someone in the defence of the Reich game, but can also lead to difficulties if there is a lot of glass about.

'Our account – accounts – of the events following are not wholly satisfactory. Yes, there is, indeed, more than one report and considerable variations in what they describe. That's why Nicholas and I hoped you'd be able to help in confirming – or not – certain important features of her visit. One version says that, having carried out her unsuccessful eye-search, she stepped forward about ten metres into the club, reached a table where a man and one of the girls were seated with a bottle of champagne and glasses. In this account of the next few minutes, Charlotte swept the bottle and glasses off the table with the side of her hand – the kind of blow taught in unarmed combat as a neck breaker. Both people who had been at the table were drenched in champagne.

'But a different tale insists that the distance covered by Charlotte was more like twenty metres, and the man, seeing the approaching danger from Charlotte, had time to lift the bottle, which was at least half full, and so saved it for use at another table subsequently. Perhaps this is not important. All narratives agree, though, that Charlotte then picked up the table, despite her being quite petite, and flung it over the bar, doing the famed damage. As the table struck, she screamed the names of two Toledo girls, Inge and Olga, along with some foul-mouthed descriptions of them and their careers. There may have been a reference to uncleanness. Then, it appears, Charlotte announced regretfully that she could not stay longer because she had left the children unattended and had to get home. Possibly one girl, Anna or Annette, received

an injury from a flying shard, though this was not thought to
be grave. So you see, Major, there are discrepancies, even
contradictions, but is this roughly how you understand things
went on?'

'All kinds of gross rumours about,' Valk said.

'But the mirror did get destroyed,' Baillie said.

'No doubt of that, surely,' Fallows said. 'The glazier's lorry
outside the next morning at six a.m., remarkably prompt.'

Valk said: 'Where do your reports come from?'

'It sounds the kind of club that, when not under attack in
this way, I think I'd like,' Fallows replied. 'Possibly this kind
of incident is rare in the Toledo. On the whole, it seems a
warm, welcoming place, with piano music for dancing, and
we're told some walls are decorated with genuine Spanish
bullfighting posters, though bullfighting has been a bit off-
and-on during the civil war. Yet, atmospheric.'

'We wondered about repercussions,' Baillie said.

'In which regard?' Valk said.

'It could be good for you, couldn't it, Major, if they kick
Knecht out of the leadership? There might be a call for you
to take over,' Fallows said. 'Surely there would be. I've heard
that one thing Herr Hitler deplores above all is that kind of
infection in his star people. You can see why this is. It under-
mines general policy. If Joe Goebbels is conscientiously
making films about Jews breeding like rats, the case is badly
weakened should people know some of Hitler's main people
are incubating crabs.' English for a moment: '"First cast the
what-you-call out of your own eye," isn't it?'

'I don't know anything about Colonel Knecht's private life,'
Valk said.

'Not so very private now,' Fallows said.

And, yes, Valk realized Fallows might be right. There could
be a leadership vacancy very soon.

'We chose the big Daimler with the extra fold-down seats
because we thought there'd be three of you,' Fallows said.
'Our information said a V Mair and BL Schiff accompanied
you.'

'My colleagues are looking into some more general issues
to do with the visit,' Valk said. 'We have to divide our efforts.
Our time is limited. I'd have liked to do this drive along the
route much earlier in my programme.'

'Which general issues would those be?' Fallows said.

In fact, Valk had not seen or spoken to Mair and Schiff for at least twenty-four hours. They didn't sleep at the embassy last night. Perhaps they'd discovered good material about Paterin's extramarital carry-on and had decided to follow up some hints. It would be typical of that pair to take over command of their work. 'For instance,' Valk replied, 'distances from all points in the procession to a hospital. This has already been examined by one of our medical teams, but we must also do our departmental checks. You have heard of German thoroughness, I expect – thoroughness to a possibly comical fault, but applied almost automatically just the same.'

'Thoroughness is no fault,' Baillie said. 'Absolutely not. It is when this thoroughness becomes compulsive that matters might turn unhealthy: obsessive compulsive neurosis, as it's known. Not the case here. The motive for making doubly sure of hospital access is clearly rational and even necessary – though, in another sense, we hope not necessary at all, because there will be no attack and therefore no injuries or worse. We know our king would be very distressed if Herr Hitler were shot while sitting next to him in a processional vehicle. The king is sensitive and has a strong feeling for decorum.'

Baillie drove, Valk alongside him in the front passenger seat. Fallows leaned forward from the back to do what he could in taking over the conversation with his mocking summary of the Toledo drama, etcetera.

'This book depository,' Valk said as they slowly approached.

'Yes, one can see just from studying the ordnance survey it could be problematical,' Baillie said.

'And that green island there, almost a grassy knoll,' Fallows said. 'Liable to bring the pace of the procession down further yet.'

'We told the depository owners we'd like to look at some of the upper rooms and windows today with our special German guest or guests,' Baillie said. 'They are entirely willing, but there were some formalities. That accounts for the delay in setting up this drive.'

But Valk wondered. He thought the delay might have been meant to unnerve and humiliate him. Why did the Führer and Knecht admire these devious British so much? Baillie and Fallows seemed the kind who would enjoy playing foolish, lordly jokes so as to annoy people. Perhaps Bilson had put them up to it – Bilson, who hadn't even bothered to meet him, despite the Somme link.

At the book warehouse they took a lift to the sixth floor. A manager escorted them. Few staff seemed to work in these higher parts of the building. Valk, Fallows, Baillie and the manager walked a wide corridor with locked doors on each side. Naturally, the manager knew why Valk and the others were there, and he unlocked several doors to rooms on the left. These had a view of the processional route. They were storerooms stacked with new books on shelving that reached up to about six feet on all walls.

Valk went to a window and looked down. To him it seemed a superb position for a sniper. There was a wide arc of fire, and the open vehicle would be in the rifle sights for at least a minute, maybe even two. 'These are books not in strong demand, so they are kept up here, away from the main flow of sales,' the manager said.

Fallows picked out a novel called *Howards End*, by EM Forster. 'Ah, only Knecht,' he said.

'What?' Valk said.

'The epigraph to this book: "Only connect,"' Fallows said. '"Only connect: the prose and the passion."'

'Which passion?' Valk said.

'It concerns girls with a German surname, as a matter of fact,' Fallows replied. 'The Schlegels. One of them gets put up the duff by somebody unsuitable.'

'The doors to all these rooms would be locked on the day, would they?' Baillie asked.

'They are almost always locked,' the manager said.

'But opened, should you have an order for one or more of these books?' Valk said.

'On a normal day that might be so,' the manager said. 'But if the procession takes place and passes here, it will hardly be a normal day. I don't imagine many sales would go through. Staff will wish to watch and cheer the procession, like everyone else, myself included. It isn't often we see a Führer and a king together. The storerooms would be out of play, I think.'

'Excellent,' Valk said. 'This is the kind of public response we seek.'

'Assured,' the manager said.

'But these locks,' Valk said. 'Of fairly standard make?'

'They serve,' the manager said. 'However, we're not the Bank of England.'

'Anyone with a set of special keys could open the doors, I expect,' Valk said.

'Twirls,' Fallows said.

'I don't understand,' Valk said.

'Twirls. Special keys,' Fallows said. 'Burglar's lingo.'

'We've never had such a break-in,' the manager said.

'Burglars probably don't go for books,' Fallows said. 'Difficult to carry enough away to be worth the trouble. Imagine a set of burglars sitting down after the break-in to share out copies of *Howards End*.'

'There has probably never been such an extraordinary day as this day will be,' Valk said.

Fallows said: 'Mr Manager, Major Valk is very thorough, in the style the Germans are so justifiably admired for. It's why they've sent him in person to oversee arrangements. He can, and notably does, connect the prose of these precautions with the potential passion and joy of the processional day.'

'We're into cliché territory here,' Baillie replied. 'Perhaps that thoroughness is not so much special to Germans as to ex-army officers, who have had the detailed running of operations during the war, regardless of nationality. That becomes ingrained. This would clearly apply to Major Valk, and it is also true of our own chief.'

'Whose name must not be mentioned, on pain of a flogging around the fleet,' Fallows said.

'He had those wartime burdens, too,' Baillie said. 'He retains that same thoroughness, although British. In fact, the thoroughness sometimes reaches a pitch with him when it becomes a mental state we were talking of earlier – obsessive compulsive neurosis. It's probable that he, too, has identified this building as potentially a prime hazard. He was, after all, an ace sniper, before being commissioned in the field. I see it as very possible that on the day of the procession he would be obliged by some inner urge to come here and vigilantly patrol these upper floors himself. That is the kind of extreme, unrelenting commitment we speak of. As Major Valk has said, door locks of this calibre would not be a great obstacle to trained people. Our boss might feel absolutely obligated to ensure no danger originated from these rooms.'

'Do you mean he would be free to move about here as he wished?' Valk replied.

'Not "as he wished",' Baillie said. 'Rather, as he felt required to, as he felt forced to, because of the onus on him.'

'Because of his overriding duty,' Fallows said. 'The making of history will be in his care.'

'As it will be in yours, Major,' Baillie said.

Valk still felt unsure of the tone of this conversation. Did they mean simply, factually, to describe Bilson's personality? Nicholas Baillie had an interest in psychology, didn't he? Or were they still teasing him, scaring him, with the thought of a neurotic Section chief in one of the rooms carrying a rifle, and brilliantly skilful in using it? Was this why Bilson wouldn't meet him – because he felt ashamed of the duplicitous role he would play? It was not like the honest enmities of the battle-field, but furtive, ignoble. 'Couldn't this building be closed down completely on the day?' Valk said. 'Perhaps the staff will be given a holiday, for the occasion.'

'Difficult,' the manager said. 'They will probably want to come in because the procession passes here. And they'll be getting paid to be spectators!'

TWELVE

Back at the embassy in Carlton House Terrace, after the alarming book depository visit and the rest of his Daimler trip, Valk wrote full notes on what he had seen. He would put these in front of Knecht immediately on return to Berlin. But then he realized that Knecht might not be in his current post any longer when this operation ended. The offensive British intelligence officer, Fallows, could be right, and Knecht would get displaced because of his sexual indiscretions, and his wife's response to them. It had been a habit of mind in Valk to regard all his work as ultimately monitored by Knecht. It disturbed Valk to realize that this might not any longer be so. Perhaps someone else would be running the Department now. Perhaps, as Fallows had suggested, he, Valk, might be put in charge. Should he rid himself of this instinctive sense of subordination to Knecht? That unsettled him a little, but also thrilled him. Possibly, he would at last escape this middling rank and its fetch-and-carry obligations.

He completed his notes all the same. Even if he won his step up, he would still have responsibilities for the Führer's life. And that life could be regarded as yet more precious to him, if it were the Führer's personal order that Knecht should be chucked out and Major Andreas Valk substituted.

He was reading over the notes when he had a message asking him to see Claus Weigel in so-called Passport Control. Valk went at once. There might be further news about Knecht and matters to do with the Department. It had irritated him to hear Baillie talk of Bilson earning his commission in the field, as if that were better than entering the army already an officer cadet, as Valk had. And, although Baillie had not mentioned it, Bilson had come out with a higher rank than Valk's. Well, perhaps he would himself get promoted in the field now: the peacetime, diplomatic field.

Weigel very looked bad. 'Something?' Valk said.

'Andreas, I stress this is unconfirmed so far,' Weigel said.

'Understood.' Valk was not going to become grandiose and haughty because a rumour said he had been pushed up to Colonel following Knecht's disgrace.

Weigel said: 'The fully clothed bodies of two males in the twenty–thirty age group have been recovered from the sea at Milford Haven – the Cleddau estuary – in South West Wales.'

Valk was standing near Weigel's desk and felt some of his balance go for a few moments. 'Yes?' he said. 'Is this in any way to do with us?'

'They were carrying German passports in the names of V Mair and BL Schiff. There was also an overturned small boat. In two capacities I get to hear of this – Passport Control and the other.'

Valk had very little voice to play with for a moment. 'But not confirmed, you say,' he muttered.

'It will be.'

God, those two, with their cheek and insolence and deter-mination to supply their own orders! He had been right to regard them as dangerous fools. Would their mad actions besmirch him, as their commander? Might this prevent his step up? 'Milford Haven?' he said. 'What, who, is at Milford Haven?'

'Their corpses were,' Weigel said. 'The information, as I have it, is they seem to have been attempting a landing at one of the Victorian stone forts on islands in the Haven. Apparently, there have been rumours around among the local population for a while that secret rearming of these installations is in hand to repel possible invasion. It's rubbish, but the suggestion is, Schiff and Mair had been sent to spy on such preparations and report. Being unfamiliar with boats and currents and so on, they had an accident.'

'Victorian forts? On a western coast? It's absurd.'

'That's the yarn.'

'I gave no such order,' Valk said. 'How could I give such an order? They were supposed to be amassing a case against Lionel Paterin so Goebbels can throw shit at him if things turn unpleasant. Drowned in Milford Haven?'

'I didn't say drowned in Milford Haven. The bodies and the boat were *found* in Milford Haven. Quite different.'

Now, Valk's breath went for a moment. He sat down. 'What is it you mean?' he said. 'Drowned elsewhere? Not an accident? Drowned by others? Deliberately killed?'

'It's a possibility, as I'm told. And perhaps you'll have difficulty arguing they couldn't have been there to carry out that operation because you mustn't say, must you, what they were really at?'

'I've said they were handling other aspects of the visit.'

'Were you believed?'

'How can anyone tell whether they're believed when talking to those insulting people from Bilson's Section?'

'And I'm told Mair and Schiff didn't come back to their embassy quarters overnight.'

Valk wondered now whether he could define what had baffled him before – the tone of Baillie's and Fallow's conversation not long ago. Had they already known, somehow, about the deaths of Mair and Schiff? Yes, somehow. God, *somehow*. Baillie, Fallows – both in the past involved with unexplained deaths, according to the dossiers. They had seemed sceptical when he spoke of what Mair and Schiff were doing, and where.

Beyond the sceptical? He'd suspected again that they were teasing him. Or perhaps it had been more than teasing. This time he had more evidence. Ridiculing him? The British enjoyed games. They'd deliberately alarmed him with the prospect of Bilson at the book depository on the day of the procession, because they'd known there would never be any procession. Otherwise, would they have alerted Valk to the likelihood of their chief standing – obsessively compulsively – at the perfect high window to annihilate Hitler? By talking about it they'd have jeopardized the plot. No. Baillie and Fallows had known there could be no state visit after the Milford Haven discoveries. The publicity was sure to shatter that plan. Germany would look disgustingly scheming, hostile, two-faced, deceitful.

'I'd assumed Mair and Schiff had gone to a pleasure house for the night,' Valk said.

'Others assume differently,' Weigel said.

And the next morning Valk saw early what others assumed. Discovery of the bodies was headlined in every national newspaper and most likely in the regionals, also:

Revealed: a dirty spy operation behind the smiles.

Munich accord destroyed by spy deaths.

German spies drown seeking secret fortress facts.

Jerry spies dead in coastal defences drama.

No state visit after dead spy scandal?

A leading article in the *Daily Telegraph* said: '*Even while preparations were well advanced for the state visit of the Führer, Herr Hitler, next year, his country was apparently conducting an operation to probe the defences of Great Britain. To what purpose? Only one seems possible: Germany expects to make war against us and attempt an invasion, and is systematically charting the locations and quality of possible resistance so that such resistance can be nullified as part of a concerted attack. The French carried out a farcical landing in this area of Wales during the Napoleonic wars, although it is the far coastline from the continent. The implication of these spies' activities is much graver, even if their doomed forts expedition was prompted by false rumour of rearmament there. Their behaviour and the behaviour of those who sent them is gross duplicity. This is flagrant cynicism, perhaps made the more abominable by occurring so near to Christmas.*

*It is difficult now – in fact, impossible – to conceive how
a state visit by Hitler to this country could take place. The
people of London, indeed of Britain, would not want it; would
find the notion intolerable. That reaction is certain, despite
the king's apparent continuing wish to achieve a lasting friendship with the Führer. In this, the king is deeply at variance
with the bulk of his people. They will now wish the government to do everything it can to put this country into a condition
of readiness for possible war with a treacherous potential
enemy. The Munich agreement may have looked solid, positive and hopeful at the time. That time has gone. Henceforth,
only a war footing for Britain is feasible.*

THIRTEEN

K ale-Walker finally opted for the sea, not an aircraft.
He considered it safer, given tolerable weather. Mount
had wondered about that. Did the North Sea ever give
tolerable weather in winter? How well was the coastline
patrolled? But north from the mouth of the Elbe on a cloudy
early January night a submarine, HMS Masthead, surfaced
just ahead of the motor inflatable carrying Mount, Toulmin,
Kale-Walker and its three-man crew. Kale-Walker had reas-
sured Mount: Masthead, he said, routinely carried out such
undercover, underwater-salvage operations. Its officers and
men were expert in very tricky navigation and manoeuvring.
Kale-Walker and the rubber dinghy crew weren't bad at it,
either. The embassy must contain all sorts of talents. The boat
drew closer to the submarine.

The Masthead's conning tower opened, and a couple of
seamen came swiftly down on to its deck. One of the dinghy's
crew hurled a line. The dinghy's engine idled. A submariner
caught the rope, and the two of them pulled on it and drew
the smaller vessel alongside. Mount shook hands in farewell
with Kale-Walker and the crew. Another man from the submarine brought leather harnesses fixed to safety-lines and threw
the harnesses into the motor boat. Toulmin and Mount fixed
these on over their life jackets. The weather was 'tolerable',

in Kale-Walker's opinion. He'd probably use the word as long as the dinghy was not swamped. But a worrying swell would make the transfer difficult. Kale-Walker said: 'I and the rest of the embassy will probably follow to Britain soon, but in an orderly, protected, official withdrawal at the start of the war.'

'Whatever your decision on the Steglitz apartment, I've left it clean and in proper order,' Mount replied.

'The chair count is right again,' Toulmin said.

'Well, yes, I know,' Kale-Walker said. 'Didn't Equipment, London arrange for—?'

'Oh, certainly, all present and correct,' Mount said.

'The three of us saw to that,' Toulmin said.

'Which three?' Kale-Walker said.

'Olga, Inge and myself.'

'Those names? Knecht apparently got something from a girl called Inge,' Kale-Walker replied. 'Or it might be Olga.'

'I've told Sam to give himself some careful scrutiny,' Mount said.

'We'll try to bring any of your family out who want to get to Britain, Sam,' Kale-Walker said. 'But it's hard to know how the German government will behave. Your family might not suffer, just as the Kordts haven't suffered, though they constantly criticize and try to undermine the regime.'

'Well, everything seemed all right at my brother's wedding,' Toulmin said.

'Yes, that might be a good omen,' Kale-Walker said.

The motor boat's engine picked up, and she moved closer still. When the swell was right, Mount leapt on to the Masthead's hull. A pair of her seamen heaved on the safety line and pulled him up on to the deck. Toulmin followed. An officer in the conning tower with a megaphone called: 'Careful, now, we don't want another accident like that very nasty, almost unbelievable, tragedy at Milford Haven, do we? Yes, almost unbelievable. Which of you is which?'

'This is Toulmin,' Mount said.

'Toulmin – that's the name of an ancient clockmaker, isn't it?' a sailor said. 'Is that his trade?'

'Not quite,' Mount said. 'We'll have to find him some other kind of job in Britain.' He and Toulmin climbed into the conning tower and went down into the vessel. She began to move. A bell sounded. The order came to dive.

FOURTEEN

'I am speaking to you today from Buckingham Palace. It is my final broadcast to you as your king. These have been a turbulent two years. I had thought at the end of 1936 that the worst of those difficulties had passed, and that the country had finally accepted me and my dear wife, as she now is. The public enthusiasm for my coronation last year and for our wedding seemed to confirm this.

'But I now see this is not so. Certain very considerable differences continue between my people and me. Foremost among these is my wish to secure lasting goodwill with Germany. I hoped to dispel an enmity which began nearly twenty-five years ago. This wish I now know is not shared by the people of Britain. It is a barrier between you and me. In these circumstances it would be perverse of me to continue as your monarch. I shall therefore abdicate forthwith, and my wife and I will leave this country. My dear brother, Albert Frederick Arthur George, formerly Duke of York, assumes the kingship. He will be a new king for this coming new year, 1939, and many years that follow, using the title George VI, in honour of our late father, George V. God bless you all.'

FIFTEEN

Back in the Section, Mount said: 'Did you two have anything to do with that Milford Haven episode? Those two – Mair and Schiff – they were trying to dig dirt about Lionel Paterin, weren't they?'

'A strange business, wasn't it?' Baillie said.

'And with quite considerable consequences,' Fallows said.

'Yes,' Mount said, 'but—'

'It's the kind of situation you might have feared when you were in Germany, Marcus,' Baillie said. 'I mean, that a spy

imbroglio would tear to bits relations between Germany and
this country. But it has happened in reverse, hasn't it? The
spy mess-up is here in Britain, and it has badly darkened our
relations with Germany. No visit.'

'Perhaps,' Mount said, 'but how did—?'

'I'm pretty sure SB wants a chat with you urgently,' Baillie
said.

And when Mount and Bilson talked, facing each other from
armchairs in SB's suite, he said: 'A good operation over there,
Marcus.' And he did look cheery. 'Also, we have developments here as well, of course. On two counts now, the state
visit is obviously impossible. First, the German security apparatus is in a mess after that Knecht scandal and the Milford
Haven episode. Knecht has been removed. It was expected
that Major Valk would take over, but now he is tainted by the
Milford Haven disaster, though he claims to have no knowledge of it. Berlin could not risk exposure of Hitler here when
there is no outfit organized properly to defend him. As you'll
know, there are constant rumours of plans to assassinate him,
perhaps on German soil, perhaps on ours. They apparently
feared a sniper attack. Crazy, really, wouldn't you say? I'm
sure you would. How could such an efficient and committed
sniper be found? And secondly, of course, the country
absolutely rejects the idea of a state visit, following Milford
Haven and the natural reaction of the Press to a spy campaign
disgracefully linked to a gesture of friendship.'

'It seems odd that those men should have been trying to
get into an eyesore Victorian fort on the wrong side of Britain,'
Mount said.

'Yes. Stack Rock Fort,' Bilson replied. 'Of course, Milford
Haven has a venerable place in Britain's past. Henry VII came
back from exile in France via Milford to claim the throne.
Nelson and Lady Hamilton were often there.'

SB did this sometimes when a subject was sensitive: start
diversions. History could help. Mount gave him some back:
'I gather these installations were known as "Palmerston's
follies" even at the time they were built – he being Prime
Minister and in favour. Now, more folly?'

'The fort, forts, were considered to have a modern defence
potential, I believe.'

Mount thought he recalled that a while ago now Baillie –

or was it Fallows? – had been in a Danish incident about local defences; a death? Fallows. 'Surely, no secret rearming is taking place in the forts.'

'Jerry's mistake, clearly.'

'I hear rumours that they didn't actually drown in the Haven, sir, but might have been dumped there, already dead.'

'As we understand it, they were drowned in an accident – having no experience of the sea and boats,' Bilson said.

'I reported to you from Berlin that they were after smear material about Paterin, I think,' Mount said.

'Yes, you did, you did, Marcus.' And Mount deduced that this was not a topic to continue with. 'The country's morale is very good now,' Bilson said.

Had that depended on the death of those two? They'd been committed to inquiries that someone had decided should be stopped. Who? Bilson? Fallows and Baillie acting independently? It looked as though nobody was going to discuss this. Occasionally, such office secrecy did operate, especially when unexplained deaths were involved. Perhaps Mount had been abroad for too long and seemed like a bit of a stranger to them all here now. They were guarded?

'Morale is crucial, you know, Marcus. Ask any officer who has seen battle.'

'Munich is corrected, isn't it?' Mount said.

'Very inept boatmen,' Bilson replied. 'Such skills might not have been part of their training.'

'Shall we see war now, sir, do you think?' Mount replied.

'Germany has turned away from us, and vice versa. Hitler will go for the agreement with Russia. I can visualize some of the newly urgent Berlin telegrams, can't you? "There exist no real conflicts of interest between Germany and the USSR." "The way seems open for a new sort of future for both countries." Your and Toulmin's excellent work has consistently pointed in that direction. Once this pact is secured, Germany will go into Poland.'

'We can't permit that. Not even Chamberlain would allow it uncontested.'

'I'd say we'll have world war two by August or early September.'

'Yes?' Mount said.